FIRST CONTACT . . .

The M'threnni—I guessed that it was a mature male, although from human perspectives the alien had an androgynous air—sat rigidly upright in the passenger seat, staring towards us.

The spherical skull was completely hairless, the nose broad and flat (the nostrils, two horizontal slits, dilated minimally as he regarded us), the mouth thin and lipless, the chin and forehead recessed. These smooth facial contours gave his countenance an infantile, doll-like character, an impression which was wholly countered by the fearful intensity of his eyes. The eyes; I left them until last, but they were what immediately drew the onlooker's gaze, those black circular orbs embedded in the skull like precious and terrible jewels, holding at their center the tiny white star of the retina. The eyes repelled and hypnotized.

"The woman is dead," I said loudly . . .

Capella's Golden Eyes

CHRISTOPHER EVANS

SF
ace books
A Division of Charter Communications Inc.
A GROSSET & DUNLAP COMPANY
51 Madison Avenue
New York, New York 10010

CAPELLA'S GOLDEN EYES

Copyright © 1980 by C. D. Evans

First American Edition

An ACE Book

First Ace printing: June 1982
Published Simultaneously in Canada

2 4 6 8 0 9 7 5 3 1
Manufactured in the United States of America

to F. D. Kelsey
a small token
and to my mother and father
with love

Chapter One

When we were in junior dorm, Annia, Jax and I used to take the dawn shuttle into Helixport on our free days and go window-shopping along the heat and bustle of Albany Avenue. We always paid freight fare, a token ten checks, and the steward, Naree, would lock us in the hold amongst the crates of oranges, roseplums and nectarines which were in transit to the market in Capitol Square. The hold was cramped and dimly-lit—a single ultraviolet lamp set high on the roof—and we would huddle together, our bodies perspiring, and talk of what we were going to "buy" that morning from the stores which served the rich clientele of the city. Sometimes, if it was very hot, we would discard our clothing and Annia would allow Jax and me to inspect her developing breasts. If we prompted her sufficiently, she would manipulate us both, watching with a completely dispassionate fascination as our ardour grew and finally burst into liquid fruition. The journey seemed endless in those days, and our games helped speed the interminable passage of time.

Finally we would hear the hiss of escaping air as the shuttle began to decelerate, feel the tug on our stomachs as it dropped earthwards. We would stand, brush the dust from our clothes, and brace ourselves as the craft touched down with a shuddering and a bump. Then there would be further waiting, our hands covering our eyes in anticipation of the flood of sunlight which would mark the opening of the hatch. Naree would be standing there smiling as we scampered down the ramp on to the terminus, the fine city dust blowing about our feet.

"Don't be late," she would call to us. "We leave at sunset."

I vividly recall the last of our pilgrimages to the city, on Midseason's Day in Summer 29. All three of us were past our fifteenth season, approaching our majority ceremonies, and we were aware that this was perhaps the last time we would visit Helixport together. We had jealously hoarded our work-checks over the past six months in order to sample as many of the delights of the city as possible. Albany Avenue was always the starting point for our excursions, its crowded walkways and its shops offering all manner of goods a constant source of fascination to us. Musicians, puppeteers and pastry-vendors plied the street; beggars mingled with the rich; the air was alive with the babble of voices and a variety of different smells. We, three children from the remote and rural High Valleys, were in our element.

Our first port of call was a small trinket shop on the corner of the avenue where we spent an hour exploring dusty shelves and boxes for any objects that might be of interest to us. I purchased a ten-centimetre object lens for the refractor I was constructing back at the commune; Jax bought a copper snake-ring which was too large for his fingers but fitted snugly on the thumb of his right hand; Annia eventually emerged with a M'threnni gasglobe, a crystal sphere awash with smoky ribbons of red and brown. She held it fondly in her cupped hands and said: "Isn't it beautiful?"

Jax and I stared at the globe, perplexed. We saw a swirling fog, muddy and bloodstained, lacking form and colour.

Annia had often coveted the globes on previous visits, but we had never supposed that she would actually buy one.

"How much did it cost?" I asked.

"Fifty checks."

"Fifty! You must be mad."

Annia laughed and thrust the globe towards us.

"Feel," she said. "It's warm."

Jax and I retreated, somewhat in awe of the object. It was rumoured that the globes caused ill-luck if touched by a human hand, and although we were old enough to be scornful of superstitions, we nonetheless felt it wise not to tempt fate.

"Cowards," Annia said with a grin, dropping the globe into her belt-pouch.

"You're a hybrid," Jax observed. "Your mother was a M'threnni."

"Then why haven't I got a bald head and funny eyes?"

"You've got your father's eyes and hair. Or maybe it's a wig." He tugged her pony-tail, then frowned: "It could be glued on."

"With your flat nose, you look more like a M'threnni."

Jax made his arms and legs rigid and opened wide his eyes. He began marching down the walkway in some imagined parody of the aliens' gait.

"Halt!" Annia called, hurrying after him, mimicking the brisk officiousness of a militia woman.

She faced him. "It has come to my attention that you are a M'threnni. What are you doing outside your tower?"

"I-am-lost," Jax droned. "Take-me-home."

Annia shook his head. "You've been out in the sun too long," she said gravely. "Your skin's turned black."

Jax threw up his hands in horror. "Bring-me-whitewash. I-must-paint-myself."

They continued with their banter as we wandered down the avenue. We mocked the aliens, I thought, because we knew so little of them and because we secretly feared them. I did not know, then, that the M'threnni were soon to intrude upon our lives and forever destroy our cosy camaraderie.

It had grown extremely hot, and the avenue was emptying of people. Capella was approaching zenith and many of the shops had already closed. I watched as the sun-dousers were activated on the façade of a furnishings store, marvelling at the way in which the windows turned grey and opaque in the wink of an eye.

We retreated into the arcades, those narrow, shadowy streets which branch like tributaries from the main thoroughfare. We stopped at a café and sat in the cooled air, drinking iced lime juice. Ice! We plucked the cubes from our glasses and ran them over our foreheads, across our cheeks, down our necks. The patrons of the café looked on, stern and disapproving. We ignored them.

It was almost seven hours, and the pools would be opening with the onset of zenith. We left the café and made our way down to the Dome Baths at the southern end of Sussex Street. The vestibule was empty, but as we passed through, dropping our clothes into the numbered bowls, Jax nudged me gently in the ribs with his elbow. A swarthy, overweight youth some seasons older than ourselves stood at the entrance to the pool. He was staring at Annia, assessing her body with a salacious gaze. He looked as if he was about to approach her, but Jax and I hurried forward and led her away into the humid, boisterous air of the pool.

We had discovered the baths on our first visit to the city three seasons before. While adults sleep or lounge in cafés over the four hours of zenith, the youth of Helixport expend their energies in watersport. At the Dome the lighting is subdued and the water cool and bracing. The three of us clasped hands and ran towards the deep end, plunging in with a splash. I swam off towards the bottom of the pool, down into the blurred, serene silence. I tried to sit on the bottom, flapping my arms frantically against the buoyancy of the water, looking upwards towards the surface, a fluid sky alive with the movement of bodies.

After we had exhausted ourselves in swimming we lay at the side of the pool, Jax and I assigning breast-sizes to the girls who passed by (the imminence of our majority ceremonies had instilled in us a growing interest in the female form). Annia lay beside us, studying the globules of water on the azure-tiled floor.

Finally tiring of our sport, Jax and I lay back and closed our eyes. The warm, moist air induced a drowsiness in me; the babble of voices grew distant, a hypnotic undercurrent of sound. I drifted in that twilight zone between true wakefulness and sleep.

Sometime later, a blunt, nasal voice interrupted my reverie: "Hey, you."

I opened my eyes. The fat boy whom Jax had previously pointed out to me was standing in front of Annia, looking down at her. His arms were folded across his chest and I could see the hint of an erection beneath his swimming trunks.

"Hey," he repeated.

Annia looked up at him, squinting in the dim light.

"I want you," he said, his hands jerking on to his waist.

Annia opened her mouth, but it was Jax's voice I heard: "She's not going with you."

The fat boy peered at Jax. "Oh?" he said. "Who says so?"

"I do."

The boy crouched with surprising swiftness. "Do *you* say so?" he asked Annia.

"Yes. I don't want to go with you."

"She's below majority," I said.

Annia glared at me, as if by explaining I had compromised her dignity.

"A virgin, eh?" the boy said. "That's even better."

"She doesn't want you." There was an edge of anger in Jax's voice. His dark body was tensed, as if he was about to spring to his feet.

"How would you stop me taking her if I wanted to?"

"There's two of us."

"Two of you," the boy said scornfully. "Two kids. Think that'll be enough?" He straightened, his fists clenched.

Jax rose slowly and moved between Annia and the boy.

"Get a steward," he told her, but she didn't move.

Suddenly the fat boy swung at him. Jax ducked, evading the punch, and butted him in the stomach. The fat boy lost his footing on the wet tiles and crashed to the floor. Jax turned away, but before he could register his triumph, from behind a pillar there appeared another boy, his right forearm tattooed with an ornate letter K, who leapt upon him and forced him to the ground.

I could see that Annia was about to move to Jax's aid. I sprang forward, grabbed a handful of the boy's hair, and tugged back his head. In the periphery of my vision I could see the fat boy stumbling to his feet. Before I could turn, he jumped on my back, dragging me away. He was much heavier than me, and, pinning my arms to my chest with one hand, he began hitting me in the face with the other. I writhed and twisted beneath him, avoiding some of his blows, sometimes flinching as red pain blazed across my face. With a great effort I thrust him away and began to rise, but he was already preparing to launch a kick into my face.

Just then Annia came between us, approaching the boy with her arms limp at her sides and a resigned smile on her face, as if she was offering herself to him. Surprised by this, he paused momentarily, and Annia knotted her right hand and punched him in the testicles. He shrieked with pain and staggered back, bent double. With a gentle push, Annia sent him tumbling into the water.

I looked around. Jax and the tattooed boy were rolling on the tiles, trading punches. Jax was short but stockily built; what he lacked in seasons he made up for in physical strength and the tattooed boy was finding him difficult to subdue. I was about to add my weight to the struggle when two tall, white-uniformed stewards burst through the crowd of onlookers who had gathered around us.

We were taken to the office of the pool manager, a bald, muscular man whose physical presence I immediately found intimidating. He sat behind a dark blue polypropylene desk, the deep V of his shirt revealing a chest thickly matted with hair. The stewards seated us on metal stools, Annia, Jax and I to the manager's right, the two older boys to his left.

The manager inspected each of us in turn, then rested his elbows on the edge of the desk.

"Who will speak first?"

Cautiously we eyed our opponents. The fat boy was still screwed up with pain, his hands covering his crotch. The tattooed boy looked calm and unafraid; he gazed at us with ill-disguised malice.

The fat boy looked up imploringly at the manager.

"I'm hurt," he moaned.

"Fetch Mauris," the manager told the steward who was standing at the door. The steward exited.

"Well, who will speak?"

"It was not our doing," Jax said. He indicated the injured boy. "He wanted intercourse with Annia."

"And you refused?" he asked her.

"Yes."

"She has not reached majority," I explained. "We were defending her right to remain inviolate."

"You are from the High Valleys?" he asked, correctly assessing our accents.

"Silver Spring commune," I told him.

The tattooed boy murmured inaudibly.

The manager turned to him. "We have not heard your side of the story."

"It was two on to one. Three if you count the girl. I was helping to make it equal odds."

"Three on to one? How old are you?"

"Nineteen."

"And you?" he asked the fat boy.

"Eighteen."

To us: "And you three are all under majority?"

"Yes," said Jax.

"And you consider that equal odds?" he asked the tattooed boy.

"Harri wanted the girl. If she had gone with him there would have been no trouble."

"Come here," the manager said sharply.

Reluctantly, the boy rose and went over to the desk. The manager's hand suddenly shot across the desk-top and grabbed his wrist.

"Now I am many seasons older than you," he said, squeezing. "How does it feel to be bullied?"

The boy gritted his teeth but did not reply. The manager squeezed harder. "How does it feel?"

He was visibly in pain now. "It hurts."

The manager released his grip and ordered him to sit down. At this point the steward returned with the doctor who knelt beside the fat boy and removed his hand from the injured area. He slipped his own hand into the fat boy's shorts and prodded his groin in several places; the fat boy winced and looked up at us in pain and embarrassment.

"No permanent damage," the doctor announced. "The pain will ease in a few hours. Try soaking it in cold water."

I bit my tongue to stop myself laughing. The doctor left and the manager addressed the steward: "Their birth numbers."

The steward took each of us in turn by the right ear, pulling back the lobe to reveal the eight-figured numerals impressed on the underside. These he called out to the manager who duly wrote them down.

This done, he said to the fat boy: "You are aware that it is illegal to seek intercourse with someone below the age of majority? Was it not explained to you at your own ceremony?"

The fat boy shrugged but said nothing.

"I'm aware that youth delights in flaunting tradition," the manager said. "But not in *this* establishment. What you do privately is your own business, although I would suggest that you would be better served if you told your warden of your difficulties in finding partners of your own age."

"I've had plenty my own age," the fat boy said indignantly. "I thought the girl was toying with me."

The manager dismissed this lie with a contemptuous glance.

"I cannot allow this sort of unruly behaviour at the baths," he said. "Consequently, you two are hereby banned from all pools in the city for the space of one season. Should subsequent inquiries reveal that you have violated this ban, I will personally make arrangements to have you brought before a sub-adult court on charges of attempted rape."

The two boys were obviously stung by the severity of their punishment, for it was exile indeed to be denied access to the pools.

The manager turned to us. "I am satisfied that on this occasion you three were victims of an unprovoked assault, and therefore I do not propose to penalize you. However, your birth numbers have been noted, and should you be involved in any similar disturbances during the next season then you, too, will suffer the same penalty. Is that clear?"

We nodded numbly, our sense of victory muted by the conditional nature of our acquittal.

Released from the baths, we decided that a prudent retreat would be advisable in case the two older boys were harbouring thoughts of revenge. We hurried away down the narrow sidestreets, pausing at each turn to ensure that we were not being followed. At length we reached the river bank and flopped breathless on to a promenade bench. Annia hugged Jax and me, inspecting our battle scars with some relish. Jax's lower lip was swollen and my left eye was bruised.

"My brave warriors!" she cried, kissing the tender spots.

"You struck the fatal blow," I observed with a grin.

She laughed. "It will be days before he is able to go chasing girls again." She hung her arms over our shoulders. "What a team we make!"

Our exertions had left us hungry and we stopped at a stall and bought pies and bread rolls to supplement the fruit and hard-boiled eggs which we had in our pouches. When our hunger was appeased we wandered down the promenade until we came to a saloon where we knew from past experience the proprietor was no respecter of youth. We took a table in a secluded corner of the forecourt. Annia went inside and presently emerged with a carafe of rice wine. While we drank it, we recounted our experiences at the baths, exaggerating them disgracefully as the wine fired our imaginations. We left the saloon with giddy heads and bright eyes.

We hired bicycles and rode eastwards along the river bank. The Tamus was at ebb-tide, broad stretches of glistening black mud being visible on both banks. Here and there a yacht adorned the waters. To our left were the red-roofed villas of the rich which stared grandly out on to the river, ivy clinging to their walls and lush green shrubbery visible through the arched entranceways. Annia was captivated by the villas and I was intrigued by the variety of purely decorative plants in the gardens. In the High Valleys we cultivated only what could be eaten or sold.

We crossed Estuary Bridge and rode southwards along the old concrete causeway which ran parallel to the shore. Jax had wanted to continue eastwards to the harbour so that he could inspect the trawlerfoils, but Annia and I had indulged his passion for boats on previous occasions and he was outvoted.

About two kilometres south of the river the causeway veered towards the beach and our path was blocked by the perimeter fence. We dismounted and went down to the fence, thrusting our fingers through the wire-mesh and staring out at the glittering blue-grey ocean. It was a cloudless afternoon and the distant horizon was barely distinguishable from the sky. Two women were wandering along the beach scooping speckled jellyfish into leather sacks with long-handled, flat-bladed instruments. Their activities mystified us; were they attempting to clear the beaches so that they could be opened to the public? It seemed unlikely, for the coastal waters were infested with the creatures and such piecemeal efforts would make no impression whatsoever. There was something furtive about their movements which suggested that their activities were illicit. When their sacks were full, they went down to the water's edge and launched a small rowing boat. They set off in a southerly direction and were soon lost to sight around the curve of the coast.

We sat down on the crest of a dune, facing the ocean. Annia traced patterns in the sand with her foot and invited us to guess what she was drawing. Jax prodded a nest of sand-ants with a piece of fence-wire. The twin suns hung vast and golden over the city to our backs, and a cooling breeze blew off the water, tempering the late afternoon heat.

I suddenly found myself thinking that this was a precious moment which I would always look back on with fondness. I wanted to grasp the entire scene in my mind's eye, to make a mental photograph of it, absorbing every image so that it would forever be imprinted on my memory: colours, pos-tures, contours, light and shade, the smell of the air, the pressure of the breeze on my face, the grainy sand beneath my palms. I felt compelled to record everything in as much detail as possible; yet even as I did so, the idea struck me as strange, for it seemed that I was less involved in experiencing the present than in shaping a fragment of the future— ossifying experience into memory even as it occurred.

On the return journey we rode three abreast, discussing what we should do next. Various possibilities were consid-ered: a trip to the theatre to see a mime-play; a visit to Monmouth Stadium to watch the soccer tournament; a return to the saloon for further bottles of wine. We could not decide. We had done all these things on previous visits and we wanted to try something new. Usually, when there was no consensus, we let Annia choose, but she was comparatively silent, and made no suggestions.

Surrendering our bicycles, we wandered back towards the city centre. A militia man stood at the head of Roanoke Drive, diverting traffic. A suction-cleaner was at work, thrumming down the road, drawing dust from the choked gutters into the vents along its flanks. A gaggle of young children ran in its wake, yelling with glee as a mist of water sprayed over them from the rear of the vehicle.

"Let's visit a dream parlour," Annia said.

I didn't like this idea. Erik, one of our wardens, mistrusted the parlours, claiming that they had been built under M'threnni orders to subvert human minds. Although I was sure that this was nonsense, I felt nonetheless that there must be a good reason for his censure.

"Well, David?" Jax said.

"We aren't old enough," I said.

"We could still get in."

"What about money? We don't have enough."

"It's a public holiday," Annia said. "Admission prices have been reduced."

"I don't know. Erik warned us not to go near them."

"Who's going to tell him?" Jax said.

"Come on," Annia said. "Let's give it a try."

I took out my purse. "I've only got seventeen checks."

Annia and Jax emptied theirs. They had worked longer and harder in the fields than I and had earned more money. Between us we had seventy-seven checks.

The Vista Dream Parlour was a large establishment in an arcade off Columbia Street. Entrance prices had been reduced from sixty to twenty-five checks and there was a queue of about twenty people outside the door. Most of the people were from the poor quarters of the city, their faces thin and etched with weariness.

We took our places at the end of the line. Annia released the clasp on her pony-tail, letting her blonde hair fall about her shoulders. It had the desired effect: she looked two or three seasons older than she was. Jax and I leaned against the wall with an affected casualness, but no one took any notice of us and within a half-hour we were at the entrance.

The doorman sat in a cubicle to the left of the turnstile, looking dishevelled and bored. Annia put four columns of coins on to the counter, mostly five-check pieces, and said: "Three, please."

The doorman scooped the money away without counting it and gave us only the most perfunctory of glances before releasing the lock on the turnstile.

We stood in a lobby at the head of a long, dimly lit corridor interspersed on both sides by an irregular series of doors. The walls were painted a dour brown; the doors cream. Street-dust littered the sallow parquet-tiled floor, and the air smelt faintly of stale sweat.

"You are all together?"

The question, delivered in a harsh, resonant tone, came from a speaker in the centre of the ceiling.

"Yes," said Annia.

"Your age?"

"Sixteen seasons."

"This is your first admittance?"

"Yes."

"Your names and birth numbers please."

Annia winked at us, then gave the names and numbers of three dorm-mates who had recently attained majority. Jax grinned back, enjoying the game; I prepared to bolt for the exit.

"Cubicle fourteen," the voice said.

We went down the corridor and found the appropriate door (both numerals were missing but we could see their imprint). The cubicle was small and unadorned. Three metal couches stood along one wall, and above each was a hemispherical headpiece connected to an instrument panel set high on the wall.

"Please lie down on the couches and put the headpieces on," the voice directed us in its neutered, expressionless tones.

I took the middle couch, Annia the one to my right, Jax the one to my left. I pulled the headpiece down. It was too large for me, but some inner band of metal contracted until it fitted me snugly.

"Please close your eyes and relax," the voice said.

Already the neon globe at the centre of the ceiling was dimming.

I squeezed my eyes shut and tried to compose myself. The headpiece began to exude a subtle vibration which at first increased my uneasiness. But then the tension ebbed away to be replaced by feelings of warmth and security. I wanted to look at Annia and Jax, but it was too much trouble to open my eyes or turn my head. I felt languid, drowsy; my thoughts blurred, began to dissipate . . .

I floated in a sea of pearly mist, like a disembodied swimmer moving through deep water. I had no impression of physical presence; I was a spirit, restless, searching. After a time, the mist before me began to thin and I saw two dim, naked figures. One was a man, the other a woman, and they stood, hands clasped, shrouded in a vaporous haze so that their features could not clearly be discerned. I had the impression that I knew them, yet simultaneously I was aware that I had never seen them before.

They opened their arms to me and smiled.

"Welcome, child," they said in unison. "Welcome."

"I greet you," I replied, in words which did not seem to be mine.

"We are pleased to see you."

I was about to reply: "And I you." But this wasn't what I wanted to say, so I pushed the impulse aside and instead asked: "Who are you?" My voice boomed through the mist.

"We are your parents. The givers of the sperm and egg from which you were conceived."

I peered harder, but I could not make out their faces.

"What are your names?"

"We have no names. Father and Mother. Mother and Father." Their speech was slow and precise, as if they were addressing a very small child.

"You must have names," I insisted.

They merely smiled back at me. I felt a desire to approach them, to draw them to me and bury my head in their breasts. I did not move.

"Won't you come to us?" they echoed. The mist played about their faces, continually blurring their features.

I hesitated, then moved fractionally forward. Their faces grew closer, but still they were hazy, as though viewed through frosted glass. Their smiles seemed hollow, devoid of any real emotion.

I drew back.

"Come," they said, beckoning again.

"You are not real."

"You don't believe in us?"

"I cannot *see* you fully!"

"First you must believe."

"No," I said. "You don't exist."

I retreated further and their images receded, grew fainter.

"Come to us," they implored, stretching out their arms.

"You are phantoms," I cried.

The vision dissolved into blackness.

I opened my eyes and looked around me. The cubicle was still in darkness but the instrument panel above my head gave off a bluish glow which enabled me to see Annia. She was still asleep, and a faint smile played on her lips. Jax, too, appeared to be experiencing pleasurable dreams. I removed my headpiece and sat up, waiting for them to wake.

Perhaps fifteen or twenty minutes passed. I was beginning to grow concerned about the safety of my sleeping friends and was about to remove Annia's headpiece when the cubicle began to lighten.

Annia and Jax roused in distinct stages. First they opened their eyes and simply lay there, blinking occasionally. Then they sat up and looked around the cubicle as if they had never seen it before. Gradually they seemed to become aware of their surroundings. They removed their headpieces, peered at me, at one another, smiled. Their movements were measured and tentative, like blindfolk exploring unfamiliar surroundings.

The cubicle was now fully lit, and the voice said: "You may leave."

As I ushered them out, they moved like sleepwalkers, but by the time we had emerged on to the street they seemed fully recovered, though still possessed by a kind of reverential glow.

The alleyway was filled with dusky shadows.

"What time is it?" I asked the doorman.

"Seventeen-thirty," he said without consulting his watch.

A half before sunset! We had lain in the cubicle for the good part of an hour.

"It was wonderful," Annia said, as we hurried along the streets to make our rendezvous at the shuttle terminus. "I met the M'threnni and talked with them. They were just like human beings, only calm and friendly. Their homeworld is covered with forests and lakes and streams.''

"I went fishing,'' Jax announced proudly. "I was the captain of a fleet of trawlerfoils, and we sailed right across the ocean to the Antipodean Isles. My crew were three beautiful women and each of them was so strong they could pull a net in singlehanded.''

"The M'threnni live at the centre of the galaxy,'' Annia said. "At night, the skies of their homeworld are ablaze with stars so it's never dark.''

"I fought with a sea-monster,'' Jax countered. "It rose from the depths but I speared it with a harpoon.''

They exchanged further details of their dreams until my silence became obtrusive.

"What did you see, David?'' Annia asked.

My stomach was hollow. "I saw ghosts.''

"Ghosts?''

"Yes. They were not real, Annia. Your M'threnni, Jax's crew. All dreams conjured up to entertain us. What were the M'threnni called? What were the names of your crew, Jax?''

Jax eyed me curiously. "We *know* they were just figments, David. But it was still fun to dream.''

I bowed my head, embarrassed. Why *was* I so upset? I knew that the parlours merely enhanced fantasies conjured up by the dreamer's mind. Had I expected some great revelation? Had I imagined that hidden truths would be revealed?

"David wears an armour of reason which nothing can penetrate,'' Jax observed wryly.

Annia smiled, and touched me on the arm. "It's a shame you would not let yourself dream, David. Sometimes surrendering to what is not real makes us appreciate more what is.''

The last passengers were boarding the shuttle when we arrived at the terminus. Naree was standing at the foot of the gangway.

"Just in time!'' she called as we approached. She peered closely at us and noticed my black eye and Jax's swollen lip. "What mischief have you been up to?''

We told her the story, hastily but without embellishment. At its conclusion she clapped her hands together.

"Gallant heroes!" she cried. "I wish that I had had two strong men like yourselves to defend me when I was a youth."

Although there was a hint of good-natured raillery in her tone, Jax and I both revelled in her description of us as "strong men."

"I think I should reward you for your bravery," Naree said. "Come closer."

We huddled around her and she began to whisper. "Two of our passengers have decided to extend their stay in Helixport. So, there is a vacant seat for the return journey. Do you think the three of you could squeeze into it?"

We nodded eagerly.

As soon as we were airborne, we undid the seatbelt and pressed our faces against the window. All our previous visits to Helixport had been made in the enclosed hold, and now, for the first time, we were able to see the city stretched out beneath us, its roofs and towers tinged gold by the dusklight. As we passed over the river, we gazed in wonder at the alien freighter terminus on Round Island, dominated by the white spiral tower of the M'threnni which had presided over the city since its birth and in whose honour the city had been named. There the mysterious aliens resided, hidden from human eyes. It was the first time we had had a clear view of the tower, and we stared at it as if we would never see it again. Little did I realize that before too long both the tower and the aliens would loom large in my life.

The shuttle banked over the Tamus estuary, passing above Needle Point, the southern lip of the rivermouth, then bisected the harbour which nestled under the hooked nose of the northern coastline. We headed inland, westwards over the hinterland plain. Soon the land of the cereal farmers lay beneath us: fields of green, fields of cream, fields of brown, a great mosaic of fields, crossed by canals and dotted with commune buildings.

Darkness was falling rapidly, and by the time the shuttle

had begun to climb the foothills of the Low Valleys, only the gleaming thread of the Tamus and the occasional solitary light burning atop the entrance to a dorm building could be seen.

I dozed sporadically, sometimes waking when the shuttle stopped to disgorge passengers. A litany of names flittered through my half-conscious mind: Dulcet, East Bend, Camden Heights, New Kentucky, Dennerton, White Mountain, Milesville. The shuttle continued to climb, zigzagging up the valleys. Finally I heard Naree say: "Silver Spring. Last call."

She was addressing the three of us, for all the other passengers had debarked at previous stops.

Annia and Jax were both sound asleep. I shook them gently and said: "We're home."

Chapter Two

The toll of the morning bell drew me from sleep. Caril was moving down the central aisle, swinging the bell with a deft movement of her wrist, as if she was brushing dust from the air. I stumbled from bed, still feeling tired; it had been well past midnight when we had arrived back at the dorm and I had had less than ten hours' sleep. Wearily, I pulled on my shirt, watching as Caril stopped at Tim's bed opposite and tapped her bell against the metal headrest. Tim, who would sleep all day if given the opportunity, sat bolt upright with a start.

"Dawn," said Caril with her gentle, mocking smile.

Jax had already departed for the dining-room. I tidied my bed and went after him. I could not see Annia amongst the stragglers who were emerging from the girls' sleeping quarters, but when I arrived at the dining-hall I saw that she was sitting next to Jax and that they had reserved a seat for me.

Over breakfast I was morose and uncommunicative; the prospect of spending the morning labouring in the fields was distinctly unappetizing after the delights of Helixport. Annia too, seemed somewhat subdued, whereas Jax was as boundless in energy as ever, attacking his food with gusto and

giving everyone within earshot a detailed and glamorized
account of our battle with the two boys at the baths. No one
else in junior dorm had ever visited Helixport, and they
always greeted Jax's tales with a mixture of awe and rever-
ence. He painted a picture of a city filled with thieves, rogues
and bullies, and it is little wonder that the younger members
of the dorm regarded him (and, to a lesser extent, Annia and
me) with the admiration one would afford to an explorer of
strange lands. His swollen lip and my bruised eye added an
extra touch of drama and veracity to his tale on this occasion.

As much as I disliked working in the fields, I was glad
when breakfast was over and we dispersed into the compound. I went down to the perimeter fence and looked up the
valley towards the snow-capped peaks of the Crescent Mountains. A veil of mist was retreating up the mountainsides
under the ripening heat of the suns, revealing the chequered,
sun-bleached fields and plantations. Olives, russets and
golds predominated, the colours of our Summer fruit crops.
In Autumn, when all the oranges and butterfruit had been
harvested, the darker shades of red and brown prevailed as
berries and vine plants cloaked the hillsides. During Winter,
when rainstorms harried the valley, the fields lay ash-brown
and fallow, and our work was primarily maintenance: tend-
ing seedlings in the cloistered, humid atmosphere of the
hothouses; spreading fertilizer; collecting water for storage in
the cisterns. In Spring we would plant root-crops and
legumes, and the valley would blossom with a hesitant
greenness before Capella sucked the soil dry once more.

"Gather! Everybody gather!"

Erik had emerged from the dormitory and was crossing the
compound, clapping his hands together. He was a short,
overweight man, his burgeoning girth the subject of much
surreptitious humour amongst the youth of the dorm. He
stood at the centre of the compound, waiting for the knots of
children to disperse and reassemble into five ragged lines,
according to their season. Erik and Caril had been wardens at
junior dorm for over four cycles. I preferred Caril to him, for

she was gentler and more appreciative of the individual, but he treated everyone fairly and was no ogre.

I joined the tail of the senior line which had formed next to the gate. Erik waited until everyone had stopped fidgeting and utter silence prevailed.

Whenever I look back on my childhood, my principal memory is of how regimented commune life was. In primary dorm we were once required to write an essay on growing up in Silver Spring, and I still recall the text which I produced: "Babies are brought from the city," I wrote, "and grown in the nursery until they are five. Then they go to primary dorm until they are eleven. Then they go to junior dorm until they are sixteen and have majority. They stay in senior dorm until they are twenty and made into adults."

I think I anticipated my discontent in that succinct and unconsciously damning paragraph. The dorm system, with its wardens specially trained to meet the needs of the age-group of which they have charge, was originally established to ensure a speedy growth in population following the initial colonization of Gaia. It is not a harsh system, but, being tailored to the needs of the community at large, it is not conducive to individual growth. Caril and Erik regularly had charge of eighty to ninety children, and Silver Spring is one of the smaller communes in the High Valleys. In Helixport, smaller units of around thirty children are favoured, and greater freedom of expression is encouraged. In defence of the communes, though, it must be said that the valley settlements are relatively impoverished compared with the city, and a sturdy childhood discipline is essential to prevent a wholescale migration to the coast.

But apart from my twice-seasonal sorties to the city, at fifteen, commune life was all I knew, and I was quite content to bear the drudgery of the fields in exchange for the camaraderie and sense of belonging which the dorm system provides. It was only on occasions that I resented what seemed to me to be an overzealous insistence on punctilio.

"I hope you are all rested after your holiday," Erik said at last. "Rested and refreshed." He rubbed his pudgy hands together. "But relaxation is like sleep. If we have too much, we want more, and we become slothful."

"If we eat too much, we become fat," Meryl, who was standing in front of me, murmured.

"So let us tackle our tasks with renewed vigour in this second half of Summer," Erik was saying. "Today we begin harvesting the butterfruit crop." He smiled broadly, as if this was some pronouncement which should cause us great delight.

"Hooray," said someone, with a studied lack of enthusiasm.

Erik took a notebook from the breast-pocket of his shirt and proceeded to give us our field allocations. Annia, Jax and I had been assigned one of the smaller plantations on the slopes below the Provisions Centre (the one concession which the commune planners allowed their youth was the freedom to work with one's friends). We departed, Jax leading the way down the mountainside, treading a sinuous path through the denuded, thorn-strewn terraces of the roseplum briars, dun-brown and sere in the sunlight.

For the next six hours we laboured in the ever-increasing heat, plucking the golden fruit from their stalks and dropping them delicately into bamboo baskets until our backs ached with a leaden, unlocalized pain and our hands were sticky with juice. The ripe fruit was extremely tender and would easily rupture under finger pressure; no matter how careful we were, we invariably ended up with at least half a basket of spoiled fruit, most of which was used for fodder.

Jax moved with a seemingly inexhaustible energy along the rows of plants, stripping them of their fruit with such adriotness that he filled two baskets to every one of mine. Jax possessed the happy capacity to adapt to any physical task, however odious, with a good humour and a desire to excel. Annia worked more slowly—she disliked fruit-picking as much as I did—but she was quietly efficient and uncomplaining. I found it impossible to concentrate my full attention on my work. Sometimes my thoughts would wander so that I would imagine myself back in Helixport, ploughing through the cool waters of the Dome Baths; sometimes I would watch the bees gathering at the spoils baskets, attracted by the sweet, oleaginous aroma of the bruised fruit; sometimes I would engage Annia and Jax in feckless conversation as a pretext to temporarily stop work; sometimes I would simply sit beneath the glossy bronze-green foliage, making no attempt to disguise my boredom and my distaste for fruit-picking.

I always followed the progress of Capella across the skies and became adept at judging when she was nearing zenith from the oblateness of the twin shadow of my outstretched arm. Zenith meant release from the fields, a retreat to the coolness of the dining-room. A bell would ring, at first distantly, hardly perceived, then drawing closer as Erik or Caril moved through the fields summoning everyone to midmeal. The morning bell, that rude interrupter of dreams, was a vexation, but the zenith bell was always music to my ears.

That morning Erik approached from the upper slopes. Since we were working close to the stream we were among the last to be summoned, and I had been anticipating the bell for over ten minutes before I actually heard it. Hurriedly we gathered our baskets together and awaited his arrival. I had filled only six baskets compared with Annia's ten and Jax's thirteen—they constantly outdid me in their labours—but by the time Erik had reached us, Jax had transferred two of his baskets to me so that the evidence of my sloth was not so blatant.

Although he walked at a moderate pace, Erik was red-faced and breathless when he arrived. He surveyed our baskets and made an entry in his notebook. He indicated that we could leave, but as we collected our towels and water-bottles, he said to me: "Not you, David. I want to speak with you."

Annia and Jax departed, casting curious, knowing glances at me. Erik upturned two empty baskets and invited me to sit down. He put the bell between his legs, unconsciously creating the effect of an artificial phallus.

"How did you get that?" he asked, indicating my bruised eye.

"Just an accident," I said.

He frowned, but evidently decided not to press the matter.

"It is almost five seasons since you entered junior dorm," he said, dabbing at his sweat-filmed brow with a striped rag cut from an old pillowcase. "As you may know, when we receive a new nursery intake from the incubators in Helix-port, the authorities provide us with a list of conception dates. It is commune policy to conduct majority ceremonies on the very day an individual reaches his or her sixteenth season."

I nodded; already, in the first six months of Summer, half of our season-mates had left for senior dorm, and Annia, Jax and I had been on tenterhooks throughout sixth month, afraid that one of us would be called away to majority before our final visit to the city. Luck had been with us.

Erik took a small white plastic card from the buttoned waist-pocket of his shirt and passed it to me:

HEREWITH NOTIFICATION THAT ON
8.7 SUMMER 29
A MAJORITY CEREMONY ON BEHALF OF
DAVID 52211419 SILVER SPRING COMMUNE
WILL BE HELD IN THE CENTRAL COUNCIL
HALL AT 0230 HOURS

"The majority ceremony represents formal recognition that one has passed beyond childhood," Erik was saying. "You must be prepared from now on to shed the frivolities of youth and begin to accept the responsibilities of maturity. It is a time of transition, perhaps the most important time of your life."

Erik said the words by rote; it was obviously his standard speech. He folded the rag into quarters and slipped it into his breast pocket.

"Are you nervous?" he asked.

"I don't know," I replied, though in truth my only feeling

was that of satisfied curiosity: I now knew my precise date of conception.

"Have you decided on your choice of vocation for the future?"

"I didn't think we were allowed a choice."

"It is true that the elders reserve final judgment, but part of the purpose of the ceremony is to ascertain for what duties one might best be fitted. If you have a preference for something, they will try to accommodate you."

This hardly seemed a concession; the choices were limited. Although accession to senior dorm generally meant a release from fruit-picking, the duties were still primarily manual: sorting and packing fruit; planting seedlings; extending areas of cultivation, and so on. Nothing of this nature appealed to me.

"Most youths of your age have already discovered their interests," Erik said. "Surely you must have some ambition?"

I stared hard at the ground, pretending to think.

"No," I said finally. "I don't know what I want to do."

"Between now and the day of your ceremony I suggest you give the matter some serious consideration. It is far better to be assigned to some task which you find only moderately interesting than something which you actively dislike."

Annia and Jax both congratulated me on my forthcoming ceremony, but there was a hint of sadness in their reactions which was echoed in my own feelings. Although there was no reason why we should not remain close friends when I left for senior dorm (after all, they would be joining me there before the end of the season), we all sensed that we had reached a watershed in our relationship, that somehow things would never be the same again. We had become close friends in our first season at junior dorm, and the dorm itself was central to us. By leaving it, we risked destroying the nexus, the foundation on which our friendship rested. At the time, of course, none of us was capable of understanding or articulating these feelings, but they manifested themselves as a vague apprehension nonetheless.

The next six days passed slowly. I busied myself in the fields, doubling my usual quota in a burst of activity designed to stave off thought. Although I knew that the majority ceremony was little more than a formality to mark one's ascent from childhood to adolescence, a prelude to the attainment of full adulthood at twenty, I nonetheless grew increasingly nervous as the appointed time drew near. The physical activity of the fields was a blessing at this time, and I volunteered for extra field duty in the evenings—much to the surprise of Caril and Erik. Morning and afternoon work was compulsory and unpaid, but evening harvesting carried the lure of a one check per hour payment; Annia, Jax and I had subsidized our visits to the city in this way.

In the classroom over zenith I was restless and unable to concentrate on my lessons. The dim, humid atmosphere and the droning voices of our tutors was oppressive. In the past I had excelled at schoolwork, adept at mathematics and abstract theory, intrigued by the principles underlying plant hybridization and soil management, keen to learn all I could of our history on Gaia. Jax, averse to all things academic, often relied on my help to complete the written assignments which were periodically given; in this way I repaid the debt I owed him for his help in the fields. But the prospect of the ceremony now loomed before me, obliterating all my attempts at concentration. The truth was that I did not want to leave junior dorm.

I completed the construction of my telescope two days after our return from Helixport and was given permission to mount it on the roof of the dorm. One afternoon during zenith I focused on Lesser Capella, and, using a rectangle of white plastic to display the image, observed the transit of one of the minor suns across its face, a black spot embedded in a brilliant golden sphere. After sunset, Annia and Jax joined me on the roof and we surveyed the planetary bodies of our solar system: Argus, our nearest neighbour, shrouded in dense, bluish-white clouds; Tyche, the seventh planet of our system, a mottled, olive-brown globe; Hecate, the distant gas-giant, a huge grey-green world, hostile and forbidding.

Jax had little interest in astronomy, but Annia was fascinated by the amount of detail which was visible through the crude instrument, blurred and tinged with spectral hues though the images were. The next day I borrowed the *Star Atlas* from the library and that night I focused on Sol, our ancestral sun, the central jewel in the constellation of The Crown. It was an unremarkable star, a flickering gold-white point of light somewhat dimmer than its neighbours.

At last the day of the ceremony arrived. I watched my dorm-mates leave for the fields and for once I longed to accompany them. Caril was with me and she seemed to sense my disquiet. She kissed me lightly on the forehead and said: "It will soon be time. We must prepare."

I took a long bath and put on a clean shirt and shorts. I combed my hair, brushed my teeth and drew patterns in the misted mirror with my finger until Caril called me. She had discarded her shirt and pants for a long white robe, belted at the waist. She looked radiant and serene, like a figure from a dream. Then, as if to dispel this impression, she burped loudly and winked at me. I grinned and followed her out into the bright morning sunlight.

We crossed the arched stone footbridge and began to climb the asphalt pathway which wound up the northern face of the valley to the white stuccoed council building which stood aloof and imposing on the upper slopes. As we climbed I looked backwards down the hillside to where my dorm-mates were toiling in the fields, crouched white figures amidst the foliage. Suddenly I was glad that I was ascending the mountain rather than grubbing in the dusty earth.

"Come," Caril called. She was beginning to outpace me and I quickened my stride.

My body was prickly with heat by the time we reached the hall, but the vestibule was cool and I lay back against the stone walls and closed my eyes. I felt peculiarly composed, even eager for the ceremony to begin.

I had expected some delay, but minutes after we arrived, Philip, the elders' secretary, emerged and informed us that we should enter.

The austerity of the hall surprised me. It was a simple stone chamber, unadorned except for the commune symbol, the letter S embellished in silver on the chimney flue. The sunlight, entering through the chamfered windows, laid a series of bright rectangles along the concrete floor. The elders— there were over twenty present—sat at a long mustard-coloured table in front of the empty fireplace, all dressed in white robes, all looking curiously alike, their faces dark and sun-seamed. Facing them was a single, empty chair. I had always supposed that the council hall would reek of grandeur and ancientness, whereas it seemed empty and impersonal, a place where people meet but do not linger.

Caril led me forward and sat me down on the chair. She stood behind me and rested her hands on my shoulders.

The elder Robert, seated at the centre of the table, addressed me:

"You are David 52211419?"

I nodded, puzzled; Robert knew me well.

"Please reply."

"Yes. I am David."

"Caril?"

"I confirm," Caril said.

"You are aware of the purpose of this ceremony?" Robert asked.

"Yes."

"You have now reached the age of majority, sixteen seasons. To achieve majority is to begin the transition from youth to adulthood. From now on, no longer will your deeds and misdeeds be judged as would a child's; no longer will you be cosseted by your wardens. You will be expected to behave as a responsible individual whose main objective is to carve out a permanent and fitting role in society. Therefore, much of this ceremony will take the form of an evaluation of your potential and a consideration of how your talents may best be employed for the benefit of the community at large. Is this clear to you?"

"Yes." Robert had merely reiterated more solemnly what Erik had told me.

"Very well." He paused to scratch the back of his neck, then said: "Tell me what you know of the economic basis of our commune."

Thus began a series of questions which were designed to test my knowledge of all aspects of commune life. Practically all the elders posed at least one question. Arthur was concerned with agronomics and the search for suitable hybrids which would improve soil fertility by fixing atmospheric nitrogen; Guy concentrated his questions on the financial aspects of trade between the communes and the city; Leah was particularly interested in the historical factors which had determined the present social order; Rila went even further back, asking me what I knew of Earth. I answered all their questions as well as my memory allowed but it was difficult to judge whether my responses were satisfactory, for the elders would merely nod at the end of each and jot down notes on the pads before them. Only Pamila, sitting stooped and wizened to my far left, inquired as to how *I* felt about commune life. I replied that I could find no cause for complaint. There were no further questions.

Robert studied some papers on the table in front of him.

"I have here your manual and academic records," he said. "Your performance in the fields is not good. Your daily quotas have been well below average—" he peered at me over the top of the sheet "—despite surreptitious help from your friends. Do you deny this?"

I shook my head; everyone knew that the wardens deliberately overlooked the basket-swapping designed to equalize quotas, but they were obviously aware of the capacity of each worker.

"Do you have any explanations?" Robert asked.

"No."

"Then you accept that your labours have been below standard?"

"Yes."

He seemed surprised by my admission. Well, I thought, it was true. I did not accomplish as much in the fields as my dorm-mates.

"Do you have no regrets about this?" Rila asked.

"I am sorry that I could not fulfil quotas," I told her. "But it was not through laziness that I failed."

"Then why?"

"I don't know. I dream a lot in the fields."

"Dream?" said Robert. "Of what?"

"Just daydreams. When it gets very hot, I dream of cool water and the night. I get bored in the fields."

To my surprise, Robert did not treat this admission with the distaste I had expected.

"It may be that you are simply not suited to manual duties," he said. He referred again to the papers before him. "Were you aware that your record at tutorials was also being monitored?"

"No," I replied, though this was not strictly true. Periodically we were given written tests, and while the results were never released, I had often suspected that they were used as an indicator of academic progress.

"Then I can inform you that you have attained consistently high grades in all aspects of your classwork."

I was unable to hide my pleasure. Pamila returned my smile, and I felt the gentle pressure of Caril's fingers on my shoulders in surreptitious acknowledgement of my success.

"Furthermore," Robert continued, "the quality of your studies so impressed your tutors that they submitted your reports to the Institute of Higher Education in Helixport. The Institute has since confirmed that your studies have reached an acceptable level for admission to their preliminary course currently in progress. Should you wish to attend the Institute and should you then execute your studies to the satisfaction of your lecturers, you will be given the opportunity to enrol in a more advanced course of study lasting three seasons and ultimately leading to a Certificate in Advanced Studies in the subject of your choosing."

I was dumbfounded. Each season the Institute accepted no more than twenty students from the High Valleys, and it was sixteen seasons since Silver Spring had last provided a candidate.

I looked at Pamila, who was one of my tutors and who had attended the Institute herself perhaps fifty seasons before. Had she arranged for my work to be forwarded to the Institute? Her smile told me that she had had some part in it.

"Do you understand what I am saying?" Robert asked. "The Institute is prepared to offer you a scholarship."

Still I sat mute. It was inconceivable. I had always been aware of my aptitude for schoolwork, but I had never imagined that I was capable of producing work of sufficient quality to interest the foremost educational establishment in Gaia.

"Are you prepared to accept the offer, or do you wish to consider it for a day or so?"

"No. I mean, yes. I accept."

The rest of that day remains in my memory only as an after-image following a sudden flash of blinding light. I dined with the elders, a sumptuous meal of roast chicken, vegetables and sweetcorn, followed by a mélange of cheese, red peppers and soya beans, then a fruit salad drenched in honey, and finally sweetmeats and minted ice confection to finish. I was sated. The elder Arthor suffered from a digestive imbalance and his stomach rumbled vociferously throughout the meal, although he insisted on sampling each course. His discomfort was the subject of some levity amongst the elders, and for the first time I saw them as ordinary human beings rather than remote, imposing figureheads.

Later, when the effects of the meal had subsided somewhat, I was taken to the surgery, subjected to a rigorous physical examination, then left alone in a tiny room furnished only with a bed. A senior girl from a neighbouring commune came to me and we spent several hours together while she instructed me in the art of lovemaking. This, my first exploration of the secrets of the female body, was an event I had long anticipated, and yet it seemed merely a postscript to a far greater revelation: I was going to the city to live!

Afterwards I returned to the hall and was presented with my majority card, a hand-sized rectangle of plastic similar to that which had announced my impending ceremony, only pale green and filled with encoded information. The cards, though seldom used, contained the necessary legal proof of one's status.

"You have been presented with a rare and special opportunity to further yourself," Robert told me. "At the Institute you will receive the finest education which Gaia can offer. Do not let this chance slip by. Embrace what knowledge and experiences you can. Reflect on them and learn from them so that when you attain full adulthood you will be ready to use your skills for the benefit of others."

The other elders filed out from behind the table and I passed along their ranks, engaging each of them in the archaic handshaking ritual of our ancestors. Pamila, at the end of the line, gripped my hand with especial vigour and whispered: "You'll do us credit."

The day had passed swiftly. Leaving the hall, I saw that it would soon be sunset. Only the isolated worker was still abroad in the fields, and deep shadows were spreading down the valley. I found Annia and Jax at our favourite hide-out, a gaunt outcrop of white rock overlooking the Communications Centre. They were tossing stones on to the corrugated roof and ducking from sight whenever Lenard, the radio officer, emerged from the building. I squatted beside them, breathless after my climb, and they assailed me with questions. I told them everything of my ceremony, reserving the news of my scholarship to the Institute until last.

"Apparently I did well in class," I said, unsure of whether to sound pleased or solemn. "My work was forwarded to the Institute and they have offered me a place. I've accepted."

For a moment there was silence. Then Annia grinned widely and said: "David, that's marvellous!" She sprang forward and hugged me.

"I'll be sorry to leave you both," I said.

"You have to go." She squeezed my arms. "Just think of it. A chance to live in the city. When do you leave?"

"In five days' time. I have until the end of Summer to prove my worth. If I succeed, I'll be able to enrol for three more seasons to obtain my Certificate."

"I always knew you were a genius," Jax said, tossing a handful of gravel into my lap.

"Hey," I protested, rising to brush the dusty rubble from my hitherto unsoiled shorts. Jax flicked a stone over my head and I heard it skitter on the roof below. Lenard darted out of the building and caught sight of me. He raised his fist and began to ascend the incline.

"He's coming!" I cried, and with a mixture of laughter and panic we scurried off up the slope.

Since I had only five days left at the commune, I had assumed that I would be allowed to stay in junior dorm until I left for the Institute. The following morning, however, I awoke to find that most of my personal effects had already been transferred to senior dorm. I remonstrated with Caril, pleading with her to be allowed to stay amongst my friends. Caril was sympathetic but powerless; she had anticipated my complaints, but had been unable to obtain the necessary permission for the move to be cancelled.

"Tradition takes no account of the individual," she told me sadly. "You must grin and bear it."

After breakfast I was taken to senior dorm and introduced to the warden, Uri.

Uri was a cheerful, effusive man who glibly ignored my sullenness with a ceaseless stream of chatter as he led me around the dorm. The only obvious difference between senior and junior dorm was the partitions between the beds in the sleeping quarters—a concession to privacy which the seniors, free to indulge in sexual gratification, doubtless welcomed. At my own request I was assigned a bed at the end of the dorm, rather than in the middle, as was the normal practice with newcomers. Although I was acquainted with most of the senior youth, I knew none closely, and I saw no point in attempting to cultivate friendships in the short time which remained to me.

I saw little of my dorm-mates in any case. I was excused from further work in the fields to concentrate on my studies. During the next four days I spent over fifty hours in the dim,

sequestered library of the schoolhouse, attended at different
times by all six of the school's tutors.

My lessons focused predominantly on aspects of city life,
an area of study which had received scant attention in normal
classes. I learned of civil ordinance and administration, of the
judicial and executive functions of city law, of commerce, of
the rights of the citizen, of modes of taxation, of traffic
regulations—the list was endless. It was all, I felt, unnecessary. Surely, I protested, I will discover all this when I am
living in Helixport. But my tutors were resolute; I think they
wanted to ensure that I had a good grounding in urban affairs
before I departed so that I would not appear naïve to the
Institute authorities. Each evening I would emerge from the
library like a drunkard from a saloon, my head reeling with a
welter of ill-digested information. I would then rendezvous
with Annia and Jax at our hiding-place.

With my departure imminent, we had abandoned our tradi-
tional pursuits of chasing rock-burrowers or aggravating
Lenard; we simply sat and talked. I cannot remember what
we discussed, although I suspect that we indulged ourselves
in those rambling, quasi-philosophical reflections which are
often the propensity of youth. When the sleep bell finally
tolled and we departed reluctantly for our dorms, I remember
feeling a vague sense of dissatisfaction, as if I was not
making the most of the time I had left with them. At night, a
female or two would come to my bedside, but I turned them
all away; too much else was occupying my mind.

A proctor from the Institute arrived late at night on the
fourth day and I was roused from bed a good two hours before
dawn the following morning and introduced to him. His
name was Rayner and he was a tall, gaunt man of middle age
who spoke little and wore a dour expression.

My tutors scurried to and fro, proudly showing him the
schoolhouse, while the elders gathered for an early breakfast.
The meal was lavish, in keeping with the established custom
of culinary hospitality towards strangers, but our guest was
not happy to be the focal point of the celebrations. Although
he asked me several general questions about my lessons, he

did not seem particularly interested either in the commune or in his prospective student. Strangely enough, I found his impassive manner somewhat comforting; it made the pressure of the occasion easier to bear.

At dawn we stood on the edge of the landing strip, buffeted by waves of air from the descending shuttle. Six elders were present, in addition to Caril and Erik, and Annia and Jax. My stomach was a knot of trepidation as each of the adults embraced me and gave me their good wishes.

Then Jax gripped me by the arm and said gruffly: "Good luck. I wish I was going with you."

He turned and strode off before I could reply, taking the pathway back towards the dorm. Over a cycle would pass before I was to see him again, and under circumstances beyond my wildest imaginings.

Annia approached, carrying a package. She handed it to me, kissed me on both cheeks, and whispered: "We'll visit you."

I said nothing; I could not move. Finally Rayner took my arm and led me towards the shuttle. We walked up the ramp and as we entered the craft the door slid shut behind us with a resounding thud.

Chapter Three

The Institute was a much larger complex than I had envisaged. It lay in the northern suburbs amongst the sprawling estates of the middle-income workers, the main administrative building a pyramidal structure built of yellow sandstone and glass. A maze of classrooms, lecture theatres and laboratories surrounded it, all interconnected by covered walkways. The campus boasted wide stretches of well-watered grass interspersed with shrubs and rock-gardens. Outside the main building a large, black rhombohedron had been mounted on a plinth. It was so dark that it seemed to be sucking in light, a crystalline black hole. Intrigued, I asked Rayner what it was, but he merely replied: ''An artifact.''

The proctor maintained a leisurely pace as he led me around the various departments, expounding at length on their history and function. Soon I was intolerably bored and was grateful when he finally took me to the students' residence hall on the eastern side of the campus and showed me to my room.

The hall was a squat, cylindrical building, four storeys high, and I had been allocated a room on the third floor with a splendid view out over the campus. The room was surprisingly large, containing a desk, a data screen and cassette machine, a large bed, an oddly warped reclining chair, and—best of all—a private bathroom which made the toilet facilities of the commune look primitive.

Rayner gave me the door-key and said: "Dinner is at sixteen-thirty. I will call for you."

Alone, I lay back on the bed and contemplated my surroundings. The entire building was air-conditioned and I luxuriated in the coolness. This was to be my new domain: a white, immaculate chamber, bathed in sunlight, yet sequestered from the outside world. It was in complete contrast to the noisy humidity of junior dorm, and I relished it.

After a while I went out on to the balcony. In the mellow light of evening, groups of students were lounging on the grass, and a gardener attended the flowerbeds in the shadow of the black crystal. Beyond, a thread of smoke drifted lazily into the air from the chimney of one of the laboratories. The whole scene had a tranquil, idyllic quality, a sense of ample time for the accomplishment of objectives, and suddenly I felt very happy. Here was the opportunity to give my life a new direction, at my own pace and to my own design.

I took a long shower, standing under the cold water until my skin was numb, then vigorously towelling myself down until it glowed. I lay back in the reclining chair, but I could find no position of comfort in its warped contours so I abandoned it for the desk chair. Later, I unpacked and mounted my telescope on the desk. Although it was not ideally suited to terrestrial observation, it still enabled me to conduct a fairly detailed visual examination of the neighbourhood. The main north-south highway ran past the entrance to the Institute, although the traffic on it was sparse. Later still, I sat down on the bed with Annia's parting gift to me. It was the latest edition of the *Star Atlas* which I had borrowed from the library, and it was the first book to grace the empty shelves on the wall beside my desk.

The Institute dining-hall, which also doubled as a viewing

theatre and conference room, was filled with people by the time Rayner and I arrived. The air was replete with the babble of voices; everyone sitting at the long tables seemed either to be expostulating at great length on some subject or studiously attentive to the argument while mentally framing a suitable reply.

Rayner led me to a table occupied by several youths the same age as myself. It transpired that they were also preliminary students who were hoping to gain full scholarships at the end of Summer, and they immediately put me at ease with their enthusiasm for the Institute. A girl named Wendi sat opposite me, small of stature, but intense and extroverted. She had a head of curly, jet-black hair, and the darkest eyes I had ever seen.

"You're from the High Valleys," she said.

"Yes."

"Which commune?"

"Silver Spring. You're from Helixport?"

"Not quite. The Plains, although my commune is less than ten kilometres from the outskirts of the city. It's quite suburban."

"How long have you been here?"

"Three months. You'll like it."

"I hope so. Is the work hard?"

"It shouldn't be. After all, we're supposed to be fledgling geniuses, aren't we? Otherwise we wouldn't be here." She grinned. "What's your subject?"

"My subject?"

"What do you want to study?"

"I haven't decided yet."

"Mine's medicine. I hope to become a doctor. Have you just passed majority?"

"Five days ago."

"Were you a virgin? I made love several times before my ceremony."

Embarrassed by her candour, I peered around the table, but no one seemed to be paying particular attention to our conversation.

"Tradition is strong at our commune," I murmured. "You risk punishment if you break the rules."

"I've always wanted to visit the High Valleys. Is it really much cooler up there in the mountains?"

"A little. Mostly at night."

"Do you like mutton?"

"Yes. Why do you ask?"

"It's on the menu tonight. I had a friend once who was allergic to any kind of sheep's meat. She came out in a cold sweat and trembled a lot. Food allergies are quite interesting; they're not very well understood. I'm lucky, I can eat practically anything."

As if in emphasis, she scooped a large spoonful of chilled cucumber soup from the bowl in front of her and swallowed it whole.

"I've forgotten your name," she said.

"David."

"I used to know an old man called David. He travelled around the communes selling herbal remedies. Most of them were just coloured water or perfumed lard, but occasionally he'd come up with something that really worked. He gave me some ointment, once, for a sprain, and it cured it within hours. You have to keep an open mind in everything." She pushed her unfinished soup-bowl aside and turned to the main course which had just been set in front of us. "Do you believe in astrology?"

In this desultory fashion we continued our conversation as we ate. Rayner was called away on some errand before the meal was over, and when Wendi offered to give me an unofficial tour of the campus, I accepted gratefully. I had seen enough of the lugubrious proctor for one day.

As we wandered around the grounds in the fading light, I noticed that the black crystal was emitting a faint, pearly light. Wendi explained that it was some kind of M'threnni art-form which absorbed light during the day and re-emitted it at night. Dusk fell quickly, and the crystal glowed brighter, its ashen light casting a dolesome pall over the grass and flowerbeds. I found the crystal even more eerie and unsettling than Annia's gasglobe. I felt that it had been put on display to satisfy some morbid fascination with the bizarre; it lent a wholly unwelcome strangeness to the arboured landscape.

Wendi showed me the tennis and basketball courts, the golf range, the swimming pool and the gymnasium—facilities which Rayner had not deemed worthy of inspection during my earlier tour. Although the Institute was academically orientated, it evidently did not neglect those of an athletic bent. Following this, she took me to the recreation room in the basement of the residence hall, a long, low-ceilinged chamber, dimly lit and sultry. A small bar sold a variety of drinks, and students sat at rounded tables playing board games (chess, backgammon, merels) or simply talking. Wendi was greeted by several youths, and even as I was being introduced, a glass of wine was being thrust into my hand.

It must have been four or five hours later before we emerged from The Cellar (as it was popularly known). I felt somewhat light-headed after numerous glasses of wine; all evening, drinks had been freely supplied to me by the other students.

"Did I pass the test?" I asked Wendi as we rode upwards in the elevator.

"You did all right. The last fresher was carried out unconscious."

"You could have warned me."

"That would have spoiled it. We have to find out what sort of person you are."

"So, what sort of person am I?"

"I haven't completed my research yet."

When we reached my room, Wendi immediately kicked off her sandals and sat down on the edge of the bed.

"I hate shoes," she told me. "On the farm I always went barefoot."

I sat beside her. "You never got bitten?" I asked, recalling the time when Jax, who also disdained footwear, had inadvertently disturbed a burrower's nest and paid the penalty with a grossly swollen foot.

"Lots of times. But I'm immune to burrower venom." She showed me her feet. A tracery of white scars ringed both her ankles.

"I think they liked the taste of my flesh." She took the *Star Atlas* from the shelf. "Is this good? I never read, apart from course manuals and textbooks."

"I use it to find my way about the skies," I said, pointing to the telescope on the desk-top.

"Oh, you're a star-gazer." She flicked briefly through the pages then closed it. "I had my fortune told the other day. Carl in first grade specializes in it. He plots the positions of the stars and planets at your conception date, and is able to predict from them what the predominant influences in your life are going to be."

"Did you get a favourable prognosis?" I asked, thinking the whole idea silly. We had already had quite a verbal tussle over the merits of astrology at the dinner table, and I think she was trying to bait me again.

"Mixed," she said. "My stars were auspicious for wealth and career, but unsettled emotionally." She put the *Star Atlas* back on the shelf. "Have you ever visited a dream parlour?"

"No," I said, inexplicably.

"It's very interesting. I dreamt I was a bird that went soaring all over Gaia, swooping out over the ocean, then back, far up into the Crescent Mountains until the air was so cold and rare I had to come down again. It was exhilarating. The parlours are very effective in providing a controlled access to one's fantasies."

"I've heard it said that the experience is somewhat hollow, ultimately."

"No, not hollow. A little stage-managed, perhaps, but at least the experience mirrors one's subconscious preoccupations. An easy way to wish-fulfilment."

She rose, went over to the window, and pulled down the blinds. Turning to me, she said: "Shall we make love now?"

She crossed her hands at her waist and pulled her vest over her shoulders. Her shorts fell to the floor at her feet. Stepping out of them, she went over to the reclining chair and her hand reached beneath it. The chair seemed to move subtly, like a piece of pliant plastic, but I immediately dismissed the idea as a quirk of my over-stimulated imagination.

I undressed hastily, tossing my clothes on to the bed, discreetly appraising Wendi's body—the rich, sleek brownness of her skin, the surprising fullness of her breasts, the swell of her stomach, the ebony wedge of hair between her thighs.

I straddled her, placing my arms on her shoulders, and once again the chair seemed to shift slightly, as if deformed by the weight of my body. Before I could react or comment on the effect, however, Wendi slid her arms around me and drew me on to her. Her body rippled beneath me, and this time I was sure the chair was moving with us. Wendi took my grunt of surprise as an expression of excitement, and her hand moved to my groin. I was torn between curiosity and passion, but then she arched her thighs and slid on to me.

At my initiation to lovemaking, my partner had impressed upon me the necessity of foreplay before the ultimate act of union. Males must stay their quicker flood of passion, she had told me, until the female is raised to the same pitch. How often is theory betrayed by fact! Wendi's assault had found me only half-prepared, and it was some moments before I overcame my surprise and began matching her rhythm.

Wendi's lovemaking was frantic and animalistic, so different from the relaxed passion of my initiation. She heaved, grunted, attacked my flesh with her nails, my shoulders with her teeth. At first I was surprised and somewhat shocked by her aggression; then it began to excite me. I made no attempt to match her frenzy, though, being content to watch her as, embroiled in her private lusts, she raised her pitch, thrusting, panting, moaning, the chair (it *was* alive!) in dynamic equilibrium beneath us. I came, and seconds later Wendi reached climax too, clenching her teeth and letting out great hisses of air through her nostrils as she gripped me tightly and shuddered to completion.

Spent, the chair stilled, I lay slumped across her, her breasts a warm pillow beneath my head, the viscid dampness of our thighs the sole residuum of our passion. Several minutes passed in stillness and silence, then Wendi slid from under me and retrieved her vest and shorts from the floor. The chair had moved when she had risen, and when I shifted my position, it moved again.

I jumped to my feet. "What is that thing?" I asked.

"A contour couch," she replied, buttoning her shorts. "It adapts to your posture." She slipped her vest over her head. "Much better than a bed for lovemaking."

She picked up her sandals, went over to the door and opened it. I followed, stumbling over my own sandals which lay at the centre of the floor.

"My room's just along the corridor," she told me. She put a finger to her lips, pressed it to my forehead, and left without another word.

I went back to the couch and lay down, experiencing a weird pleasure as it moulded itself to the curvature of my spine. I found the button on the underside, pressed it, and moved. The couch remained static. I pressed the button again and rolled over. The warm plastic undulated, distributing my weight evenly throughout its length.

Compared to the rigours of commune life, the timetable of study at the Institute was leisurely. Classes began two hours after dawn and continued until seven hours. There followed a four-hour recess over zenith, when we were free to pursue our own interests (though as preliminary students we were naturally expected to use this free time to expand and intensify our studies). We then reconvened for a series of seminars which ended an hour and a half before dinner. Our evenings were again our own. But the most surprising and welcome aspect of the timetable for me was that every fifth day was a free-day which could be devoted to study or leisure, as one pleased. Not here the remorseless sequence of days unrelieved by rest. The Institute encouraged extra-curricular study, but did not demand it.

I had found my métier. The freedom and atmosphere of intellectual endeavour which prevailed on campus were perfectly suited to my needs. The breadth of subjects which we covered was large. At Silver Spring, my studies had had a marked utilitarian bent: anything that did not focus in some way on commune life was neglected or often ignored. At the Institute the courses were structured in such a way that new students were exposed to a host of different disciplines so that when the time came to specialize, they were fully aware of the options available to them. The approach was extremely eclectic; there was no rigid division of subjects, so that it was possible to begin a seminar discussing political theory, then progress through philosophy, history, psychology and thence to biochemistry, genetics, eugenics, and back to politics. This is not to suggest that our studies were undirected; whenever we appeared to have exhausted one particular line of inquiry our tutors would present us with additional facts or offer new perspectives in order to keep the discussion alive. In this way, the raw information which we had been given in the more formal morning classes was not swallowed as a lump of undigested dogma but assimilated slowly in a healthy atmosphere of scepticism and debate.

Socially, too, I thrived. Although I soon discovered that Wendi's generous welcome was a service she performed for many incoming male students, she seemed to take a special interest in me, and through her I found myself active in chess tournaments, basketball games, drinking competitions—the whole gamut of leisure-time pursuits which students employ to mitigate the pressures of academic life. However, my bias remained solitary and introspective; while I cultivated friends on a superficial basis, there was no one I felt close to, no one who possessed that inner seriousness of emotional purpose which I deemed necessary for true friendship.

On the first and eleventh days of each month I visited the

postroom to collect the lettertapes which Annia sent with faithful regularity. A great distance separated us, but she always addressed me as if I was standing beside her, her tone at once gay and purposeful. She kept me abreast of all the happenings at Silver Spring, and although the news was predominantly frivolous, it was as important to me as the details of governmental policy might be to a member of the City Senate. Occasionally, Jax, too, would add a few words of his own, but he preferred live conversation, and generally relied on Annia to express the good wishes of them both.

I treasured the tapes, and never failed to reply the same day, duplicating my own tapes so that as the months passed and my collection grew, it was possible to play them through in sequence and imagine that we were sitting in the same room, talking face to face. I was happy at the Institute, but I missed the sheer familiarity and the company of those I had known all my life.

Nursery intakes at Silver Springs are received once-seasonally from the city incubators and are moved through the dorm system *en masse* until they reach the age of majority. Annia, Jax and I had often speculated on who was the eldest amongst us, and I had won a modest five-check wager by obtaining my "promotion" to seniority first. The rivalry now devolved on Annia and Jax alone. By tenth month, over three-quarters of junior dorm had achieved majority, and it was clear that they were both growing increasingly frustrated by their enforced dalliance amongst the thinning ranks of the juniors. "Caril and Erik are intolerably cheerful," Annia complained in one of her tapes. This was only to be expected, of course, for they now had less children in their charge than at any other time of the season.

At the beginning of eleventh month, I learned from Annia that her ceremony was to take place on the 5th. The day after this, I received an unexpected tape in which Annia informed me that she would be visiting Helixport on the 15th. My tutors were accommodating when I asked to be excused classes for the occasion, stipulating only that I utilize my next free day to catch up on the studies I would miss.

Owing to a traffic delay on the south-bound highway, I was almost a half-hour late on arrival at Central Terminus. Annia was sitting outside the main exit gate and when she saw me, she rushed forward and embraced me.

"I'm sorry I'm late," I said. "The bus got caught in a jam."

"It's all right. I knew you'd come." She ran a finger across my eyebrows, sweeping away the beads of sweat which had gathered there following my dash from the bus-stop to the terminus.

"How is city life?" she asked.

"It's fine," I said.

I held her by the waist. She was wearing a yellow, short-skirted tunic, very feminine. Her hair was drawn back in her familiar pony-tail, short coils of hair framing her forehead, and a hoop of gold hung at each ear. I leaned forward and kissed her gently on the lips.

We disengaged and went out through the exit gate.

"Jax sends his regards," she said.

"Oh, yes. How is he?"

"Annoyed. He hates the idea of being the youngest of us." I smiled, then touched one of her ear-rings. "A present?"

"Jax made them in metalwork class. He's become a fiend with a welding torch."

"Real gold?"

"Cupro-nickel," she said with a grin.

Nonetheless, they were finely crafted. I made a show of examining them and murmuring my approval; an obscure jealousy nagged at me.

"I've got something for you, too," I said, rummaging in my pouch and producing the object, a cerulean pebble the size of a chicken's egg.

She took it from me. "A skystone. It's beautiful. Where did you get it?"

"From the geology lab at the Institute. I told them I needed it for a project."

Somehow this confession made the gift seem unworthy; compared with Jax's handiwork, it was nothing.

"I haven't got anything as permanent for you," Annia said, slipping the stone into her pouch and producing a lunch-box. She passed it to me. Inside were six freshly-baked éclairs. They had always been my favourites; Martin, the junior's cook, had a special recipe and I had often pestered him to bake me some.

We stopped at a café near the riverbank and ate an éclair each.

"How was your ceremony?" I asked.

"It went well," Annia said, wiping cream from her lips. "Like you, I have escaped the fields. The elders were suitably impressed by my record of voluntary service in the nursery and they've made me a trainee warden there. I hope to become a wetnurse eventually."

"That's marvellous," I said distractedly. From nowhere, an image had come to me of Jax sneaking over to senior dorm at night and slipping into Annia's bed. I was appalled with myself for entertaining it.

"Shall I get us something to drink?" Annia asked.

"No, it's all right," I said, hailing a passing waiter. He came over and I gave him our order: a pot of butterfruit tea, unsugared.

"You're already the sophisticate," Annia remarked, half-mockingly.

"Nothing's changed," I said with a vehemence which surprised me. Then, lamely: "Has it?"

A flicker of puzzlement crossed her face. "What do you mean, David?"

I shook my head, my cheeks hot with embarrassment. "Nothing. I didn't mean anything." I looked up at her. She waited.

"I feel . . . cut off. From you and Jax. You know?"

She reached over the table and gently punched my hand. "I came today, didn't I?"

The tea arrived. We continued to talk, but only half my mind was occupied with the conversation; the other half berated me for my churlishness, my unkind thoughts, my lack of charity. What was wrong with me? Annia was here, and she was the same Annia I had left at the commune. Perhaps that was it: perhaps I had expected something more of her now that she had reached majority, some deeper token of friendship, or perhaps something more than friendship. . . .

I was aware of a silence. Annia was staring at me over the top of her cup.

"You were far away," she said.

"I'm sorry." I shook my head. "I don't know what's wrong with me."

She set her cup back in its saucer. "You promised to show me the Institute and that fine room you have." Her expression betrayed nothing.

"What time is it?" I asked.

"Almost seven hours."

Across the street, the blinds had been drawn on the windows of a sauna. The streets were deserted. Sheltered under the parasol from the brunt of Capella's heat, I had not noticed that it was nearly zenith.

On the bus, Annia sat close to me, her arm through mine, peering out the window and asking me what I knew of this building, of that monument. She always gauged my mood well, responding with gaiety whenever I was sullen. Try as I would, however, I could not shake my gloom. I thought: Annia is acting this way out of pity for me, not because she really wants to; she feels obligated to make me happy. By this warped and tortuous reasoning, I further darkened my mood.

The bus deposited us opposite the main entrance to the campus. As we were walking through the subway, Annia stopped me and said: "David, what is it?"

"I think too much," I said.

"No," she replied. "You just waste your thoughts on irrelevancies."

We emerged from the tunnel. There was little traffic on the highway, but as Annia and I approached the main entrance, we noticed a small floater with darkened windows approaching in the inner, south-bound corridor. The floater moved quite slowly, wavering slightly as if the driver was inexperi-

enced or unsure of the route. As it drew past us, the vehicle
pulled off the corridor and drew to a halt less than twenty
metres from where we stood. The door slid open and a figure
stumbled forth. At first we took it to be an old man, bald and
stooped, but then we saw that it was a woman. She was very
old, eighty, perhaps ninety seasons, and it was clear that she
was in considerable distress. She took several hesitant steps
forward, then collapsed.

Annia and I rushed to her side. Her aged face was con-
torted with pain and she appeared to be having some difficulty in breathing. I noticed that she was not just bald, but
lacking eyebrows too. I loosened the clasp at the neck of her
garment, a long, loose-fitting robe of a copper-coloured
material unlike any fabric I had ever seen before. Annia
cradled her head in her arms. Her face took on a purplish hue.
We watched, helpless, wondering what to do. Her eyes
fluttered open briefly, green eyes dulled with pain, then
closed again. A ragged breath issued from deep within her
throat and her body went limp.

I searched for a pulse.

"She's dead," Annia said flatly, staring down at the
unmoving head, laid like an offering across her forearms.
Gently, I lifted her body, then lowered it to the ground. I
straightened her limbs and tidied her gown. Death had
brought an immediate softening of features, revealing a face
almost devoid of the wrinkles of age.

I looked up. Annia had gone over to the floater and was
staring incredulously inside. I followed her. Sitting in the
passenger seat of the vehicle was an alien, a M'threnni.

Although the M'threnni had not been seen abroad in
Helixport since the city was built, it had long been rumoured
that they made brief, covert excursions from their tower.
Accurate portraits of the aliens were few. Some aged photo-
graphs taken by one of the original colonists revealed a race
of tall, frail-looking humanoids but no real details (the
cameraman had been some distance away from his subject).
Numerous crude sketches were also extant, but of dubious
verisimilitude since they tended to caricature. The most fam-

ous portrait, and the one from which practically all subsequent reproductions had been taken, was a watercolour of a M'threnni male painted by Thomas Kaufman, the leader of the original colonists and the first mayor of Helixport. Kaufman had been the first person to confront the aliens soon after they had landed, and legend had it that he had actually spoken with them, though this was hotly disputed. He had obviously striven for accuracy in his depiction, but he was not a natural artist, and his portrait (of which I had seen only a reproduction), while capturing something of the strangeness of the alien form, was stylized and inevitably anthropomorphic.

The M'threnni—I guessed that it was a mature male, although from human perspectives the alien had an androgynous air—sat rigidly upright in the passenger seat, staring towards us. He was tall and pale-complexioned, and he wore a reddish tunic of the same shiny material as the old woman. His torso and limbs were attenuated: an indented chest, a narrow waist, spindly arms draped limply across his lap—but his face belied the weakness which seemed to reside in his body, for he wore an expression of implacable aloofness and inscrutability; his features, thrown into eerie halfrelief by the violet glow of the floater fascia, bespoke a face which had been moulded by an evolutionary process uncannily close and yet so far away from that which had produced homo sapiens.

The spherical skull was completely hairless, the nose broad and flat (the nostrils, two horizontal slits, dilated minimally as he regarded us), the mouth thin and lipless, the chin and forehead recessed. These smooth facial contours gave his countenance an infantile, doll-like character, an impression which was wholly countered by the fearful intensity of his eyes. The eyes; I left them until last, but they were what immediately drew the onlooker's gaze, those black circular orbs embedded in the skull like precious and terrible jewels, holding at their centre the tiny white star of the retina. The eyes repelled and hypnotized.

Apart from the evidence of his breathing, he made not the slightest movement as we stared at him; it was as if he was the product of some inspired but crazed holo-sculptor. And yet the eyes were active; without moving, they absorbed everything, encompassing the whole field of vision through the floater door. They stared at us, yet did not acknowledge us; we were just another feature of the landscape, of no more interest than a stone or a patch of grass.

Annia was transfixed by the alien's gaze. I drew her to me, turning her head away.

"The woman is dead," I said loudly.

Nictitating membranes darted across the M'threnni's eyes, clouding them momentarily, then vanishing. Seconds crept by. Then slowly the alien began to turn his head towards the control panel. He extended his arm and touched a button. A series of strange violet shapes began flashing on the panel, and I realized that this was no human-built floater, but a M'threnni duplicate.

The door slid shut with a sigh, and the engine caught. The sounds were faithful to a "real" floater. The pitch of the engine heightened, and the floater lifted and glided out on to the transit corridor, picking up speed rapidly. Within a minute, it was out of sight.

I held Annia tightly, as unnerved as she. I buried my head in her shoulder and we rocked one another gently, drawing comfort from our closeness. At length, I heard another vehicle approaching. The floater, painted deep-blue and bearing the gold stylized I of the Institute, drew off the highway and pulled up outside the gates. The driver emerged and I saw that it was Margret, the registrar. She noticed the old woman's body and hurried over to us.

With an explosion of words, I told her what had happened. She nodded at intervals, looking increasingly grave, and when I was done she knelt and examined the woman. Then I helped her load the body into the trunk of the floater (Annia was still numb with shock) and we drove into the campus and pulled up outside her office in the west wing of the main building.

She led us inside and said: "You are to wait here until I

return. Under no circumstances are you to leave or open the door. Do you understand?''

I nodded.

She went out and a key turned in the lock. Moments later, I heard her floater depart.

I sat Annia down on the couch which lined the wall opposite the window. I took a decanter at random from the drinks cabinet, filled a glass with the brownish liquor it contained and passed it to Annia. Sipping at the drink, she unwound a little, but she would not speak. I tucked my arm around her and she laid her head against my shoulder. Soon, to my surprise, she was asleep.

An hour passed. Two. My arm had long grown numb but I didn't want to move for fear of disturbing Annia. Occasionally she shivered in her sleep, as if experiencing a nightmare. Where was Margret? She had been possessed of an urgency when she had left, and yet she was allowing us to languish here alone. While I waited, I mulled over the incident with the M'threnni innumerable times; its eeriness lingered on.

Finally, after almost three hours of waiting, Margret returned. I woke Annia. Although calmer now, she was still subdued and silent.

"I'm sorry to have kept you," Margret said, "but Lionel is a busy man and was at a meeting when I went to look for him. He's ready to see you now."

Lionel was the principal of the Institute. Evidently our encounter with the alien was receiving attention from on high.

I held Annia's arm as we followed Margret up stairways and along corridors, heading towards the apex of the building where Lionel's office was situated.

We waited in the lobby for a further hour. I stared out through the window, down the slanted, glass-faceted front face of the building, alternate panes golden bright with the sunlight. Zenith was over and the campus was all but deserted. I tried to ignore the rumblings of my stomach, but my impatience seemed only to heighten my appetite. At last the door opened and Lionel was ready to receive us.

"I do apologize for the delay," he said to Margret as we entered. He was a tall, heavily-built man, with bushy eyebrows and a thick, though well-trimmed beard. He sat down at his desk and offered Margret the seat opposite. Annia and I were obliged to stand beside her.

"Paperwork," he said, regarding the sheets on his desk with distaste. "I'm overwhelmed with it. Now, where were we?" He looked up, and only then did he acknowledge the presence of Annia and me. "Ah, yes," he said; then, brusquely: "Well, what happened?"

Unnerved by his abruptness, I stammered out the story. Occasionally he looked at Margret and I had the distinct impression that she had fully briefed him on the matter. All this, the waiting and the ultimate absence of chairs for Annia and me had been engineered to discomfort us. But this awareness did not help me at all; it only served to increase my unease. I stumbled on, and finally I was done.

Lionel was frowning and tapping his thumbs together.

"This is a most unfortunate incident," he said. "Most unfortunate. You are to say nothing of this matter to anyone, is that clear?" His eyebrows, joined at the bridge of his nose, formed a shallow V.

"I am not a student," Annia said stonily. "You cannot order me around."

His hands came together, flat against one another. "My dear, this is a matter which goes beyond the bounds of this campus. You must understand that."

"Since you have explained nothing, how can I?"

Lionel peered at her for a moment, then sighed. "Very well, let me outline the situation for you." Suddenly his tone was one of persuasive reasonableness.

"The aliens occupy a—ah—delicate position in our society," he said. "They are our patrons, and we are greatly in their debt, but their motives remain unknown to us. It is well known that there is a widespread clandestine fear of the M'threnni, but most people are comforted by the knowledge that they choose to isolate themselves on Round Island and not interfere in human affairs. It would be injudicious to make it known that they have been seen abroad in Helixport proper." ᐧ

"But there have always been rumours to this effect," I said.

"Rumours are one thing. A verifiable incident is another. We could not predict the consequences of such a revelation. No M'threnni have been seen on public view since the foundation of the city, and until such time as they choose to manifest themselves, we must respect and protect their privacy. This is why I must have your oaths of silence."

"Where was the M'threnni going?" Annia asked.

"Who can say? The motives of the aliens are unfathomable to us. We must simply accept their presence and their right to move anonymously through the city if they so desire. All I can say is that the evidence suggests that such excursions as you witnessed today are exceedingly rare."

He put his elbows on the desk. "Now I must have your word that you will tell no one of it." The threatening tone had returned to his voice.

"Who was the old woman?" Annia asked, completely unintimidated by his posturing.

Lionel sighed. "She was a servant of the M'threnni. A Voice."

"A Voice?"

"In the early days of the colony the aliens took several human beings into their tower, and the practice has persisted. We call these people Voices since it was originally assumed that they were to act as interpreters for the M'threnni."

"They live with the M'threnni inside the tower?"

"Yes."

"Of their own free will?"

"Yes. We think so."

"How are they chosen?"

"We have no idea."

"How many are there?"

"Who knows? Estimates of number vary from ten to a thousand. There is no way of being certain."

"But surely the authorities must have some idea."

"People disappear all the time. We have no means of telling how many of these become Voices."

"Why do the aliens need them? Do they conduct their business for them?"

"No. They remain inside the tower just like the M'threnni. We cannot fathom their function." There was an edge of exasperation in his voice.

"Will you give me your oaths of silence?" he asked impatiently.

I was prepared to submit, but Annia shook her head, whether in puzzlement or refusal, I could not say, but Lionel's expression darkened.

"Enough," he said. "My patience is at an end. Unless you both agree to keep your counsel on this matter, I will arrange for you to be taken into custody for treatment which will erase all memory of the incident."

I did not know if this threat was a real one or not, but it had the desired effect: a silence fell, and I saw that Annia's resistance was broken. After a moment, she mumbled her assent, and I was only too eager to echo her.

Lionel's manner immediately softened. He asked Margret if she had anything further to add. Margret, who had not moved or spoken throughout, shook her head curtly. It was clear that she wanted to end the interview as quickly as possible.

"Good," said Lionel, with evident satisfaction, and (I thought) not a little relief. "I will respect and rely upon your oaths." He eyed us meaningfully, then said: "No doubt you are both quite hungry."

"Famished," I said involuntarily.

He switched on the intercom atop his desk and a crackly voice said: "Yes?"

"A table for three, please."

We travelled down through the heart of the building in the staff elevator and got off at the first floor. Margret left us to return to her duties; I suspected that she had eaten while

Annia and I had been incarcerated in her office. The staff restaurant was empty, everyone else having eaten hours earlier too, and the chef emerged to fuss around Lionel and advise him on the menu. Although we were undoubtedly treated to the best food the restaurant had to offer, I cannot remember what we ate. The appreciation of good food, as Erik (himself something of a gourmet) was wont to say, involves the mind as well as the taste-buds; and I was only too aware that the meal was just a sop to our silence. At one point, Annia took my hand momentarily under the table and squeezed it tightly as if affirming our bond of shared and secret knowledge.

Afterwards, Lionel insisted that Annia be given an official tour of the campus—a belated courtesy which we were unable to refuse. The arrangements were protracted, eating away another hour, and when finally our guide arrived, it was none other than Rayner, po-faced and dour as ever. I bit my lip in frustration as he led us around the campus at an even slower pace than on my first day, his toneless voice like the droning of bees. By the time the tour was over, I was numb with boredom and scarcely aware of my surroundings. We were standing at the main gate, and I heard Rayner say: "I suppose you will want to be getting back to the terminus now."

"What time is it?" I asked.

"Almost seventeen hours. A bus is due."

An hour before dusk; the entire afternoon had been consumed. I heard Annia murmur somewhat half-hearted thanks, and then the proctor was striding off up the driveway, back towards the main building.

"He's so gloomy," Annia said with a grin. "Does he ever smile?"

"Never. Everyone calls him Grim Death."

"Is that a M'threnni stone?" she asked, indicating the black crystal. Rayner had scrupulously avoided the object during our tour.

I nodded. Annia stared at it for a moment, then looked up the highway. The bus was approaching.

"I'm sorry about this afternoon," I said.

"It wasn't your fault. Besides, it's not every day that you get to meet an alien."

"Did it scare you?"

She shook her head. "I'd rather not talk about it."

We took seats at the rear of the bus and talked instead about Annia's next visit to Helixport at the end of the season. Jax would also be accompanying her, and I planned to introduce them to the delights of The Cellar. I would organize a celebration with my student friends for them; we would concentrate on adolescent fun, steering clear of the authorities.

We sat in the forecourt of the terminus, listening to the harsh, electronic voice of the annunciator and the whine of taxiing shuttles. Annia rested her head on my shoulder; my arm was around her waist. Despite the frustrations of the day, my mood had lightened considerably for I knew that my geographical separation from Annia and Jax had not affected the strength of our friendship. We hardly talked as we sat there; we were content in our closeness.

Finally the annunciator gave details of the impending departure of the High Valleys shuttle. We rose, hugged one another, and then Annia was off, running towards the departure gate. As she stopped at the barrier to surrender her ticket for inspection (no more travelling in the hold now that we were seniors), she turned and waved, and then she was gone. I waited until the shuttle had lifted and banked out of sight over the rooftops before finally making my way back towards the bus-stop.

I received no lettertape on the first day of twelfth month, but I took no account of it, assuming that Annia had considered it unnecessary so soon after her visit. Ten days later, however, there was still no word from her, so I hastily dispatched a tape of my own filled with facile chatter but suffused with a certain anxiety and the implicit question: why haven't you contacted me?

At this time, my workload was heavy since I was studying for the admission examinations which were scheduled for the last three days of the month. I had also initiated some extremely covert investigations into the M'threnni, my curiosity over my encounter with the alien outweighing my fears that Lionel might be monitoring my activities. To my surprise, however, I discovered that the Institute ran a course entitled Alien Studies which was specifically concerned with elucidating aspects of M'threnni culture from the material evidence which was available on Gaia. I postponed any further research, resolving to pursue my interest less conspicuously by enrolling in the course that Autumn.

Several days passed and there was still no news from Annia. Huddled in my room, I contemplated mounds of textbooks and the bright print-outs of my data screen. Personal concerns would have to wait until the examinations were over. I could not allow myself to fail.

On the evening before the first exam, I retired to bed early. I could not sleep, however, and had been tossing and turning for over an hour when there was a vigorous tapping on my door. Answering it, I found Wendi standing outside, wearing only a short, sleeveless vest.

"Hello," she said. "You've become a bit of a recluse lately. I thought perhaps you'd given it all up and gone back home."

"I've been studying," I said, stepping aside to allow her entry.

She stood on tiptoe to kiss me on the chin; the faint aroma of wine emanated from her.

"You've been drinking," I said. "The day before the exam."

"It loosens me up."

"Are you worried?"

"No. I just like to relax with a little physical pleasure before exerting my brain." Her hand slithered towards my lower regions.

"I have to sleep. You'll be hung-over tomorrow."

"Oh no." Her hand had located its target. "Lovemaking concentrates the mind wonderfully. You'll see."

I was in no position to argue.

Afterwards I went into the shower, letting the tepid water wash away the sweat, the saliva, the seminal juices of our bodies. Then, above the hiss of the water, I heard a female voice speaking in a conversational tone. Hurriedly I stepped out of the cubicle and returned to the bedroom. Wendi was playing one of Annia's tapes.

"Turn it off," I said angrily.

She complied.

"Are you no respecter of privacy? Is nothing sacred to you?"

She was staring at me quizzically, but she did not speak.

"Well?" I said, my anger made even more intense by her silence. "Is this how you behave in the rooms of others?"

"I pressed for music," she said quietly. "The tape was in the wrong slot."

Suddenly I felt foolish. I had been playing one of Annia's tapes earlier that evening and had forgotten to remove it from the machine. Wendi had not been prying.

"I'm sorry," I said, feeling too embarrassed to explain my outburst further. I went back into the shower, turned the water to cold, and stood under it until I had regained my composure. When I emerged, Wendi was gone.

The examinations came and went. I felt confident that I had acquitted myself well enough to attain a full studentship. But while everyone else gathered in The Cellar on the evening of the 20th to celebrate their ending, I retired to my room and spent the evening scanning the skies with my telescope. Tomorrow was Newseason's Day, and Annia and Jax were due to visit Helixport. But I had received no word from them in over a month, and now, released from all academic pressures, I began to worry. Would they come?

I arose early the following day and took the bus into the city centre. I whiled away the morning in the cafés and shops along Albany Avenue. When the High Valleys shuttle came in from the west I was standing on the fan-shaped balcony of the city's premier art gallery not far from the terminus. The gallery had organized a "spontaneous paint," and a prominent artist was applying somewhat random dabs of colour to a canvas. I almmost knocked over a pot of paint in my haste to exit.

The shuttle had only just landed as I arrived, and when the passengers began to debark I scanned them eagerly, but there was no sign of Annia or Jax. Eventually Naree emerged and went over to unlock the hold. I leapt the barrier, ran across to her and tapped her on the shoulder.

She turned. "David! Were you hidden in the hold? I didn't see you get in at Silver Spring."

"No, I'm living in Helixport now. Studying at the Institute."

"Of course. I had forgotten. Are your studies going well?"

"Well enough. Naree, were Jax and Annia aboard?"

"Jax and Annia? No, I haven't seen them." She called to a forklift driver to be more gentle with his handling of a butterfruit crate. "Yes, it's Newseason's Day, isn't it. You always travelled to the city on holidays." Again she remonstrated with the driver. "No, I'm sorry, David, they didn't get on at Silver Spring."

I went directly to the radio booth in the forecourt of the terminus. I had only thirty checks in my pocket, but it would suffice for a five-minute call to Silver Spring. I fed the machine with coins, then punched out the number. The screen flickered briefly, then stabilized; Lenard's gaunt, ascetic face looked out at me.

"Hello, Lenard," I said, knowing that he would remember me from the skittering of stones on his roof.

"Good morning, David. How is life at the Institute?"

"It's fine. Do you know if Annia and Jax made any plans to visit Helixport today? It's holiday time and we always . . ." My words trailed away as I saw a flicker of discomfiture across his face.

"What's the matter?" I said.

"I think you should speak to Robert," he said hastily. "I'll connect you."

Before I could reply, the screen went blank and in the

ensuing pause apprehension gnawed at me.

It was over a minute before Robert's face appeared on the screen. He was sitting in his private chamber and he looked grim.

"What's happened?" I asked.

"I have tragic news, David. Annia is dead."

I stared hard at his brown, withered face.

"Dead?" I said finally, more unnerved by my apparent lack of reaction to his words than by their actual content.

Robert's voice seemed to come from afar. "She took ill with a fever, only two days after she visited you. She was dead within hours."

"A fever? What sort of fever?"

"We don't know. It was a virus of some sort. It left the doctors mystified. We had to commit her to the fires almost immediately to minimize the risk of infection. Fortunately, there have been no further cases."

It was some time before I responded.

"And no one saw fit to notify me," I said hollowly.

Robert looked uneasy. "We saw no reason to add to your burdens, knowing that you were soon to take your examinations. It is important to us all here that you do well."

"Annia was important to me!" I cried. "She was my friend."

He looked abashed, but said nothing.

"I want to speak to Jax."

Robert shook his head solemnly. "I'm afraid that won't be possible, David. Jax has disappeared. He was obviously deeply upset by Annia's death, and the day after she died we found that he had vanished from the commune. Our attempts to locate him have so far been unsuccessful. I am sorry."

I wanted to punch the screen, to smash his face into a thousand pieces. Instead, I merely reached forward and blanked the connection.

I must have wandered aimlessly through the streets for over an hour. A dust storm was developing, and the wind whipped eddies of fine sand along the gutter. I sat down in the empty forecourt of a café, its windows shuttered against the storm, and contemplated my knuckles. The grit-laden wind made tears well in my eyes, and I shivered. Above my head, a loose shutter tapped rhythmically on a first-storey window, a metronome for the storm.

Some time later something touched me on the shoulder and I turned around. A middle-aged woman stood before me, dressed in an expensive gown which was creased and grimy. In fact, her entire appearance suggested affluence gone sour. Her elaborate hair-do was in disarray beyond the ravages of the storm, and her face seemed drained of all vitality despite the plumpness of her cheeks. She wore an expression of blank bemusement, like a child lost in some foreign place. Her hand still rested on my shoulder, but lightly, as if she was afraid that I would suddenly break away, or as if she was not sure that I was really there.

"A drink?" she whispered. "Do you have some water?" The wind tugged at the whorls and waves of her hair, drawing them across her face.

I stood up, took her arm and led her down the street to the nearest faucet. She followed like a docile animal.

I pointed to the faucet but she stared at it without comprehension. I retrieved a paper cup from the flotsam pinned to the grille of a drain by the wind and washed it under the tap before filling it with water and handing it to her. She held the cup in both hands and drank in gulps, water dribbling down the front of her dress. When her thirst was finally slaked, she let the half-empty cup drop on to the sidewalk, exploding wetly at her feet. She stared at me for a moment, as if about to speak, then wandered off down the sand-swept street.

Chapter Four

Two days later, the results of the examinations were posted in the main hall. Ninety-eight of the one hundred and twenty preliminary students had been accepted for further study. No marks were given, but it was clear that the order of names suggested the degree of scolastic excellence. My name was fifth on the list; Wendi's, I noted, was second.

My academic success was the only bright spot in a period of intense personal bleakness. I was informed that arrangements were being made for me to visit Silver Spring, but I declined the offer outright; my anger and my despair were channelled into resentment and recrimination against the elders of the commune. I hated them for not having informed me of Annia's death and Jax's disappearance, and I suspected that they were keeping something from me. I grew convinced that the mysterious virus which had caused Annia's death had been contracted in some way from our encounter with the M'threnni Voice. Annia had been leaning over the woman when she had been in her death throes, and it seemed likely that she had been exposed to some alien organism which was virulent to ordinary humans. Annia's reaction to the encounter had been more extreme than mine; she had been drained by it. This was readily explainable as the initial reaction of her body defences to the attack of an unknown organism, and it also clarified Lionel's obsession with secrecy: the authorities knew that the M-threnni and their Voices were potential plague-carriers and were afraid that if this knowledge became widespread there would be a mass panic. I guessed that the commune elders were embroiled in the cover-up and that Jax's disappearance was in some way connected with the deception. Had they killed him to ensure his silence? No, that was taking my scenario too far. Jax was still alive, I was sure; throughout most of first month I fully expected him to turn up at my door, having somehow made his way to the city, but he never appeared. I shared my speculations on Annia's death with no one, since I still felt constrained by my oath to Lionel. But I brooded, deeply and blackly.

During this period I became almost maniacally devoted to my studies. The exigencies of day-to-day life no longer mattered to me; I drew relief only from the certainties of the printed page and screen. I took no part in the social life of the Institute, spending my evenings and free days locked in my room, engaged in further study or in "star-gazing." Although my academic performance rose to new heights during this period, my tutors were obviously aware that I was under a considerable strain, and I was finally obliged to visit the student counsellor, a woman named Elise.

Elise was an intense, gruffly spoken woman who took a dynamic interest in my problems from the outset. I spoke little during our first few meetings, but Elise, undaunted, would question me relentlessly and take voluminous notes whenever I made some kind of response, however brief, before launching into an exhaustive series of speculations on the import of my words. As the sessions progressed, I began to feel somewhat abashed at the degree of attention I was receiving. Elise homed in on the meagrest of utterances, leaving me surprised and impressed by the wealth of meaning which she was able to extract from them. Soon I was approaching each session not with a timid hope of impending emotional catharsis, but rather as one would anticipate a chess game against a difficult opponent. I began to make random, elliptical comments designed solely to test her ingenuity; I invented; I embroidered; I made contradictory statements practically in the same breath. Elise responded to this challenge with equal verve, her powers of interpretation and analysis rising to new heights. Before long I was actively relishing each new encounter with her.

Towards the end of our twelfth session, Elise uncoiled herself from her chair (she always sat with her legs crossed and her right instep tucked behind her left ankle) and went over to the fish tank atop her book-case.

"You have not mourned," she said, and it was as if she was addressing the overfed goldfish which were basking in the bright green water. "You are bottling your sorrows within."

This was hardly the revelation which her tone would have me believe. She sat down again and leaned across the table, awaiting my response.

"There is no one I wish to share them with," I said lamely.

"There need not be. You must reveal your sorrows to yourself." Her wire-frame glasses shone in the light of the desk-lamp like strange and sinister moons.

"Accept your sorrows and you will be free of them," she said. "I can do no more for you."

Was this to be her ultimate pronouncement? I could hardly believe it.

"I'll try," I said, striving for a tone which suggested resolution.

It seemed the least facile response I could make.

One evening several days later there was a tapping on my door. I recognized the staccato immediately and was loath to answer it. But the knocking was persistent and when I finally opened the door I was surprised to see that Wendi had come, not in aggressive near-nakedness but fully clothed. Since the incident with the lettertape our relationship had been stiffly formal and we had tended to avoid one another. Yet now she stood outside in an attitude of defensive politeness, as if prepared to make peaceful overtures but expecting a rebuff.

"Can I come in?" she asked in a small voice.

"What do you want?"

"Only to talk for a few minutes."

"I don't really feel like company just now."

"A few minutes, that's all."

"I'm tired. I was about to take a nap."

"Please, David."

I shrugged and let her in.

She sat down on the desk-top, I seated myself on the contour couch. She crossed her legs and put her hands in her lap, a demure and wholly uncharacteristic posture. She wriggled her feet and her sandals dropped to the floor.

"I came to see how you were," she said.

"You've seen me at classes. I'm all right."

She shook her head. "You're a walking corpse. Everybody's noticed. You haven't left your room in two months."

I said nothing.

"How did she die?"

I feigned ignorance. "Who?"

"The girl. Annia." She pronounced it *Ann-e-ah* rather than *Ann-yah*.

I studied my thumbnails. "A virus of some kind."

"Were you very close?"

"She was my friend. We grew up together." I looked up at her. "How do you know about Annia? Did Elise send you?"

"No. Honest. I've been spending some time with her as part of my course. We go over case-histories but names are never mentioned. I knew you were visiting her, though; I've seen you leaving. The other day Elise was discussing a case and it occurred to me—I don't know how or why—that she was talking about you. So I sneaked a look at her notes. It was all there."

"Elise set it up. She knew you and I were friends."

"No, I don't think so," she said. "But does it matter, anyway? I came on my own free will."

Her face was a picture of ingenuousness. I believed her; Wendi was incapable of guile.

"You can't go on like this, you know," she said. "Has Elise helped you at all?"

"She's quite a remarkable woman."

Wendi smiled at the ambiguity. "She's a verbal hurricane. Did she jump on your every word?"

"It felt like every letter. Sometimes I had the feeling that if I farted she'd be able to attach a wealth of significance to that, too."

Wendi laughed. "She does the same with me, even though I'm her student not her patient. She's fascinated by what she describes as my aggressive, extroverted sexual proclivities. I told her I was molested by an elder at the age of five and she's built an elaborate theory on my lie."

I grinned, imagining the intricate edifice of misguided speculation which Elise could construct on such a basis.

Wendi got down off the desk.

"I made you smile," she said.

She slipped her sandals on and went over to the door. As she opened it, she turned and said: "I'll call in again tomorrow. Take care."

The months passed, and slowly my sorrow at losing Annia and Jax began to wane—helped, no doubt, by my developing relationship with Wendi. My studies, which for a while had simply been a means of diverting my thoughts from my grief, once again became of real interest to me.

Our courses in this first scholarship season were more structured and compartmentalized than in the preliminary session, though our tutors continued to expand our curriculum with the object of providing us with a wide basic background knowledge before we finally began to specialize at the beginning of our second season.

Although I had an aptitude for mathematics and physical sciences, my particular interest was history—not only the history of Gaia, but also of Earth. At this early stage we were

almost exclusively concerned with our own planet (and with
conspicuously little reference to the influence of the
M'threnni), so I spend much of my free time reading about
the tangled web of national and international intrigues which
characterized the history of Earth.

As a youth, I had always considered myself the descendant
of Earth-born stock without having any real notion of what
"Earth-born" meant. I soon discovered that practically all
Gaians could trace their ancestry back to two specific nations:
the United States of America and the British Federation.
Anglo-American research teams had developed the ion-pulse
drive which had made interstellar travel possible, and of the
original colonists, nine-tenths were of British or American
origin. We were the descendants of two nations, not a world.

Our history tutor, Jon, practised the maxim "Show not
tell." He arranged a series of visits to sites of historical
interest, the most important of which was the Auriga Centre
in Union Plaza. The *Auriga* had been the starship which had
brought the colonists to Gaia. After the ship had been
beached on the planet's surface, it was disassembled and its
five hexagonal units rearranged to form three sides of an open
square. It functioned now as a living museum, a vital link
with the civilizations of Earth.

We filed in through the main entrance in the central unit.
Kaufman's original portrait of the M'threnni hung in the hall.
Most of my fellow students were suitably impressed by it, but
I could only reflect on its blandness compared with the real
thing. But the portrait stirred unhappy memories and I was
glad when Jon led us off into a long room crammed with
data-banks and consoles. Stored in the banks was all the
knowledge which our ancestors had accumulated over mil-
lennia, knowledge which the pioneers had used, allied with
M'threnni aid, to construct our society. Without it, the colony might have degenerated into primitivism and would
certainly have never attained the degree of technical sophistication to which we were accustomed.

But the *Auriga* held more than just knowledge; it held life
itself. We entered a large, high-ceilinged chamber, filled

with row upon row of sealed compartments, labelled in the terse, cryptic languages of the botanists and zoologists. These were the plant and animal gene pools, containing the seeds and embryos of a host of different species, preserved under rigidly controlled conditions of temperature and humidity. Through careful experimentation, the first farmers had eventually discovered which species were capable of thriving in Gaian soil, thus establishing an Earth-based agricultural system without which the colony would have been doomed, for the native flora and fauna of Gaia were sparse.

Adjacent to this was a deceptively similar chamber whose compartments held the most important seeds of all: human reproductive cells. The incubator authorities constantly utilized sperm and ova from this reservoir to sustain a wide genetic diversity in the population of Gaia. Jon explained that the present population, now approaching a quarter of a million, less than a fifth could claim dual parentage from people who had actually lived on the planet; most were offspring of long-dead folk who had bequeathed their reproductive cells to the gamete bank.

We passed through the ship's accommodation area, which occupied three complete units. The *Auriga* had carried a complement of one thousand passengers, and the living quarters reminded me of a large but compact hostel. The sleeping cubicles were arranged, bunk-like along the walls, and the canteens, with their arrays of long, collapsible tables, had evidently provided the inspiration for the dining-halls of many Gaian communes. Elsewhere, in the recreation zones, there had been a more generous allocation of space: the extensive garden areas were a pleasing contrast to the confines of the sleeping and eating quarters, and there were spacious lounges, a number of gymnasiums and swimming pools, and even a miniature golf course. The ship had maintained an acceleration of one gravity to the mid-point of its voyage, decelerating thereafter at the same rate so that the gravity on board remained at a constant norm throughout. For the passengers, the voyage to Gaia took just under eight Earth years, or two Gaian cycles, whereas back on Earth, decades passed.

Though intellectually I knew that the theory of time-dilation at relativistic velocities was sound, I still found it hard to accept emotionally; somehow, it was not at all comforting to contemplate the idea that time itself was inconstant.

Our visit ended in the control room, a globular blister on the roof of the central unit. The viewscreen, which had once looked out on the barren darkness of interstellar space, now reflected the more prosaic vistas of the plaza: the curved walkways and benches which ringed the finger of granite marking the city's foundation. A small boy was scratching his name on the rock with a sliver of metal.

The control room was filled with a variety of electronic equipment, all now deactivated. I tried to imagine the ship under full power: a semaphore of multi-colored lights flashing on the instrument panels, the relentless data print-outs, the whirring of magnetic tape, the steady throb of the engines. A dramatic and unrealistic view of the voyage, no doubt, but a potent one, nevertheless.

"Once the survey teams had verified that Gaia was fit for human habitation," Jon was saying, "the colonists were ferried down to the preferential site of settlement at the mouth of the Tamus. Each shuttle was designed to double as a temporary housing unit until permanent buildings could be constructed. When everyone had been landed safely, a skeleton crew brought the *Auriga* down. Unfortunately, during the descent there was a systems malfunction involving the retrojets which resulted in the ship touching down at a speed of two hundred kilometres per hour. The ship sustained only minor structural damage, but the crew was killed outright."

He indicated a copper plaque which had been set into the centre of the floor:

IN MEMORIAM:
FRANCES TAYLOR
RIKKI ALVAREZ
JANIS MARTIN
ROGER UMBACH
DONALD SPENCER

"They were the first humans to die on Gaia," Jon said. "Their bodies were committed to the river, and the colonists honoured them by christening the river the 'Tamus,' an acronym of their surnames."

Jon pointed to an array of screens high on the wall opposite the observation blister. The screens transmitted the perspectives of various scanners set into the engine chamber walls. The ship's propulsion system was complex beyond our understanding, but there was no mistaking the awesome power which the now-defunct ion-pulse units had once possessed. To accelerate such a massive craft as the *Auriga* to velocities approaching that of light-speed was a supreme accomplishment indeed. But the ship would never fly again; it had been grounded almost thirty cycles ago, and it was now an immovable monument. The first colonists had irrevocably committed themselves to establishing a new life on Gaia.

The remainder of the history course that season concentrated on the development of the colony from its initial base. M'threnni aid was acknowledged but not directly discussed. It was only when I began to attend the Alien Studies seminars midway through the season that the M'threnni became the focus of attention.

It was a subsidiary course, and only twelve students had opted for it, reflecting the general attitude that the aliens were best ignored or paid as little attention as possible. We convened in a small conference room in main block. Jon was again our tutor, and he prefaced the first session by saying: "This will be a short course. About a quarter of it will be fact, the rest just intelligent guesswork. We know little about the aliens, despite their proximity and their influence on Gaia, and it would be foolish of me to pretend otherwise. Regard these seminars as exercises in speculative xenology."

He went over to the window and pulled up the blind. The black crystal dominated the lawn. Jon had brought with him no notes or visual aids, but the M'threnni artifact was a more potent reminder of our subject matter than any holocube or ill-taken photograph.

"Let me deal first with the historical facts," Jon said. He sat down at the head of the table and put his feet up on an empty chair.

"The colonists," he began, "had been on Gaia only one season when the M'threnni came. At this time, their settlement was little more than a few crude buildings dotted around the *Auriga* on the northern bank of the Tamus, although a small fishing fleet was also operating out of the harbour. But the settlement was in serious difficulties. Crop failures and the general difficulty in adapting to an alien environment had resulted in many deaths, and the total population had only increased by five per cent in that first season, despite the overall success of the agricultural programme and the introduction of the incubator system. Then, at midnight on the last day of second month in Summer, the M'threnni arrived.

"Their ship, a torus of light, dropped out of the sky and landed on Round Island, which at the time was nothing more than a barren, uninhabited rock. The colonists were naturally awestruck. Being defenceless and not knowing what to do, they simply waited. All through the night the island was alive with mysterious activity—vague shimmerings of light, and eerie, barely audible sounds. As dawn broke the following day, the dumbfounded colonists saw that an entire terminus—everything that exists on the island today—had been constructed overnight."

Jon stretched his arms and put them behind his head. A faint smile played on his face as he absorbed the expectant silence. He was obviously enjoying the drama of the story as much as we.

"Shortly after dawn," he went on, "a craft left the island and crossed the river, landing at the centre of the settlement. Several aliens emerged. Kaufman attempted to communicate with them, but if they understood human speech, they were unable or unwilling to use it. The M'threnni—the name, by the way, is believed to be a corruption of a fragment of alien speech overheard by Kaufman—merely stood there, surveying the ramshackle buildings and the terrified humans. Then, without apparent provocation, several people stepped out of the crowd of onlookers and went over to them. No words were exchanged as far as we know, but they accompanied the aliens into their craft, which then returned to Round Island.

"The day passed without further incident. Again that night there was activity on the island, and another ship landed. The following dawn, the humans returned and explained that the aliens had proposed to supply the colony with the raw materials necessary for its survival. The first consignment already lay waiting on the terminus. Kaufman listened to the terms—Round Island must remain sacrosanct to the aliens, and the aliens in turn would eschew direct intervention in human affairs—and, after hasty discussions, agreed. The Voices then returned to the tower. Kaufman anticipated further discussions, but they never appeared again. A bridge was built to the island to facilitate the transport of the goods, and that, more or less, is the way things have remained ever since. M'threnni freighters deposit their cargo on Round Island at regular intervals and the haulage people move in to pluck it away and deliver it into our grateful hands." He leaned forward. "Questions?"

Everyone's arm was raised.

"Why did these people go with the M'threnni?"

"We don't know."

"Were they ever seen or heard from again?"

"The Voices emerge from time to time to watch the loading operations at the terminus, but they remain at a distance and do not attempt to communicate with the haulage teams. There has been no direct contact with the aliens or their voices since they met with Kaufman."

"So why do the aliens need the Voices?"

"Again, we don't know."

"How many Voices are there?"

The questions were the same as those that Annia had asked Lionel.

"We believe that every M'threnni in the tower has a human companion, though naturally we can't be sure of this. Estimates of the number of aliens vary, but it is certainly more than ten and probably less than a hundred. We also believe that a male M'threnni always takes a female Voice, and vice versa. We have no idea why."

This concurred with my own encounter with the alien, I thought. The dying Voice had been female, the M'threnni male.

"Do the Voices breed?"

"There is no evidence to presume so."

"What happens when one dies?"

"A replacement is chosen."

"How?"

Jon paused, and eyed us conspiratorially. "It appears that the M'threnni travel secretly through Gaia to seek out suitable candidates. What their criteria of choices are, no one knows, but there is no evidence to suggest that people are spirited away to the tower against their wishes. Those chosen always seem to accept their calling without demur; as far as we know, no prospective Voice has ever spurned the aliens. It's most mysterious." He paused again, then said quietly: "In view of the general feeling of mistrust towards the M'threnni, however, I would ask you to keep this information to yourselves. The authorities have always turned a blind eye to the M'threnni excursions, while at the same time seeking to ensure that the populace at large is not aware of them. There is no telling what fears might be kindled if the knowledge of the aliens' 'recruiting missions' became public."

There was general agreement that we would say nothing. Jon's candidness was far more appealing than Lionel's threats.

"Are the M'threnni immortal?" someone asked.

"Again, it is impossible to be sure. Highly unlikely, I would say, although they may possess considerable longevity. The Voices, too, appear to live to quite an advanced age by human standards."

The questions went on, and Jon answered them as best he could. It was clear, however, that precious little was known about the aliens or what life was like for the Voices inside the tower. The Voices served the M'threnni until they died; none had ever emerged from the tower to tell their tale.

In subsequent seminars we went on to discuss the various raw materials and artifacts which the M'threnni had supplied to Gaia. The bulk of the supplies were building materials and raw ores which were in short supply on our planet, and these alone provided few clues about M'threnni culture or its level of technological development. But the aliens had also shipped to Gaia various artifacts such as the gasglobes and the black crystal which had no obvious practical use but were nevertheless the products of sophisticated processing techniques. Detailed studies of many of these artifacts had been undertaken, and while it was not possible to draw any sweeping conclusions from them (as Jon put it: "You cannot infer the whole of a civilization from a handful of trinkets"), one salient fact emerged: many of the artifacts derived their effects from the emission or absorption of radiation in the lower visible and infra-red regions of the spectrum. Allying to this the speculation that the aliens disliked strong sunlight (a speculation derived mainly, though not wholly, from the fact that they conducted their freighter operations by night) it seemed likely that the M'threnni were accustomed to radiation less intense and of a slightly longer wavelength than that of Gaia's suns. This suggested that their home-world orbited a dim, red sun. The M'threnni's attenuated physiques indicated also that it was a lower-gravity world than Gaia. Thus environmental difficulties might be strong factors in the aliens' self-imposed exile in the tower.

Of the M'threnni level of technological development, all that could reasonably be inferred was that it was extremely advanced, possibly beyond our understanding. The gasglobes apparently worked their colour changes through some photosensitive process which could not be elucidated, while the black crystal absorbed light via complex sub-atomic interactions which were equally unfathomable.

"We are like children attempting to understand the workings of a radio set," Jon told us. "We simply lack the sophistication of thought to grasp the complexities involved. Countless papers and articles have been written on the subject of the M'threnni, but they are all inconclusive. We are groping in the dark.''

It was true; I had read most of the literature which Jon had recommended and found only a web of incomprehension and blind speculation. As the course drew to its end, I began to realize that all my fond hopes of learning the secrets of the M'threnni were doomed to frustration.

By the time we gathered for the final seminar, the mood of anticlimax was manifest amongst those of us who remained in the class (five students had dropped out). Jon, however, appeared to be in a jaunty mood as he sat down at the head of the table.

''I can appreciate how disappointing the contents of this course must have been to you,'' he told us, ''but I offer no apologies. One cannot build elaborate theories on a shortage of facts. However, to conclude matters, I'd like to present you with a few speculations of my own—speculations which are probably as wildly inaccurate as anyone else's but which may, at least, give you food for thought.

''Firstly, why did the M'threnni come to our aid? Because we are rational beings, a fellow intelligent species? Perhaps, but we must not presume that the M'threnni regard us as their peers. Their civilization is so far in advance of ours that it is more likely that they view us as we might a primitive society—with affection and curiosity, and worthy of preservation for its novelty value alone.

''Secondly, why is their aid so limited? Why do they not offer more direct help? Their reasons could be diplomatic— they are aware of the natural human fear of aliens—or cultural—they only want to keep the colony alive and not dictate its form—or ethnic—they may possess some racial instinct against direct intervention.

''Thirdly, why do the aliens maintain a presence on Gaia at all? Why not simply ferry in all goods automatically, as their technology would surely allow? We can only conclude that they wish to observe the progress of the colony at close quarters, to be in the midst of it, yet apart from it. Perhaps we are under constant scrutiny from the tower. The aliens may be looking into this room at this very moment.''

There was a murmur of disbelief which Jon quieted with a wave of his hand. ''Remember the unimaginable sophistication of their technology. Animals are unaware of the presence of radio waves in the air. The M'threnni may be monitoring us by methods which we are equally unaware of.''

He waited a moment, then smiled broadly. ''For what it's worth, I consider that to be one of my wilder speculations.''

A few people shuffled with evident relief; it was not a pleasant thought.

''Finally,'' Jon said, ''what do the M'threnni hope to gain from this arrangement, if anything? My answer would be: they are simply entertained by it. I believe that our colony is, to the aliens, little more than a sophisticated zoo. At best, the aliens in the tower are equivalent of anthropologists, studying the activities of a primitive species. Now admittedly this is not an ennobling idea, but we must not shy away from it because of that. Humanity is far too anthropocentric in its outlook; it's time we learned a little humility.''

A contemplative silence ensued. John smiled ruefully, as if disappointed that his provocative views had not raised a stir. When it was clear that no one was going to speak, he said: ''One question remains. Why do the M'threnni need the Voices? In the light of my preceding scenario, two possibilities suggest themselves. Perhaps the aliens simply desire human companions in the way that humans desire pets. Or it could be that the Voices function as laboratory specimens which the M'threnni can observe at close hand. Choose whichever seems preferable to you.''

I had remained silent through most of the course, afraid of showing too much curiosity in case Jon had been informed of my encounter with the M'threnni. He had shown no indication that this was the case, however, and I decided that the time was ripe to test my own hypothesis.

''It could be,'' I said, ''that the M'threnni restrict themselves to the tower for fear of exposing the human population to alien microbes. Perhaps the Voices are experimental animals in this sense. Perhaps the M'threnni are seeking to immunize humans against M'threnni diseases.''

Joh nodded his head reflectively.

"An interesting proposition, David,'' he said. ''But an unlikely one. There is simply no evidence to suggest that the M'threnni are carriers of organisms harmful to humanity. Indeed, at their level of development one can safely assume that they will have eliminated all native diseases.''

It was clear that Jon thought the idea preposterous. I said nothing further.

The seminar was near its end, and Jon began his conclusion. ''Remember that most of what we have discussed today is pure speculation. It may be that it is impossible to attain an understanding of M'threnni motives in human terms. I spoke earlier of anthropocentric viewpoints, and these are precisely in what I have been indulging myself. The M'threnni are the product of a different evolutionary process from us and it may be unreasonable to suppose that their preoccupations are similar to ours. All we can do is to try to imagine *from human perspectives* what their likely motivations are. As such, our vision is blinkered by the very apparatus which we use for our imaginings—the human brain.''

Autumn passed and gradually I grew more content. Wendi and I consolidated our relationship and by the end of the season we had begun to function as a couple in liaison, spending most of our free time together and eschewing copulation with others. On our free days we took to roaming the nooks and crannies of the city—all the places Annia, Jax and I had never deemed worthy of a visit (we had been tourists, content to seek out only the most obvious areas of interest). We would take a bus at random, getting off at the terminus and exploring our immediate surroundings for the remainder of the day. Helixport was a sprawling, loosely peopled city, continually changing its character from area to area. There were the heavily industrialized sectors of the north-east, the canal-laced regions of the west, the artists' quarters on the fringes of the city centre, the casinos and pool halls on the rocky hills above the harbour. But the most interesting area to us became the South Bank of the city—primarily because it was so different from the rest of Helixport—and it was here that we spent most of our free time.

The South Bank was the city's poor quarter. In contrast to the broad and elegant avenues of the city centre and the placid suburban estates of northern Helixport, the South Bank was dirty, ramshackle and noisy. Here the streets and alleyways had not been built to some preordained design but had grown up haphazardly in blithe disarray according to the whims of its inhabitants. Tin-roofed shacks and squat adobes lined the narrow, twisting thoroughfares where the sunlight seldom penetrated and dogs barked incessantly.

Most of the inhabitants of the South Bank were refugees from the Plains and the Valleys who had migrated to the city hoping for higher wages and improved living conditions. They found neither. Helixport was under a slow, controlled expansion and there was no place for unsolicited labour. The citizens of the South Bank had thus found it necessary to construct their own social order. Handicrafts such as pottery and weaving were popular, and often the quality of the goods was excellent. Links with the harbour were strong, and it was frequently possible to buy fish which was as fresh and far cheaper than that sold in the market at Capitol Square. Mostly, though, life revolved around semi-legal pursuits such as gambling, prostitution and drug-trafficking. By far the greatest amount of revenue was obtained from the processing of the drug euphorin, an opiate derivative extracted from the macerated bodies of the speckled jellyfish which infested the coastal waters of Gaia. The women Annia, Jax and I had seen on the beach during our last visit to Helixport had been collecting creatures for that very purpose. The authorities had made half-hearted attempts to stamp out the trade (such as fencing off the beaches) but the militia made few arrests, primarily because the prospective recipients of the drug were the rich and influential citizens of Gaia (only the rich could afford to indulge themselves, for the market price for the purified drug was over ten thousand checks per gramme).

Euphorin, as its name implied, was a mood-enhancer and hallucinogenic. It was reputedly non-addictive and free from side-effects, though Wendi, who was studying pharmacology, told me that psychological dependence was common and that prolonged usage could cause personality disorders. The current vogue amongst the rich was to visit a dream parlour under the influence of the drug, and the consequences of this were frequently dire. The blissful dream-states evoked by the combination of drug and brain-rhythm modulation eventually proved more attractive than reality and resulted in schizoid withdrawal. The woman who had accosted me outside the café the day I learned of Annia's death had been such a drug-parlour freak—a ''zombie'' slowly surrendering to the formless mists of catatonia.

The South Bank was also the cradle of a variety of different religious sects and political groups whose unorthodox views could find no place in the secular, conservative ethos of Gaian society at large. Their temples and meeting-halls— generally these were derelict buildings which had been appropriated for their use—played host to small gatherings of zealots who had evidentially discovered salvation in the contemplation of strange divinities or visions of a new social order. The sects ranged from the genuinely philanthropic to the grossly eccentric, and most of them comprised only a handful of devotees. Wendi and I were fascinated by their rituals and tenets. There were the Psychometricians, who urged that the government be handed over to psychologists who would then use their understanding of human behaviour to construct a just society; the Humanistic League, a group of disaffected radicals who viewed the M'threnni presence as invidious and dispensed pamphlets advocating that they be petitioned to leave Gaia; the Supplicants, a silent, lugubrious sect who regarded the M'threnni as gods and prayed hourly to their masters, prostrating themselves in the direction of the tower; the Children of the Divine Light, a saffron-robed sect who hated the M'threnni and saw the twin suns as the eyes of the goddess Capella who watched over Gaia and directed all

human activity; the Panpsychists, who believed that everything in the universe possessed sentience and earnestly discussed abstruse philosophical problems with rocks and hand-
fuls of sand; the Holiest Church of the Most Venerable
Latter-Day Saints, a ressurrected version of a faith which had
originated on Earth; the Harbingers of Existential Glory,
whose mythos was so complicated it must have attracted
adherents by virtue of its intellectual challenge. All these,
and more, lent a dash of colour to the grime and poverty of the
South Bank. It was refreshing to discover such a jumble of
heterodoxies, and Wendi and I always felt welcome there for
a genial attitude of *laissez-faire* prevailed amongst its inhabitants.

At the beginning of Winter we had to choose our specializa-
tions. Wendi was already embarked on her medical studies; I,
after some vacillation, finally decided on Generics, a somewhat grandiose title for what was a broad-spectrum course
which would enable me to pursue my dual interest in science
and history. Wendi and I now shared a double room on the
top floor of the residence hall and we had settled into a quiet,
almost mundane lifestyle, preferring to concentrate on our
studies and our explorations of the city than to attend the
many social events on campus. It was a fruitful, industrious
time, unmarked by any upheavals or events pertinent to this
account.

   Towards the end of the season, the rains arrived. Winter
was always a time of gales and downpours, but no one was
prepared for the severity of the storms which broke at the
beginning of eleventh month. The fishing fleets were forced
into harbour on three occasions—the first time this had happened in over five cycles—and many shuttle flights were
suspended. Then, on the penultimate day of the month, a
particularly severe storm erupted, lasting for two days. The
swollen Tamus heaved over its banks and wide areas of the
city were flooded. Particularly hard-hit was the South Bank,
whole streets of buildings collapsing as the ground beneath
them dissolved into mud. When the storm finally abated, an

eerie silence settled over the city. I remember going out on to
the balcony of my room on that first fine morning and looking
out over the campus. Nothing moved, and everything seemed
weighed down by the tremendous burden of the rain. The
suns, which now burned with a peculiar intensity in the clear
skies, fixed me with their baleful gaze.

Restoration work was speedily accomplished on the North
Bank, where the flood damage had been relatively light, but
by the time the authorities had turned their attention to the
less fortunate inhabitants on the other side of the river, an
epidemic of fever was raging there. Although short-lived, its
effects were severe: over fifteen hundred people, one percent
of the city's total population, died. Wendi and I spent several
evenings in the South Bank during the closing days of twelfth
month as volunteers with the salvage teams. The entire area
was devastated and the survivors wandered around numbly,
their faces glazed with shock. As the days passed and the full
impact of the tragedy began to register, discontent
burgeoned. Why had the M'threnni sat idle in their tower
while people were dying? Why had they not come forward
with direct aid to ameliorate the effects of the flooding and
the disease?

Newseason's Day of Spring marked the beginning of the
thirtieth cycle of settlement on Gaia, and a grand parade had
been organized to celebrate the event. In common with the
rest of the city, the Institute held a pageant. We all dressed up
in the garb of the original colonists and, an hour after zenith,
began our march from the campus to the city centre.

We were wearing the stiff, elasticated tunics of the
pioneers and the hemispherical face-masks which they had
employed to screen our possible harmful bacteria (a precau-
tion which they had soon discovered to be unnecessary). The
costumes had been faithfully duplicated from the originals—
too faithfully, for after a half-hour's marching we were all
sweating profusely. We were forced to discard the masks and
make vents in the sides of our costumes, compromising
authenticity for comfort. For the pioneers, the first few

months on Gaia must have been uncomfortable ones indeed, sealed as they were in cocoons of their own perspiration.

We continued southwards, Lionel and the rest of the staff at the head of our column, dressed in the navy-blue robes of their office. By fourteen hours we were approaching the city centre, and we joined the main parade at the northern end of Albany Avenue. The street was filled with spectators— people thronging on the sidewalks, people standing on the first-floor balconies of shops, people sitting on the roofs. At the bottom of the avenue we turned right into New Broadway with its governmental offices and its incubator hatcheries, and thence into Falkirk Street, the narrow road which finally debouched into Capitol Square, our destination. It was with great relief that we sat down and unlaced our heavy boots, for it had been a warm, cloudless day with only a hint of wind.

The square had been cleared of the majority of its stalls (those remaining had been gathered in one corner to dispense food and refreshments) and the brown cobblestones, swept and hosed for the occasion, gleamed immaculately. Banners and buntings hung everywhere in a splash of colour, the red, white and blue of our ancestor nations vying with the green, gold and black of Gaia. The rapidly swelling crowds milled about, and there was much talk and laughter. Wendi and I took a table at a café in an arcade just off the square and ordered a demilitre of roseplum wine. It was going to be a long evening.

When all the marchers had finally dispersed, a clearing was created at the centre of the square and a troupe of dancers entered, cartwheeling and leaping over the cobbles. All the members were naked, save for the flesh-coloured codpieces of the males, and they staged an elaborate, sensual ballet which drew roars of approval from the crowd at its completion. A mime-theatre came next, the actors garbed in black leotards and balaclavas. Their pantomime was full of slow, jerky movements, compelling in its strangeness, the players like shadows acting out some phantasmal drama. Jugglers, fire-eaters, singers, musicians followed, a relentless se-

quence of acts to keep the crowd entertained. We purchased
a fresh bottle of wine. The sky bronzed, reddened, slowly
darkened. Puppeteers displayed their art; a woman was
bound in chains and wriggled free within half a minute; a
fortune-teller cast dice, consulted cards, and predicted prosperity for Gaia. Incense thickened the air, intermingling with
the smells of fried fish, vegetable broth, pastries and freshly
baked bread. Wendi and I shared a bowl of soup, a hunk of
cheese and a large chicken pie. We drank more wine.

Presently, a searchlight atop the main entrance to the
square was activated, throwing a cone of smoke-filled light
on to the balcony of the mayor's residence at the centre of the
north façade. The crowd fell silent and turned towards the
balcony. Moments later, the tall, thin figure of Helmine
Orne, the current Mayor of Helixport, emerged, dressed in
her ceremonial robes and flanked by the six members of
the City Senate. The golden chain across her shoulders and
the oval lenses of her spectacles gleamed in the light as she
raised her arms to request a silence which was already complete. Wendi and I left our table and wandered into the square
to listen.

"This is an occasion for celebration and reflection," Helmine began, her unamplified voice carrying effortlessly
across the square. "We have already celebrated, so let us
pause for a moment to reflect a little."

She glanced over her shoulder, then moved back from the
balcony, and it was Nathan Davidson, the diminutive
Vice-Mayor and Helmine's prospective successor, who
stepped forward and began to speak.

"Thirty cycles ago," he said, "our ancestors landed here
on Gaia. They found a harsh and arid planet, an environment
which was not immediately suited to human habitation. But
they had made the voyage across the void of space to find a
new home and there could be no turning back. Here on Gaia
there was air to breathe and firm ground to walk upon, so they
immediately set about the task of transforming the land into
something upon which human beings could live." He spread

his arms. "The evidence of their success is all around you. In thirty cycles we have grown from an original settlement of one thousand people to a thriving community of almost a quarter of a million souls, and there is hardly a corner of the continent which we have not penetrated. We have made large areas of barren land fertile, and we produce food aplenty for all our people. We have incorporated the technological knowledge which was our inheritance from Earth to build a civilized and sophisticated society, of which this city of ours is the prime symbol."

He let his arms fall and there was a pregnant pause.

"In this time of human celebration," he went on, "let us not forget that without the city, without a coherent centre of settlement from which to expand, our colony would surely have failed. When our descendants were in direst need of help, help arrived from the skies." A murmur passed through the crowd. "Helixport was built by human hands, and it is a monument to our endeavours, but much of the materials of our labour were freely donated to us by the M'threnni." The murmur grew stronger. "They have asked nothing in return, and they have continued to supply us—" someone hissed "—with the raw materials which will ensure our future growth and prosperity." The hissing was taken up by others, and someone shouted: "Parasites!"

Nathan looked disconcerted, but he attempted to continue: "So let us give thanks—," but his words were drowned in a sea of boos and angry cries.

He stepped back and conferred with Helmine. They had obviously misjudged the mood of the populace in acknowledging our debt to the M'threnni. The torrent of hisses, boos and yells was full-blooded by now, and Helmine stepped forward and gestured towards the entranceway. The searchlight went out.

An instant later, a series of explosions erupted overhead and the night sky was rent with bursting flowers of green, gold, red, white and blue. The firework display was splendid and by the time it was over, the mood of anger had all but evaporated and everyone's attention had turned away from the now empty balcony. Dancers reappeared in the square, inviting members of the crowd to join them. Soon the festivities were in full swing again, and Wendi and I were amongst the revellers.

Chapter Five

Mayoral elections were always held at the start of each new cycle and it was the custom for the outgoing mayor to endorse a candidate. The City Senate members, having risen through the hierarchy of central government, were regarded as heirs apparent to the position, and Helmine had followed tradition by endorsing Nathan, the Vice-Mayor, as her successor. Nathan, a comparatively young man for the position (he was still in his forties), was hardly an imposing figure. Small of stature and somewhat diffident in character, his performance as Helmine's back-up had been undistinguished, his speech to the crowd on Newseason's Day aptly demonstrating his lack of political acumen. His term of office seemed assured, though, for the elections, held at the beginning of second month, had in the past been formalities: the official candidate had run unopposed. But now, for the first time, there emerged a concerted opposition to central government.

In the aftermath of the floods and the spontaneous outburst against Nathan's speech in Capitol Square, the Humanistic League, that eclectic body of radicals who had been languishing on the South Bank, had recognized the prevailing mood

of disaffection towards the M'threnni and had united under
the leadership of one Eilan Bailey, a former psychologist
once in the employ of the government, now an ardent and
eloquent voice for those who demanded that the M'threnni
leave Gaia. While the mayor and her protégé were making
bland speeches to the polite sections of the city society, the
League launched a vigorous attack against both the government and the aliens, pasting posters on prominent buildings
by night and distributing pamphlets by day.

There was nothing in the city constitution to debar anyone
from running against the official candidate, and it soon became clear that the League was attracting grass-roots support
not only on the South Bank, but also in the High and Low
Valleys, where there had never been a fondness for aliens.
Although the outlying regions had only block votes in city
elections, their influence was still strong and prospective
mayoral candidates always sought commune approval since
the Mayor of Helixport was the *de facto* ruler of Gaia and
needed a harmonious relationship with the regions in order to
be able to work effectively.

Delegates representing various communes began to visit
Eilan and her followers at their headquarters on the South
Bank, and the *Helixport Chronicle* covered a League rally in
Union Plaza. I could glean little of the League's motivations
from the report. Their platform seemed based on a mixture of
resentment towards the long-standing rule of the Senate and
an ill-disguised xenophobia towards the aliens. But Eilan was
not amongst the speakers at the rally, and when I heard that a
holoscope team from the Institute had interviewed her and
that the interview was to be broadcast in the main viewing
theatre the following day, I resolved to attend the screening.
There had to be more to the League than bombast and prejudice. I tried to persuade Wendi to accompany me, but she
had no interest whatsoever in politics, so I went alone. The
theatre was filled to capacity a good ten minutes before the
screening began.

Eilan and her interviewer confronted one another across a
small table in a dimly-lit private room. The interviewer was a

young sociology student named Francis who was well known on campus for the acerbity of his opinions. Tall and fair-skinned, he was crouched predatorily in his seat, in stark contrast to Eilan, a squat, crumpled figure of negroid origins. She looked as if she had just been woken from a nap.

Francis squared the notes in his lap and said: "This is the first time that an official candidate for the mayorship has been opposed. Could you explain briefly what brought you to make such a radical decision?"

Eilan raised herself a little in her seat. She wore a shapeless fawn woollen dress, long-sleeved and high-necked. It was Winter-wear, but she did not seem to be suffering from the heat.

"We believe," she said, "that we have made no significant social or technological progress since the foundation of the colony. Our continued dependence on alien resources has stultified human initiative, resulting in a society which is materialistic and essentially stagnant. We feel that the City Senate embody this attitude of complacency, whereas we propose to introduce reforms which will hopefully bring our colony to life."

Francis waited a moment, as if expecting her to elaborate. When she did not, he said: "This seems a remarkably perverse claim. I would have thought that to establish a thriving city and a fertile hinterland capable of supporting almost a quarter of a million people in under thirty cycles is evidence of a remarkable vitality in our society."

Eilan brushed a fly from her cheek. She was a woman well past her sixtieth season, her dark skin deeply wrinkled, her wiry ash-coloured hair parted severely at the centre of her head and drawn back into a knot at the base of her neck. Although she looked old and time-worn, she seemed to possess an inner reserve of strength which manifested itself as an apparent nonchalance: her posture was slovenly, but her eyes were intent.

"I am talking about the quality of life, not its abundance," she said. "I do not deny that in purely expansionary terms we have accomplished wonders, and I do not belittle those achievements. But we have also seen a corresponding increase in poverty and social injustice, as anyone who lives here on the South Bank will verify. A society can only truly grow if its physical development is accompanied by political reform to deal with changing conditions. We intend to introduce such reforms should we gain office.''

"Exactly what do you propose?''

"At the core of the problem is the fact that we retain a colonial mentality. We are reliant upon outside aid—the M'threnni—to support us. Thus the average individual is given no great opportunity or incentive to contribute to the well-being of the colony because the feeling is prevalent that we are being ''looked after.'' Our first objective, then, would be to dispense with M'threnni aid and take on the responsibility for our own destinies.''

"So your principal objection to the aliens is that their aid tends to militate against self-development?''

"Precisely. As long as we continue to exist in a state of dependence on the aliens there will be no impetus to self-improvement.''

This, I thought, was a complete reversal of the common attitude. Most people saw the M'threnni presence as essential to the continued development of the colony. Still, Eilan had a point. I knew from my studies that our social and political systems had hardly evolved at all since the foundation of the city.

Francis appeared unimpressed. "Your opponents would claim that your dislike of the M'threnni is really rooted in resentment of the fact that their aid is so *limited*,'' he said.

"Our opponents are entitled to misinterpret our pronouncements any way they wish. It is a common political ploy.''

"Others maintain that simple xenophobia prompts you to seek their departure.''

"Again, that is their prerogative.''

Francis nodded his head reflectively. Eilan had lost none of her initial composure in the face of his hostility and skepticism. It was clear she would not be goaded.

"What are your own feelings towards the M'threnni?" he asked, changing tack.

"Personally, I do not fear or hate them because I do not feel that they have ever posed an overt threat to our society. But neither have they shown any sign that they wish to aid us directly. Their position is an extremely ambiguous one, and, as such, is a focus for resentment and hostility. This is a further reason why I feel that our colony would ultimately benefit if they left Gaia."

"You want to chop off the hand that feeds us, as it were? Isn't that an incredibly churlish attitude? The aliens have provided us with essential supplies and have asked nothing in return except that we respect their privacy."

"To pursue your analogy," Eilan said, "how would you feel about someone who fed you but would not save you from drowning or give you medicine if you were sick? Would you expect the survivors of the South Bank floods to feel grateful towards the aliens?"

Francis did not reply. Like me, he had been a volunteer with the salvage teams after the floods and he knew only too well how much resentment and even hatred towards the aliens had sprung up on the South Bank.

"The M'threnni aid us in their own terms," Eilan said. "Terms which are unknown to us. True, we should be grateful for their help in stabilizing the colony in its early days, but does this mean that we should ignore the fact that they will let human beings die rather than emerge from their tower? Should we—"

"Despite your earlier remarks," Francis interrupted, "you *do* seem to be arguing for more direct aid from the M'threnni."

"I'm arguing quite the reverse. There are good reasons to be positively afraid of any direct M'threnni intervention in our affairs."

"What reasons?"

"Because their culture is so inordinately advanced compared to ours, and because it is an alien culture at that. No doubt the City Senate are hoping that one day the M'threnni

will emerge from their tower and bestow upon us a cor-
nucopia of alien wisdom. I believe that if this did happen, the
results would be disastrous for our society."

"In what way?"

"There are many examples in Earth history of an advanced
civilization encountering a more primitive one and proceed-
ing to pass on the 'benefits' of its culture. There are two
possible outcomes. Either the primitive society is overwhelmed by the impact and withers into extinction, or it loses
its ethnic identity by degrees until it becomes indistinguisha-
ble from the dominant civilization. What makes our situation
even more precarious in the event of direct M'threnni involvement in our affairs is that we would be involved not just
in a cross-cultural transference, but an inter-species one, too.
It would mark the beginning of the alienization of our society."

Francis looked at her with frank disbelief, but again I felt
her point was valid. The history of Earth was littered with
examples to support her case: the destruction of the Incas by
the Spaniards, the subjugation of the Red Indians by Euro-
pean migrants to North America, the dwindling of the Austra-
lian aboriginal population following the arrival of settlers
from Britain—there were numerous precedents.

"This is not just idle speculation," Eilan was saying.
"You have only to look at the Voices to see the way in which
M'threnni culture could affect human beings. Does this pros-
pect appeal to you?"

Francis considered for a moment, then said: "Could you
not be suggesting a more plausible motive for the aliens'
aloofness? Could it not be that they recognize the possibility
of culture shock and that is why they maintain their policy of
non-interference?"

"It's quite possible. And, if so, it negates the hope that one
day they will increase their aid."

"So, then," Francis said, pouncing, "there is no real
reason to fear them, is there? If they intend to remain aloof
from our society, your last point is invalidated."

"But they do not exactly maintain a posture of complete

aloofness, do they? It is an open secret that periodically they leave the tower to seek out new Voices. Little is known of these trips, but I would suggest to you that there must be an element of coercion involved when a M'threnni selects a Voice. Have you ever met anyone who would gladly commit themselves to a life inside the tower?''

This was something that had occurred to me during the Alien Studies seminars. Despite Jon's assurances, I found it difficult to believe that the M'threnni took only willing subjects. Even people who were generally sympathetic to the aliens baulked at the thought of spending a lifetime as a Voice.

"This is my ultimate objection to the aliens," Eilan said. "They may be concerned about the well-being of the colony as an entity, but they show a complete disregard for individual human beings. Our society is founded on democratic principles. We believe that all people have equal rights and privileges. The M'threnni flaunt this principle. They do as they please. They *are allowed* to do as they please. In order to build an egalitarian society, one cannot allow élite groups to exist within yet apart from the whole, be they humans or aliens. That, finally, is why the M'threnni must be made to leave Gaia.''

There was a pause. Francis seemed to have lost a little of his early assertiveness and assurance. He leafed through his notes, then said: "Assuming that the League is victorious in the elections, how do you propose to engineer the M'threnni's departure from Gaia?''

Eilan eyed him meditatively. "I think," she said after a moment, "that we will be in a position to present to the people of Gaia direct evidence that the M'threnni presence here is positively undesirable. I am not prepared to say any more than that at this juncture.''

Francis pressed her, but she refused to elaborate. Finally he moved the discussion on to a consideration of the League's proposed reforms. Eilan continued to respond courteously and candidly to Francis's often disingenuous questions, and by the end of the interview it was clear that Francis had failed in his objective of provoking her into some ill-considered remark or of uncovering some seedy aspect of the League's programme. Eilan had reasoned, concerted arguments to back her opinions, and she had the expository gift of combining clarity with brevity. She was not some greedy outsider, hungry for power; if anything, her arguments were too intellectual to have a mass appeal. But the League had other orators who used a more emotive approach to win their audience over. I was thoroughly impressed. From being a mere repository of the disillusioned, the League had emerged as a cogent political force.

When the lights came on at the end of the screening, there were none of the curt dismissals of the League which had abounded prior to the interview. A few people remarked that Eilan's cryptic comment about presenting direct evidence of the M'threnni's undesirable presence was no more than a piece of election propaganda, but there was no doubt that most of the audience had been impressed by her forthrightness and apparent integrity. She was not simply the mouthpiece for a band of rabble-rousers, but a shrewd and committed radical. And the possibility that she *did* have something up her sleeve made things all that more interesting.

As the elections drew near, there were increasing signs that the League would garner sufficient support to oust the Senate. But it was not to be. On the night of the 16th, three dream parlours in the city centre were fire-bombed and League slogans daubed over their walls (despite their popularity, the belief was widespread that the parlours were M'threnni inventions). Retaliation was swift and uncompromising. The League was declared a subversive, illegal organization and the Civil Militia moved in, arresting Eilan and one or two other prominent members of the party, and shutting down their headquarters. This action proved decisive, for the League, always a loose confederation of opinion rather than a concerted ideological movement, had little internal strength; bereft of its leaders, its adherents melted away.

The day before the election, it was announced that Nathan (still unpopular for his pro-M'threnni speech) had decided to stand down as mayoral candidate in favour of Helmine, who had been unanimously endorsed by the Senate to serve an unprecedented second term. She promised to uphold the traditions which had seen Gaia prosper and to "maintain law and order." Two days later, Helmine began her second term of office, elected without opposition.

Spring passed, and the political life of Gaia reverted to its staid, placid norm. Wendi and I graduated from the Institute at the end of the season, both of us gaining class I certificates in our respective subjects. We looked forward to secure and lucrative careers.

Wendi obtained a post at the psychiatric faculty of Helixport General Hospital, while I, after a customary period of indecision, finally began work in the Information Services department of Central Government, the deciding factor in my choice being the promise of subsidized accommodation in a villa on a select estate when I attained adulthood. In the meantime, Wendi and I took up temporary residence in a hostel, and I spent the first six months of my working life undergoing training in the basement of Central Government Complex, that great monument to the Civil Service which rises in megalithic splendour about the approach to Round Island Bridge. I worked on data storage, cataloguing and indexing reports, and updating old statistics. The work was monotonous and undemanding, but it was only a transitory post, and quite well paid for that.

The last day of third month was Wendi's maturation day. She visited her commune and returned with her lineage card. Her surname was Carver and her distaff ancestry was traceable back to a prominent feminist politician of the late twentieth century. She was now a full citizen of Gaia, with the right to vote in elections, to apply for parentage, to full protection (and liability) under Gaian law. For a while she gently teased me with her new status, calling me "young

man'' and tugging at the lobe of my ear to reveal my birth
number (hers having been erased during the ceremony). And
then it was seventh month, and my own ceremony loomed.

It was not essential to return to one's area of origin for the
ceremony, but the elders of Silver Spring contacted me by
lettertape, inviting me to return. A full cycle had passed since
I had left the commune, and my anger towards them had
abated somewhat. Besides, I wanted to see my home again. I
notified them of my acceptance.

On the eve of the 8th I boarded the dusk shuttle for the High
Valleys. I had a first-class seat at the front of the craft. When
the steward came down the aisle to check that each passenger
was securely strapped in before take-off, I saw that it was not
Naree, but a young man only a little older than myself. I
thought perhaps she had been transferred to another flight,
but when I questioned him, he told me that she had retired
two seasons previously.

"Retired?" I said. "She always claimed she'd keep going
until she dropped."

He shrugged. "She broke a leg and it never healed properly. She was pensioned off. The old ones never know when
to give up."

He moved on, and I was left to reflect that another link with
my past had been severed.

Caril was waiting at the terminus when I debarked. She
kissed me lightly on the forehead and led me up the mountainside. I knew that it was not normal custom for the warden
of a junior dorm to greet a visitor from the city, even if that
visitor was a former resident of the commune. That the elders
had foregone protocol to take account of my dislike of ceremony was evidence that they were treating my visit with
some delicacy. We talked freely as we climbed the steep
pathway to the adult dorms; it was as if only a month had
passed since I had seen her last.

"The elders will greet you in the morning," she told me as
we entered the small dorm reserved for visitors. "A drink
before you retire?"

"Yes, please," I said.

We sat in the parlour, sipping nectarine tea. I told Caril about my life at the Institute, about my new job, about my hopes for the future. She, in turn, brought me up to date with events at the commune (little had changed since my departure) and informed me that there was a girl in her second season at junior dorm who showed every sign of surpassing my scholastic attainments.

"She has a brilliant intuitive grasp of concepts," Caril told me. "Unfortunately, she's also extremely lazy, and there's a possibility that she'll waste her gifts. Aptitude is not enough; it must be combined with application."

I smiled. "You sound like Erik."

She laughed. "I've been working with him for too long; those maxims of his have begun to stick. But it's true, nonetheless. As in your case, David. You always knuckled down to your work."

"In the schoolroom, perhaps. But not in the fields."

It has her turn to smile. "You always were a poor farmer. But then you might never have left Silver Spring if you hadn't been. Have you missed the commune at all?"

"To be candid, no. I suppose I'm grateful to everyone for giving me the opportunity to further my education at the Institute, but my only real ties here were severed when Annia died and Jax ran away."

Caril took a sip of tea. "Yes, that was a sad affair. Did you ever hear of Jax?"

I shook my head.

"The elders scoured the valleys for him, but without success. We finally decided that he had run away to Helixport."

"Probably. But if he did, he never got in touch with me."

"It's always a shame when we lose track of old friends."

"Are Annia's remains preserved?"

"Yes. You'd like to see them?"

It was clear she knew I would. I nodded, and she said: "We'll visit the crypt tomorrow, after your ceremony."

I was awoken at dawn the following day by a gentle tapping on the door. A young woman entered, carrying my breakfast on a tray. Her face was vaguely familiar and it turned out that she had been in her first season at junior dorm when I had been in my last. We had never known one another, however, and she seemed pleased that I had remembered her.

Diane—for that was her name—left, and I attended to my breakfast. It was the custom to spend the morning alone in a room on the day of one's maturation ceremony—supposedly so that one could reflect on the import of the occasion—but I had grown unused to solitude, so after I had eaten I slipped out of my room and went walking, up the mountainside to the old haunts of my childhood.

On the crest of the ridge above the Communications Centre, I turned and looked down the valley. It was filled with the goldbrowns of Summer and the crouched white figures of the harvesters, just as it had been when I had left for the city. The cycle continued remorselessly, and the thought was at once comforting and vexing. I realized at that moment that I would never return permanently to the valleys as I had often vaguely imagined I would. Although they would always be my spiritual home, one cannot live amongst dreams, and the reality was that they could never provide me with the elusive sense of fulfilment which I sought.

I followed the stream westwards, climbing all the while. The sparse brown soil of the fields had long surrendered to rocky outcrops of cream and buff stone, and the valley sides narrowed and steepened in lesser imitation of the true mountains further west. The stream which fed our valley was now no more than the width of an outstretched arm; but it cut its way through the bedrock with uncompromising swiftness, and when I removed my sweat-laden shirt and ducked my head into the water, its rushing chill tugged the air from my lungs with exhilarating speed. I lay down on a flat rock and let the suns warm me again. By the time I had retraced my path to the commune, it was an hour before zenith, the appointed time of my ceremony.

Once again I faced the elders in the austerity of the council hall, and once again the elder Robert asked me to confirm my identity. He then proceeded to give the date of my concep-

tion, the date of my transfer from the incubators to the
nursery at Silver Spring, and the dates of my accession to
primary dorm, junior dorm and senior dorm. Each date was
accompanied by a reference to the pertinent Act: the Genetic
Diversity Act, the Population Distribution Act, the Child
Rearing Act, and so on. It was tedious but over with relatively quickly. Finally he gave a résumé of my childhood at
the commune leading up to my departure for the Institute. He
then acknowledged that I had reached the age of twenty
seasons and he asked me if I was prepared to take on the full
responsibilities of adulthood.

"I am."

(Of course I am, I thought impatiently. Why else would I
be here?)

This admission was followed by another tedious enumera-
tion, this time of the twenty-four main tenets of the Gaian
Constitution to which, as a full citizen, I would be expected
to adhere. I stood there, numb with boredom and hardly
listening until Robert said: "Do you so agree?"

"Yes."

"Step forward."

I approached the table. Robert opened a small metal box
and produced a device which looked like a pair of pincers
with circular pads attached to each jaw. He motioned to me to
lean forward and when I did so, he clamped the jaws about
the lobe of my right ear. I felt a brief sensation of heat and
then he removed the device. My ear lobe tingled. Robert
passed me a small oval hand-mirror and I examined the
underside of the lobe. My birth number had been eradicated.

A black-rimmed envelope lay on the table. Robert picked
it up and handed it to me. It bore the logo of the Incubator
Centre. I broke the seal and removed the card inside. The
name at the top, my name, was DAVID WHITE.

Immediately below the name was a list of encoded information detailing my blood-type, my fingerprint patterns, my
voice profile, and so on—a physical and biochemical com-
pendium of me. The back of the card was divided into two.
The left-hand side was filled with closely printed type which

gave brief biographies of my forefathers back to the time of
the colonization. My father's name was Daniel and he was
still living, a bargemaster by profession. At the root of my
family tree was the name of one William White, an agronomist
born in Gloucester, England, who had evidently gained passage on the *Auriga* by virtue of his experience of semi-arid land
husbandry. The development of high-resolution Kellman
spectroscopy at the turn of the twentieth century had enabled
astronomers on Earth to determine the approximate conditions
on the surface of Gaia long before the departure of the *Auriga*,
and the colonists had been carefully selected according to their
findings.

The right-hand side of the card contained only a few lines
of information, none of which was comprehensible to me, for
it was the shorthand of the incubator authorities. The ovum
from which I had been conceived had been drawn from the
Auriga's gamete banks; my mother was a citizen of Earth,
long dead.

Robert took the card from me, examined it, and gave it
back. He gripped my shoulders. "Welcome to adulthood,
David White."

Once again I shook hands with each of the elders, and then
we departed the hall for the feast. A sheep had been roasted
for the occasion and a consignment of new potatoes had been
received from the Plains. The elder Arthor was particularly
lavish in his praise of the cuisine. Evidently the menu suited
his stomach, for there was not a hint of flatulence about him
on this occasion.

Afterwards Erik visited me briefly. He was courteous but
somewhat remote, and I was glad when he left to attend to the
afternoon's harvesting. Later, when Caril was leading me up
the mountainside to the crypt, she explained, unbidden, that
Erik disliked the city and its inhabitants and that he had
probably been curt with me because he now considered me an
urbanite. I merely nodded; it did not really matter that much
to me.

We reached the crypt, a vault of stone set into the ground
on the lichen-crusted ridge high on the north face of the

valley. Caril and I swung back the brass-plated trap-door and descended a flight of stairs into the cool, dark air. Caril activated a strip of bluish neon beside the entrance, bringing the vault into sudden, stark focus.

Hundreds of small aluminium urns sat on ledges along the walls and on shelves which demarked three corridors down the long, narrow chamber. We walked down the central corridor and stopped halfway, where the rows of urns ceased abruptly and the shelves were bare. Caril checked along the highest occupied shelf and examined several urns (the light was poor) before finally passing one to me. It bore only Annia's name, birth number, and the dates of her conception and death. I removed the lid and peered inside. A small pile of livid ash lay at the bottom of the vessel.

I replaced the urn on the shelf and prepared to leave. But Caril took my arm and led me further down the chamber into a larger, squarer room where the darkness once again prevailed. She switched on another neon light and I saw that here the walls held not shelves but lockers.

"Sometimes," Caril whispered, "the older people request that mementoes be stored here after they die. It was once an established practice amongst the ancient civilization of Earth, I believe."

I nodded.

Caril went over to one of the lockers, took a key from her pocket and opened it. She returned with a small white plastic box which I recognized as having once belonged to Annia. She opened the box and removed a glassy orb which glowed a dim reddish-brown; it was the M'threnni gasglobe.

"I discovered this amongst Annia's belongings after her death," Caril said, passing it to me. "I knew that the elders would not take kindly to alien artifacts on the commune, so I decided to hide it here until you returned."

I rotated the globe, watching the gently swirling wreaths of colour. It *did* feel faintly warm, as Annia had once suggested.

"Will you take it?" Caril was asking. "I'd prefer to have it off my hands."

"It was worth coming today for this alone," I said.

I left the commune an hour after zenith. No shuttle was due at Silver Spring until dawn the following day, but the elders had graciously offered to provide me with transport to New Kentucky in the Low Valleys, where a shuttle departed for the city at dusk. The battered old electric wagon used by the elders for courtesy visits to neighbouring communes stood on the asphalt road outside the main adult dorm as I made my farewells. When I saw the driver, I smiled with pleasure; it was Diane.

The journey down to New Kentucky took over five hours. Neither the wagon nor the tortuous mountain road was designed for speed, so we made slow but steady progress down the valley in the mellowing afternoon light. Diane was good company; as one of the elders' personal attendants, she was privy to their secrets, and she described in graphic and amusing detail their various idiosyncrasies while the wagon purred softly along the road. Robert, for example, always felt a chill at night and insisted that a hot-water bottle be placed in his bed before he retired, no matter what the season. He was constantly plagued with heat-rashes as a result, and was fondly known as The Scratcher. Leah was obsessive about the upkeep of her fingernails; she favoured daily manicures and frequently wore gloves for the most innocuous of tasks. Fritz, whose work involved the maintenance of the chicken-coops, was so enamoured of his fowl that he often slept with them and consequently stank of their ordure. Rila was extremely superstitious and prone to bizarre behaviour which she would later explain as having been necessitated by some ill omen or auspicious event. Diane seemed to have an anecdote for every one of the elders, and while I'm sure she elaborated her stories for my entertainment, I could not help but be amused.

We made two stops, at Milesville and Dennerton, for refreshments during our journey. The steep valley sides slowly flattened and broadened as we descended, while the stream widened, was joined by other tributaries, and became a full-blooded river. Finally we rounded the crest of a hill and below us, at the confluence of the northern and southern branches of the Tamus, stood New Kentucky. It was a larger commune than Silver Spring, with a population of over a thousand. The commune buildings were mostly grouped in the fork between the two tributaries, while the cultivated fields and pasturelands filled the bowl-shaped valley further downstream. Goats and sheep graced unattended on the upper slopes.

"We have almost an hour before the shuttle arrives," I said.

"Indeed," Diane agreed with a smile, slowing the wagon.

"How about there?" I said, indicating an outcrop of white rock overhanging the road just ahead.

We parked in the shadows beneath it, climbed into the back of the wagon and strung the canvas sheeting over the frames. I made my flight with only minutes to spare.

Chapter Six

Now that we had both attained adulthood, Wendi and I
notified the authorities that we wished to enter formal liaison.
We visited a registrar, and ten days later received our con-
tract. Five days after that, we were granted accommodation
at a villa on a plush estate beside the Tamus—one of the very
houses I had admired only a cycle before during my last visit
to the city with Annia and Jax.

The villa, a single-storeyed building of mock-Roman design, was surrounded by castellated walls which enclosed a
patio at the front and a spacious garden at the rear. Soon after
moving in, Wendi developed a passion for horticulture and
she began to stock the garden with a wide variety of plants.
She cultivated the delicate mistflowers bred by Gaian grow-
ers, planting them just outside our bedroom window so that
each morning when the cupped white blossoms opened to the
sun, their fragrant, gaseous emissions drifted like wreaths
into the room to greet us from sleep; she planted the indigenous rope-ivy, which soon found vigorous purchase on the
walls, she seeded the ornamental pool with lilies. But her
particular pride were the sapphire roses which had originated

on Earth and did not commonly grow well in Gaian soil. For
Wendi, they blossomed. She laid them out in crescent-
shaped beds on either side of the pool and they were much
admired by our neighbours. Hardly a day went by when she
did not spend at least an hour in the garden, watering, pruning
or manuring. I played no part in her endeavours, for they
reminded me too strongly of the chores of my youth. Instead,
I took to the roof, converting our tiny attic into a mini-
observatory where I spent many evenings star-gazing.

My probationary period at the Complex was now over and
I was transferred from data storage to compilation. The job
involved gathering information for the endless stream of
reports and documents which issued from the Complex; I
became mobile, travelling all over Gaia. The work was
interesting and varied, since it brought me into contact with a
wide range of people from the gruff, taciturn quarryworkers
who laboured sixteen hours a day in the arid, dust-choked
ravines of southern Gaia to the rich businessfolk and high-
ranking administrators who frequented the exclusive ski-
lodges on the north-western slopes of the Crescent Mountains. After three months of this, an additional post became
vacant with the death of the previous incumbent, and I
immediately applied for it. The post was unpopular and there
were no other applicants. After due consideration, my
superiors appointed me to the position of Inventory Clerk for
Off world Cargoes.

The post was unpopular because it entailed accompanying
the haulage teams to Round Island whenever a shipment from
the M'threnni homeworld arrived; few people would submit
voluntarily to making regular visits to the island. But for me,
the prospect was enticing; I nurtured the faint hope that I
might see an alien again. It was the very elusiveness of the
M'threnni which made them fascinating to me at that time.

The M'threnni shipments arrived at intervals of twenty-
three days—an incongruous regularity believed to be related
to the rotational period of the M'threnni homeworld. The
freighters arrived at night, ghostly haloes of light which came
and went almost without a sound. Surreptitious observations

by "meteorologists" in "weather-balloons" hovering conveniently near the island and armed with infra-red viewers and cameras had failed to uncover any details of the unloading operations. As a freighter approached the terminus an opaque grey glow would envelop the landing strip, blocking off all observations until the freighter departed two to three hours later. The freighter's cargo would be stacked at the centre of the terminus in white rectangular units the size of a small room (the units themselves were constructed of a tough polymeric material which was malleable under heat and was extensively used in the interiors of buildings). At dawn, the arched portal on the western arc of the black parapet which rimmed the terminus would dilate, and the haulage teams would move in, a fleet of highly-paid forklift drivers who had been selected for their speed of work and their phlegmatic attitude to things alien. The M'threnni tower stood diametrically opposite the portal, on the eastern end of the terminus.

I had been told that the atmosphere inside the terminus was strange, and when I rode in on the morning of my first assignment, I found this to be true. There was an excessive stillness and silence inside the black-walled arena, as if the natural world had been excluded or allowed only partial access to the island. We rode in on a bright, cloudless morning, but as we stepped out on to the obsidian-like surface of the arena, Capella's light seemed muted and the sky was shaded towards grey. There was a complete absence of any wind, of any motion whatsoever, beyond that of the incoming trucks. I could not hear their engines until they were quite close; sound was dampened too.

"Is it always like this?" I whispered to Berenice, the forklift driver in whose truck I was riding; she was the senior member of the haulage team.

"Like what?" she said in an ordinary conversational tone which sounded frighteningly loud to me.

"So quiet."

"Like a crypt," she said. "Always."

The cargo units had been stacked in four neat rows at the centre of the terminus. The units had evidently been designed so that the trucks could handle them easily—evidence that the M'threnni were well aware of the exact capabilities of human technology. They were lidless and curved at their edges like rectangular wash-basins. They bore no distinguishing marks.

While Berenice manoeuvred the truck for pick-up, I stared towards the tower, but there was no sign that anyone had emerged.

"Have you ever seen any aliens or Voices?" I asked her.

"I've seen a Voice or two a few times. They stand there like dummies, just watching. They never bother us."

"Haven't you ever felt the urge to approach one of them?"

"Never," she said, slotting the forks beneath the nearest unit. "What would I have to say to one of them?"

The shipments themselves varied little in overall content. The bulk of the units contained crude metal ores and minerals, plastics, synthetic rubbers, and—most importantly—woods. Wood was scarce on Gaia, for there were few native ligneous plants and few trees of Earth-stock which grew well in our climate. Afforestation programmes in the Low Valleys had been only partially successful and the M'threnni wood—which varied from a dark mahogany-type to the aptly named whitewood—was much prized for furniture. The ores and minerals invariably required refining before they could be used—a sign that the aliens wanted to ensure that the colony had to work a little before it reaped the full harvest of the freighter shipments.

The utilitarian bias in the aliens' shipments was, however, belied on each occasion by the inclusion of a single unit containing what were essentially luxury items—*objets d'art* such as the gasglobe; miniature abstract sculptures carved in semi-precious stone or moulded in rare metals; luminous rods (the so-called lightsticks) which gave off a pinkish radiance; larger items akin to the black rhombohedron at the Institute (they came in different shapes and different, though always dark, hues); and finally—the most prized items of all—a variety of luxurious fabrics. It was the "trinket box" which demanded my greatest attention, for I was required to make a detailed list of every item within it before it was loaded on board the transporter which waited outside the terminus.

I soon discovered that the contents of these boxes were plundered by high-ranking officials and private citizens who were rich enough to forfeit the sums of money required for a unique piece of M'threnni jewellery or a length of fabric sheer enough to be made into a most exclusive gown. The more commonplace items—there were always gasglobes and lightsticks in the box—eventually found their way out into the open market.

On my third visit to the island, a dark, oval portal appeared in the tower's base and two Voices emerged. The tower stood over two hundred metres away from the centre of the terminus, so I could not see them clearly, but both were male. Frozen like holocube figures in the mouth of the portal, they simply stood there, framed by its darkness, watching us until the last truck had left the terminus.

In the middle of Autumn, Wendi and I donated sperm and ova to the incubators for compatibility studies. Towards the end of the season we spent ten days holidaying at a ski-lodge in the Crescent Mountains. Wendi was captivated by the surroundings: the pristine white landscape, the cool, rarefied air, the heady atmosphere of affluent decadence. Most of the patrons were wealthy middle-aged or elderly folk, long-established in the Gaian society, and for the first few days we felt like intruders. Then, one evening when we were dining, a white-haired man who had been sitting alone at a table near by came over and introduced himself.

His name was Theo and he was a banker in Helixport. Was this our first visit to the lodge? It was. Were we enjoying ourselves? Yes, indeed. Would we care to join him for cocktails? We would. We made small talk for an hour or two, effortlessly and pleasantly, and before he left he invited us to a "gathering" at his suite the following evening.

We arrived at the agreed time, dressed apprehensively in our best clothes. There was much wine and choice titbits which we nibbled as Theo led us around his luxurious suite, introducing us to theatrefolk, senior public officials, economists, surgeons, militia colonels, antique dealers—the affluent élite of the city. Everybody greeted us with great civility, and the men especially were charmed by Wendi's youth and gaiety. Soon I felt completely at ease.

Some time later, when my head was considerably lightened with wine, I noticed that snuff boxes were being passed around. Eventually one turned up in my hand. It contained a bright yellow powder and when I asked what it was, I was told: "Sundust."

I pretended to take a pinch and sniff it, but there was nothing between my fingers. "Sundust" was the fatuous slang-term for euphorin.

Within an hour, everyone was stretched out on sofas and cushions, smiling dreamily. All conversation, all social exchange was extinguished: every person had retreated into the private microcosm of their mind. Wendi amongst them.

The following morning we argued. Why had she, who had always deplored the traffic in the drug, compromised herself? As an experiment, she told me. Just to see what it was like. She claimed that she had taken only a small amount, less than that required for a total hallucinogenic effect. I said that this sounded like waffle to me: how could you have partial hallucinations? She replied that I was being silly, that I had always had a prejudice against any form of imaginative experience. She cited the fact that I had consistently refused to accompany her to a dream parlour. Was I afraid of my own unconscious? I stormed out of the lodge.

We were reconciled by zenith. Wendi was contrite, and she promised that she had no intention of further experimenting with the drug. I drew from her a further promise that we would not attend any more "gatherings" during our stay. We would socialize publicly, but steer clear of private functions.

As luck would have it, we received no further invites. We learned to ski (I somewhat more successfully than Wendi), gambled cautiously at the roulette wheels and baccarat tables (she somewhat more successfully than I), and spent the evenings indulging in polite conversation in the muted atmosphere of the cocktail lounge. Wendi was thoroughly enamoured of the lodge by the end of our stay, and we promised one another that we would return there as soon as time and our finances allowed.

The first rains of Winter visited the city and there was a minor outbreak of fever on the South Bank—a grim echo of the previous epidemic a cycle ago. Wendi and I received notification that our sperm-ova samples had been accepted for incubation. Two children, a boy and a girl, would be conceived some time during the next three seasons (dates were never specified in order to forestall inquisitive donors from seeking out their offspring, genetic parentage being frowned upon).

Oddly, our success in attaining parentage did not serve to cement our liaison. Since our return from the ski-lodge, Wendi had grown slowly more restless and preoccupied. Although she insisted that nothing was amiss, and made love to me as ferociously as ever as if to emphasize the fact, there was a distinct change in her behaviour. Her job at the hospital demanded that she keep irregular hours, but I soon noticed that she was spending more and more time away from the villa, especially in the evenings. Her distracted manner when she was at home reminded me of the earliest phase of our relationship, when I had been just one of her many bed-partners at the Institute's residence hall. I tried a gamut of approaches from tenderness to anger in an attempt to discover what was troubling her, but she made light of my attentions, claiming that I was projecting some anxiety of my own upon her. I sensed that a crisis was looming, and felt powerless in the face of it.

A M'threnni freighter visited Round Island on the second night of fifth month, and soon after dawn the following day the haulage teams moved into the terminus. It was a heavily overcast day and a stiff easterly wind was blowing, threatening rain. The wind died to nothing as we entered the black-walled arena, the familiar deadening of the natural world to which I had grown accustomed but not entirely inured. Capella was visible as a diffuse oval patch of light behind ashen clouds.

The cargo units were stacked, as ever, at the centre of the terminus. I had an arrangement with Berenice, who drove the lead truck, that she would always pick up the trinket box, for it was easier to complete the detailed itemization of its contents while the other units were being loaded into the transporter.

I climbed out of the truck and stood on one of the forks, which Berenice then raised until I was able to see over the top of the units. We drove along each row and finally I located the trinket box (its position varied with each shipment) at the near end of the third row. I signalled to Berenice and she began to lower me to the ground.

Suddenly there was a tremendous roar, as if a massive wave had flung itself over the parapet, and I found myself lying on the glassy floor of the arena with fragments of black rock raining about my head. I stumbled to my feet. Fifty metres to the left of the portal, plumes of smoke were rising into the air from a breached section of the parapet wall.

The last of the flying rubble skittered away across the arena and the smoke dissipated rapidly in the breeze. The explosive device had evidently been planted under the lip of the parapet for the rent was roughly V-shaped, extending two-thirds of the way down the wall. A flock of seabats, disturbed from their nesting places on the rocks outside the terminus, wheeled about overhead, screeching hoarsely.

I became aware that Berenice was knocking on the windscreen of the truck. She waved her arms as if calling me back, then pointed towards the tower. The dark portal had opened in its base.

"Come on!" I heard her cry. "Let's get out of here!"

The rest of the trucks were already hurrying towards the exit, their loads forgotten.

Two figures emerged from the tower, the one human, the other alien.

"They're coming!" I called, with a mixture of surprise and glee.

Berenice swung the truck around and drew up beside me. "Get in."

I shook my head. "It's all right. You go on."

For an instant she stared at me as if I was mad. Then she slammed the truck into gear and accelerated off towards the exit.

The silence which fell when her truck had quitted the terminus was absolute. The seabats still whirled overhead, but I could not hear their cries. I stared towards the tower, watching the two figures who were approaching.

As they drew near I could see that the Voice was a male and the M'threnni, a good half metre taller than the man, a female. She walked with a curious shuffling stride, her feet invisible under her gilded maroon robe. Her arms rested at her sides, her long fingers splayed spider-like on her garment. She had heavier hips and a thinner waist than the male I had encountered, but she was devoid of breasts and hairless, and possessed the same piercing ebony eyes. Her nostrils dilated rapidly as she moved.

The Voice walked slightly behind her, his hands dangling loosely at his sides in mimicry of the alien. He wore a copper-coloured tunic exactly like the one the dying female Voice had been wearing. He was lean and hairless, his lack of eyebrows making his forehead seem disproportionately large compared with the rest of his face. His skin was almost as pale as the M'threnni's and his utter lack of expression gave his countenance the aspect of a china mask. I guessed him to be of middle age.

The alien and the Voice came within metres of me—I could hear the female's laboured breathing—but they did not stop or acknowledge my presence. They walked on until they reached the damaged section of the parapet wall. The M'threnni's fingers wriggled restlessly at her sides as she regarded the destruction; the Voice stood at her shoulder, motionless and impassive.

It was, perhaps, ten minutes before they turned away from

the wall and began walking back towards me. They stopped about three metres away, the alien riveting me with her black stare. A series of hisses, low-pitched murmurs and throaty clicks began to issue from her half-open mouth. Her lips did not move (the inner mouth was wet and purplish) but the grey membranes flashed spasmodically across her eyes as if in punctuation.

The Voice listened in absolute stillness, his head cocked slightly towards the alien. The susurrus ceased abruptly, and the Voice looked at me and said: "You are a representative of the city authorities."

The words were delivered in a bass monotone so that it was impossible to tell whether the sentence was a statement or a question.

"Yes," I replied, deciding on the latter.

"The wall has been breached by explosives."

Was this another question? I stared at him, wondering. His face remained as expressionless as his voice. The smooth, pallid skin was like that of a young child, but the deadness of his eyes made his face seem almost unhuman.

"Why did you not leave the terminus," the Voice queried.

I was about to speak when the alien began her sibilant burble again. A rift had appeared in the clouds and a shaft of harsh, wintry sunlight illuminated the terminus; I guessed that it was this which had provoked her outburst. The alien's fingers moved rapidly as she spoke, while the Voice continued to gaze blankly at me. When she had finished addressing him, he said: "You will accompany us to the tower."

A sudden panic surged within me, but I fought it down, reminding myself that the very reason I had stayed behind was in the hope of meeting the aliens. Was this not an additional bonus? But I could not quell my fear for I knew that no human had entered the tower who had not become a Voice.

The female shuffled off and the Voice followed closely behind. Checking my stride to match their leisurely gait, I fell in at their side.

As we crossed the terminus, the only sound I was conscious of was the female's heavy intake and exhalation of air, a sucking and hissing, sucking and hissing, like an asthmatic struggling for breath. Neither the female nor the Voice looked back at me as we approached the tower.

At close range, this strange, magnificent structure looked even more impressive than when viewed from a distance. It rose over two hundred metres into the air, a gleaming white corkscrew which mocked all human architecture in its exotic splendour. There were no windows, no external features at all; just a tubular ivory coil which curved upwards in ever-decreasing circles until it diminished into a spire.

The base of the tower was the most substantial part of the building, a squat cylindrical area containing the oval entrance portal at its centre. The oval was deep maroon, almost black in colour, and although I knew that it was "open," nothing could be seen within. It was like looking into a dark, unwelcoming cave.

The M'threnni passed through the portal and abruptly vanished from sight. The Voice gently took my arm and led me forward. I felt a strange, not unpleasant tingling on my skin, and a vague tugging in the pit of my stomach, like riding upwards in a fast-moving elevator. Then the darkness ebbed away to reveal an oval corridor lit by a dim reddish light. The air was cool and exhilarating: a high oxygen content, I guessed. As we moved down the corridor I began to realize that normal human perspective was inadequate in the tower; the corridor seemed quite short, yet we appeared to be making no progress towards the dark portal at its further end. And then, suddenly and unexpectedly, we were upon it and stepping through. Again my skin tingled and this time the gut-feeling was one of falling. Again the blackness faded and we were standing in a small, low-ceilinged, oddly-proportioned chamber lit by the same ruddy illumination as the corridor. I felt giddy, and blinked my eyes to clear my vision.

The chamber was roughly rectangular in shape, but it held no angles or corners, no individual walls or floors, just a single surface which enclosed us so that it was like being inside an opaque, cuboid bubble. The smooth curves of the room admitted no shadows, and the feeble red light did not seem to originate from any single point. This lack of focus in the geometry and the lighting increased my disorientation and I felt as if I was about to fall over. The Voice must have sensed this, for he moved forward, took my arm and sat me down on a small, rounded plinth which seemed to have grown miraculously out of the floor.

Another plinth faced me, this one higher than mine to accommodate the extra length of the alien. The female settled herself upon it, her knees pressed tightly together and her arms bent backwards so that her hands rested on her shoulders—a pose which looked as queer as it did uncomfortable. There was no plinth for the Voice, and he took up a position to the female's right, sitting down on the floor.

Seconds crept by in silence. My dizziness had abated somewhat now that I was seated, and I peered around the chamber, trying to guess its normal function. But apart from the plinths, there was no other furniture or features, just the pale, smooth contours of the room, insubstantial in the dim light, and the dark portal through which we had entered shimmering faintly off to my left.

The M'threnni began her sibilant and guttural intonations, an undulating flow of unintelligible syllables, at times oddly reminiscent of a human struggling with a severe stammer, at times wholly exotic. The Voice seemed remote and distracted, as if the sounds came from far away and he had to sit absolutely still and silent in order to apprehend everything. The alien did not look up at him as she spoke; her ebony eyes were fixed firmly and disconcertingly upon my own face.

Finally she was done and the Voice showed a modicum of animation again.

"This one would know the purpose of such destruction," he said in his leaden tones.

"I do not know," I replied, my eyes darting nervously between the two of them before finally settling on the Voice's placid, less disturbing face. "We—I and my fellow workers—were taken by surprise by the explosion."

There was a pause while the Voice absorbed this information and formulated his next question.

"Do you know what persons are responsible," he said finally.

I considered, and decided on honesty. "I do not know precisely who they may be. But there are some who oppose the M'threnni presence on Round Island. It is possible that this attack was undertaken by these people."

Again several seconds passed before he replied.

"Do these people wish the tower to be abandoned and that we should come among you," he asked.

His question sent a slight chill through me, for he had said "we" almost as if he considered himself a M'threnni.

"They wish for the M'threnni to leave Gaia," I said. "They feel that we must manage our world without outside intervention." I paused, then added: "But these people are few in number and do not represent the wishes of the people at large."

This half-truth made me feel nervous as soon as it was out, for I had the sudden, irrational feeling that the M'threnni female was reading my mind. Her eyes had not moved from my face throughout the exchange, and it took a positive effort on my part not to look at her.

The Voice took even longer than usual to digest this information. Then he rose and said: "It is welcome that you have communicated these facts to us."

The "interview" was obviously over. I rose and allowed the Voice to lead me over to the portal. The M'threnni remained seated and the grey membranes now blurred her eyes.

The Voice directed me to step through the portal. I did so, and this time the falling sensation was so profound I instinctively reached out for something to break my descent. But there was nothing. My skin tingled fiercely and the black air seemed to be rushing past me. Then the darkness vanished abruptly and with it the feeling of motion; I found myself outside the tower, blinded by the sudden bright light of day. I stood still for a moment to reorientate myself, and a shiver passed through me. Rubbing my arms to disperse the chill of the tower, I began walking across the terminus to the exit portal, which was still open.

A vague feeling of dissatisfaction possessed me as I crossed the deserted landing-strip but I could not pinpoint its source. I checked my watch and discovered to my astonishment that I had been inside the tower for almost an hour, whereas subjectively it had seemed only ten or fifteen minutes. I still felt slightly dislocated, as if there was a veil between me and the world, and it was only after I had passed through the exit portal that this dream-like quality of sensation passed away.

The forecourt was deserted save for a single floater. A militia man got out of the vehicle and motioned to me to climb in. We drove across the bridge to the Complex and he led me up a narrow flight of stairs, along a corridor and into a small elevator which eventually deposited us opposite a dark, wooden door. On this he tapped three times before opening it and indicating that I should enter. Not once had he spoken to me.

I stepped inside and the door closed immediately behind me. I stood in the office of Helmine Orne, the Mayor of Helixport.

A luxurious green carpet covered the entire floor and all the furniture was of dark M'threnni wood. Potted plants decorated the window ledge, the bookshelves, the filing cabinets, and the air was redolent of their fragrances. It was like being in a garden.

Helmine sat at her desk, scribbling something on a pad. "Sit down," she said without looking up. I settled into the upholstered chair in front of her desk.

She scribbled on for a minute or so, then put her pen down and took a handkerchief from her pocket. She removed her glasses and began to polish the lenses.

"What happened?" she asked.

I blurted out my account, sparing no details. Helmine did not interrupt, nor did she look up from her incessant polishing until I had finished.

She put her glasses on, pocketed her handkerchief and said: "Is that all?"

"As well as I can remember."

She got up, went over to the window and looked out across the river towards the tower. "It's not very much, is it?" she said.

"What do you mean?"

"You were inside the tower—for how long?"

"About an hour. But it felt like a lot less."

"And they questioned you."

"Yes."

"And you didn't think to ask them questions yourself?"

Of course. That was what had been troubling me vaguely ever since I had left the tower. The questions. All the many questions I had wanted to ask had gone unasked. They had not even occurred to me.

Helmine turned away from the window. She was holding a small cactus plant, stroking the furry down which cloaked it. "Well?"

I shook my head contritely. "I don't know," I said. "I was so shocked, so surprised to even be allowed inside . . ."

"Do you realize," she said, reseating herself, "that you are the first person who has even been allowed to enter and leave the tower? Do you realize the opportunity you had? Do you realize how many people would have given a limb for such an opportunity?" Her tone was scathing.

"Why do you think I stayed behind after the explosion?" I said. "It was because I hoped to meet the aliens. It was because they intrigue me. But the tower is strange. I felt disorientated. I couldn't think straight."

Helmine was not mollified; she stared at me stonily.

"It was hardly a spying mission, in any case," I said. "I did not know what to expect and as a result did not know how to react. Perhaps if you had given me a detailed list of instructions beforehand . . ."

"Now, now, my boy, don't be petulant," Helmine said with oily propitiation. "You must appreciate that this was an ideal opportunity to discover something of our mysterious mentors.'' The rictus of a smile formed on her face. ''You showed great resolve in staying behind.''

I did not react to this platitude. Helmine put the plant down on the desk and rested her chin on her interlocked fingers. ''I'd like to ask you a favour,'' she said.

''What sort of favour?''

''I'd like you to submit to a brain-scan.''

''A brain-scan?'' I said with foreboding.

She waved her hands dismissively. ''All we do is hook you up to one of the brain rhythm modulators used in the dream parlours. We programme you to dream of the tower and we monitor the images. It's perfectly harmless and quite painless and it will provide us with a better idea of what you actually saw inside than any verbal or written account.'' She waited.

''I don't like the idea,'' I said. In fact, it terrified me.

''There's nothing to it,'' she insisted. ''The technique was developed cycles ago for monitoring the dreams of disturbed patients. No harm will come to you.''

''I don't like the idea of people prying inside my head.''

''Oh, come, come. We can ensure that you focus on the visit to the tower alone. I'm not interested in your life-history, my boy. I just want to see for myself what it's like inside the tower.''

''I've told you what it's like.''

''Telling is not enough. I have to see for myself. Can't you see how important this is to me?''

She waited again, then said: ''You understand, of course, that I can ensure that you submit to a scan whether you want to or not?''

I simply stared at her.

''Forcible scanning *does* destroy large areas of the memory. Sometimes it blanks out the entire brain.'' She sucked on her teeth, as if drooling on the thought. ''Well?''

I submitted to the scan. I remember nothing of it, except a blackness. When I awoke I was unharmed and all my memories were intact. I was allowed to return home that evening, hungry and exhausted.

Wendi was not yet home. I took a bath, cooked myself a meal and, when it was eaten, sat back and reflected on the day. What had I learned of the aliens from my sojourn in the tower? Had I learned anything? Yes, I had established that the M'threnni were not quarantined in the tower, that they harboured no mysterious viruses or bacteria likely to strike down an ordinary human being, in the way that I had once imagined Annia had been. That idea had always been somewhat preposterous, I realized; it had been rooted in my need to assign some special significance to Annia's death. No, the tower, the aliens were sterile, and Annia had been killed by some terrestrial or Gaian micro-organism. But if not quarantined, the M'threnni were certainly isolated in their tower, maintaining only a minimal interest in the affairs of the colony. The female and the Voice had apparently been unaware of the existence of the League, or indeed of the general feelings of unrest which had persisted since the floods. They were not the omniscient watchers of Jon's imaginings, but the remote and aloof beings of popular fancy. Even so, I found it hard to accept that they could be that uninterested in a colony which they had subsidized since its inception.

The tower itself was stranger than I could have imagined, but it seemed to conform to the accepted notion that the M'threnni preferred a cool, dimly-lit environment with a slightly lower gravity and a higher atmospheric oxygen content than that of Gaia. As for the aliens themselves, they remained inscrutable because they only spoke through their Voices. Suddenly I caught myself. *Only spoke through their Voices.* What if that were literally the case? The Voice had been like a doll, like a man of straw when he had been addressing me. What if the alien had actually spoken directly to me by temporarily usurping his brain? Could it be that the Voices were human puppets, worked by the telepathic hands of their alien masters?

Deep into these speculations, I fell asleep, and when I awoke it was past midnight. Wendi was still not home, but I decided to go to bed nonetheless. When I went into the bedroom I came across a note on the dresser:

David: I had to leave. I'm sorry. Please don't come to the hospital. I need some time alone to work things out.

Look after yourself,
Wendi

Chapter Seven

I contacted the Complex the following morning and asked for ten days' leave. At first my request was turned down—I was already over my quota for the season—but when I explained that Wendi had left me, the arrangements were made with a speed which only personal loss seems able to evoke.

I spent most of the day wandering around the villa. The *Chronicle* arrived at zenith and the news of the explosion on Round Island dominated the front page. There was no mention of my visit to the tower. The attack itself had been a diversionary maneuvre: while the militia's attention had been focused on the island, Helixport Penitentiary had been raided and Eilan Bailey, the former leader of the Humanistic League, had been spirited away. No arrests had yet been made.

That evening I sat in a café opposite the hospital, watching the day-shift workers depart. Finally Wendi emerged, alone, and headed off down the street. She walked slowly, with an affected casualness, as if she suspected that I might be following her but did not want to look around for fear of provoking an incident. I kept my distance, though, just in case she did. Taking a circuitous route through the backstreets, she finally entered one of the plusher hostels on President Street.

An hour or so later a floater pulled up outside the hostel and a silver-haired man emerged. I recognized him immediately: it was Theo, the banker we had met at the ski-lodge. He went into the hostel and, minutes later, came out with Wendi. They got into the vehicle and drove off.

I made no attempt to follow them. Walking without urgency, I began my return to the villa. I felt no anger, just sadness, resignation and a vague envy. There had always been implicit in my relationship with Wendi the feeling that it was provisional, that as soon as one of us ceased to fulfil the other's needs, it would be time to separate. Wendi and I had both been going through periods of personal crisis when we had come together—I, shocked by the loss of Annia and Jax; she, wanting some form of stable companionship after a spell of indiscriminate sexual activity—and we had never succeeded in transforming what began as a mutual assuagement of pain—a negation of feeling, as it were—into desire in its fullest sense. We had given freely of our passions, but there had always been some essential, elusive quality lacking between us. The quality, I suppose, of love.

And now it was over. And Wendi had looked composed, almost happy now that the stresses of our last uneasy period together had been removed. I envied her contentment, and resented it, for it seemed to mock me. No matter that I had never really loved her; we had shared our lives for over a cycle, drawn strength from one another, but now she no longer needed me. That was what rankled: she no longer needed me.

The next day I sent notice to the authorities that I wished to annul our liaison. I gave instructions that copies of the relevant documents be sent to Wendi at her new address—a fit of petulance which still leaves me embarrassed whenever I recall it.

I felt overwhelmed by the recent turn of events, and there was no one I could look to for comfort. I had no close friends or confidants. I spent a further day brooding at the villa, then decided that I would seek out my father. Although it was not customary to make contact with one's parents on reaching adulthood, it was not entirely unknown, and, besides, I did not plan to reveal myself to him. I just wanted to meet him, to see what sort of person he was. (Deeper motives than this prompted me, of course, but I was determined not to rationalize them; for once, I would act on instinct.)

I had already investigated his timetable after my return from my maturation ceremony. He operated out of Venice lock in western Helixport, supplying the north-western quadrant of the Plains. Three six-day voyages a month, on the 1st, 7th and 13th, with two days' rest at the end. Towards dusk on the 6th, I entered the *Water's Edge* saloon, a rendezvous for bargemasters out of Venice.

I cradled a large mug of salty beer for half the evening, until it was warm and flat, watching the incoming and departing strangers, but seeing no one who might be him. And then, an hour before midnight, an auburn-haired man of middle height and build entered. There was something about his deportment which seemed familiar. While he stood at the bar, I scrutinized his profile. He shared the same oblique, narrow nose, the same prominent jaw-line, the same squarish cranium. I watched as he sat down at a table and began talking with two women. His posture—the tightly crossed legs, the body hunched forward—was a favourite of mine.

I gulped down the last of the tepid beer, went up to the bar and ordered a fresh mug. After I had been served, I approached the table and stood there, watching. The conversation dwindled away and three faces looked up at me.

"Daniel White?" I asked the man.

He nodded cautiously.

"Would you spare me a few moments? Can I sit down?"

There was an empty chair at the table which he pushed back with his foot. As I sat, the two women got up, draining their mugs.

"You don't have to leave," I said.

The elder of the two wiped froth from her lips with the back of her hand and said: "We have a barge to take out. Otherwise we wouldn't."

The two women nodded to my father and sauntered off.

"My name is David Carver," I said, adopting Wendi's surname for my disguise. "I work for the Information Services section of Central Government. We're attempting to gather some data on the workings of the canal system in order that we might improve the efficiency of the service."

As soon as the words were out, I immediately regretted them. My father's initial curiosity had become faint, amused contempt.

"That is," I said hastily, "we're looking for ways to regulate and standardize our shipments from the city in order to cut down on unnecessary cargo-space and journey times so that both the bargemasters and the plainsfolk benefit."

I was blathering, but his smile was not wholly uncharitable.

"I'd like to spend a few days on the barge with you. Just one voyage."

He took a long, slow draught of beer and put the empty mug down on the table. "Why pick on me?"

I shrugged. "The luck of the draw."

He drummed his fingers on the table-top, considering.

"I promise not to interfere in any way," I said. "I simply want to observe."

He looked up at me. "You'll do more than observe. My deckhand's sick, and I'll expect you to do her share of the work." He pushed the mug across the table to me.

I smiled broadly, gratefully, took the vessel and went up to the bar.

The Plains farms lie mostly within a ten-kilometre belt on either side of the Tamus; beyond this, the land rises gradually, making irrigation impracticable. The dust-storms have more severe effects on the unsheltered plains than in the city, and soil erosion is a constant problem. I had visited a number of farms on the river plain in the course of my work, and I knew how dependent they were on the supplies of fertilizer manufactured from the nitrogen-rich algae common to the shallow coastal waters of Gaia. The entire area, a geometrically intricate grid covering tens of thousands of hectares, produced the cereal and bean crops for the whole of the lowlands and was under intensive cultivation. Served by a complex system of canals and minor waterways, the farms battled constantly for their soil against the arid winds which blew intermittently but fiercely throughout Autumn and Winter.

I sat on the prow of the barge as we headed up the Tamus that first morning. A brisk, cool breeze blew down the river and I drank it in gratefully. The muscles in my shoulders and arms ached abominably from heaving sacks of fertilizer, bags of experimental seeds, boxes of provisions and sundry other items into the copious hold of the barge. Starting at dawn, it had taken over three hours to load the vessel fully. My father stood at the tiller, a canvas forage-cap pulled down over his eyes. Apart from delivering orders, he had not spoken to me since he had roused me that morning, my head fuzzy and my mouth sour from an excess of ale.

We had left the *Water's Edge* soon after midnight, my father's co-ordinated stroll making a mockery of my drunken stumblings. I had failed miserably in my efforts to match him drink for drink at the saloon—a foolhardy venture from the outset. Immediately he had taken me on board one of the long, dark vessels moored at the lock, the gentle swell of the barge in the water had induced a nausea in me, a nausea which I was able to counteract only by swallowing great lungfuls of air like a stranded fish.

He, too, had been a little drunk, I realized, for he had insisted on showing me around the barge although I had been in no state to register anything beyond a desire for immediate unconsciousness. Finally, he had taken me into the cabin and directed me to the bottom bunk, explaining that it was normally his, but that he would lend it to me for the night since he doubted my capacity to climb into the one above. Stung by this slur on my ambulatory powers, I had, after several abortive attempts, finally heaved myself aloft, collapsing blissfully on the mattress. It had seemed only an instant later that he had been shaking me awake, the pallid light of dawn diffusing through the grime-crusted cabin windows.

It is often said that exercise is the best cure for a hangover; what is seldom appreciated is that the treatment is worse than the illness itself. Loading the vessel, with only a few mouthfuls of water inside my stomach, I had flushed hot with alarming frequency, while my head had throbbed so vigorously that it seemed at times as if my brain had been about to expel itself from my skull. I had followed my father's orders mechanically, in a trance-like state, aware only of the inner purgations which were disrupting my entire system. Afterwards, when we had cast off and I was finally able to relax, I had been surprised by the relative lucidity of my mental processes and the wholesome exhaustion which had replaced—as a student friend of mine once put it—"the grisly pulsations of crapulence." Checking the contents of the hold, I had been further astonished to discover just how much we had loaded into the barge in those few hours. Sometimes the body can work quite effectively when the brain is essentially non-functional.

We entered a straight stretch of river. My father locked the rudder, went into the cabin and emerged with two foodpacks and a flagon of water. We sat down on the belly of the barge and began to eat. There was fruit, cheese, brown bread and slices of pork, all of which I gulped down hungrily, my appetite now full-blooded. My father ate more soberly and slowly, while gazing out at the fields which were beginning to encroach on both banks.

"You did well this morning," he said without looking at me. "You were not raised in the city, I think."

"The High Valleys. Silver Spring commune."

"I thought not. There is a difference between one who has forgotten hard work and one who has never known it. You have been living long in Helixport?"

"About a cycle," I said.

And then, as if I could not help myself, I began to pour out my life story, telling him of my childhood on the commune, of Annia, of Jax, of my scholarship to the Institute, of Wendi, of everything that seemed important to me—except, that is, for my two encounters with the M'threnni, upon which my over-developed sense of obligation compelled me to silence. But I must have talked without stop for ten or fifteen minutes, laying myself bare before this total stranger.

My father listened without comment, somehow sensing that I was inviting no response. Then, when finally I was finished, he closed his eyes and said quietly: "No more talking. Get some rest."

My cheeks flushed with embarrassment. I retrieved the empty food-packs, took them into the cabin and rinsed them out. Feeling weary, I lay down on the bottom bunk to rest awhile, and when I opened my eyes again, I knew that I had slept for several hours.

I went outside. My father was at the tiller again, guiding the barge down a narrow channel. Capella was in zenith, and its components were approaching eclipse so that it was as if a great golden dumb-bell had been set in the pale skies. Insects abounded, tiny midges which whirled in diffuse clouds over the water, and ungainly black pretzel-flies which buzzed in erratic orbits about my head. Cropped fields hemmed the canal: the green stubble of soya, the olive of thistlegrain, the cream of corn. We were approaching a farm, its neat array of squat white buildings lining the bank to starboard.

We went past the farm without stopping (a few children waved to us from the bank) and continued down the canal until we came to a larger settlement at the intersection to a transverse waterway. Here there was a lock, and here we stopped. Each item of our cargo was numbered and my father checked each off against a list as we unloaded them on the wharf. No one came to greet us during this time. My father showed me how to operate the lock, and we moved off again.

"I call that farm Lazy Days," he told me. "*Everyone sleeps over zenith.*"

We made three further stops that day, lightening our load so that bit by bit the barge began to ride higher in the water.

We were served drinks and snacks at the first two, but by the time we reached the third, dusk was approaching and my father indicated that we would stay the night there.

Collinsford farm was one of the larger settlements in the Plains, with a population of almost three thousand. After we had unloaded (helped by a young blind girl who insisted on carrying all the smaller items and seemed to know my father well), we joined the adults in the main dining-hall for dinner.

The atmosphere was boisterous, in keeping with the gregarious nature of the plainsfolk. Eating here was not the solemn ritual of the High Valleys, nor the casual, desultory activity of the city. The farmers attacked their food with gusto, laughing and chattering incessantly. It was clear that my father was well-respected, for we sat amongst the older members of the commune and they talked with him as if he was one of their own people.

Enlivened by the festive mood, I ate heartily, especially of the white bread which is seldom obtainable fresh in Helixport but which here came to the tables crisp and still warm from the ovens. Several females caught my eye, and one or two smiled at me in greeting. One of the elders asked me if I was Daniel's new apprentice and, out of mischief, I said yes.

With the ending of the meal a sudden lethargy seemed to overtake everyone and the hall quickly emptied. My father left with a striking blonde-haired woman on whom he had concentrated most of his attention during the meal. Their relationship was obviously a long-standing one.

Few people now lingered in the hall and I began to cast around for a friendly face. A youth my own age with tawny, close-cropped hair came up to me, smiling widely. An array of freckles, the same colour as his hair, formed a mottled bridge across his nose.

"You're Marie's replacement?" he asked.

"Just this one trip," I said.

We introduced ourselves. His name was Mark and he worked in one of the flour mills. We sat on the veranda for a while, watching a group of young children play hide-and-seek amongst the clusters of spadeleaf bushes which lined the approach to the hall. I listened to their laughter and the swishing of the leaves as they scampered through the russet foliage.

We went down the bush-lined pathway which finally debouched into a square bordered by green-roofed dormitories arranged about three of its sides.

"You didn't want a woman?" Mark asked me.

"A woman?"

"Several females smiled at you in the hall. Didn't you notice?"

"I took it to be merely a greeting."

"Oh, no. A smile here is more than a greeting. It's an invitation."

After a moment, he added: "I thought perhaps women didn't appeal to you."

"What do you mean?"

He shrugged. "I was hoping that perhaps you were homo like myself."

"You're a homo?" I said, surprised. "They're pretty rare, aren't they?"

Mark politely ignored my boorishness. "Yes, we are few in number," he said. "Which makes it difficult to find partners."

I was intrigued. "When did you first discover it?"

He sighed, as if this was a question people were always asking him. "When did you first discover you were hetero? We grow up with our proclivities."

"But how did everyone else react? It must have caused a stir."

"My wardens were most understanding. They informed me that I was the victim of a thousand-to-one chance malfunction at the incubators. Humans are *always* bred to be hetero, they told me. I was just unlucky." He smiled without humour. "I didn't feel unlucky. I just felt different." We stopped outside a small dorm at one corner of the square. "Luckily I've always been pretty resilient and I never let it bother me. Eventually everyone got used to the idea. Everything's fine now."

"Apart from finding partners."

"That's the main problem. We have a kind of grapevine, but there are so few of us we don't get the chance to get together too often. My closest friend lives in Helixport but we see each other only once or twice a season."

He turned towards the window above our heads and shouted: "Gail!"

A moment later a female head poked through the window, a young, pretty female head with sandy, close-cropped hair remarkably similar to Mark's.

"Would you entertain a stranger on his travels?" Mark asked.

The girl appraised me briefly. "You came with the barge?"

"Yes," I said. "You were not at dinner?"

"No, I'm fasting today. It tones the mind."

"I thought not. I would have remembered your face."

She laughed. "A flatterer!" She turned to Mark: "He'll do." Her head vanished.

"She's my bond-sister," Mark told me. "We've always been very close. You'll like her."

With that he was off, strolling across the square. He began whistling a cheerful, lilting air, and after a moment I recognized it as the old American song *Yankee Doodle Dandy*.

The first day set the pattern for the subsequent days of the voyage. My father's timetable was immaculately planned so that we always arrived at a hospitable commune just at sunset. It became clear to me that my father was not merely accepted as a welcome visitor by the plainsfolk; he was, effectively, one of them. He had covered the same area for the past fourteen seasons, and with such frequency and regularity that, though his stays were only brief, they were part of the order of things; those communes that provided him with a night's bed accepted him as one of their own. He was a citizen of Collinsford, of Maitland, of Oz, and no matter that he was only "at home" for six days a month at each.

On the fourth day we began retracing our course, taking on

cargo this time at each of our stops. By now I was used to the bursts of labour followed by periods of rest as the barge puttered along the waterways. I felt relaxed and attuned to everything around me, the pressures and problems of the city pushed into the background of my mind. I had initially sought out my father with no real idea of what I hoped to gain from making his acquaintance, but things had worked out beyond my expectations. I had, simply, obtained a respite, a breathing space in which to gather my strength. I had studiously avoided reading newspapers or listening to any gossip about the city during the voyage, and now I was ready to return.

At dusk on the fifth day we stopped overnight at Collinsford, and in the morning I took charge of a letter from Mark which I promised to deliver to his friend in Helixport. A storm was developing as we cast off, and the grit-laced wind whistled devilishly through the cropped fields.

My father and I sat at the cabin for most of the day while the barge rolled and heaved along the choppy waters of the Tamus and the wind found ingress through the ill-fitting cabin door. He taught me to play poker, a game which I had never encountered before. But beginner's luck deserted me and the tally of debt which my father was entering into a notebook mounted minute by minute. When Helixport finally loomed through the murky aspect of the window, I threw down my cards in disgust and said? "I've had enough. How much do I owe you?"

"Three hundred and forty-three checks," he replied instantly.

I checked my pouch. Although I had spent nothing throughout the voyage, I carried with me less than three hundred checks.

I counted out two hundred in notes and laid them on the table. "I'll pay you the rest when I get back. Is that all right?"

My father gathered the cards together and squared the pack on the tabletop. "You don't owe me anything."

"No, a bet is a bet. I insist." I pushed the notes towards him.

He shook his head. "There are no debts. You worked for me on this trip and you worked well. I'll write off your losses. It saves me paying *you* anything." He was smiling.

"I've enjoyed it."

"And so now you will be able to write your report." There was a hint of mockery in his voice. "What improvements will you suggest?"

I pretended to consider. "What improvements would you like?"

"Ah," he said, reflecting. "An air-conditioned cabin, perhaps. Plenty of free beer. A fresh woman to ride with me each day."

"And nothing more?"

"I have simple tastes."

We reached Venice just after dark. We unloaded in the squally rain, covered our cargo with tarpaulin, and hurried across the wharf and into the welcoming warmth of the *Water's Edge*. We sat down at an empty table in one corner of the saloon and moments later the barman arrived with a small jug filled with a steaming dark red liquor. He set the jug and two porcelain cups down on the table and departed without a word. My father filled the cups and passed one to me. The liquid had a strong, minty aroma, and when I sipped it, it tasted like liquid fire; there was aniseed and liquorice, and herbs which I could not identify, pungent and stimulating on the palate; but above all there was a warm afterglow of alcohol which penetrated my entire body, casting out the chills of our stormy passage.

"It's good," I said. "What is it?"

"We call it bat's blood," my father said with a wry grin. "It's a secret recipe which Gregor would never divulge. Drink it slowly."

Not long afterwards Gregor returned with two large bowls of thick vegetable stew and a cylinder of bread. I gulped the broth down gratefully, amazed at the capacity of my appetite this past six days. The saloon was slowly filling with incoming bargemasters, each of whom Gregor served with the alacrity which he had shown us. The fluted gas-fire at the centre of the room gave off a steady heat, and with an excess of soup and bat's blood inside me, I began to feel drowsy.

A young girl of about eighteen entered. She looked about the saloon and, on seeing my father, came over to our table.

"This is Marie," my father said. "Marie, David. He's taken over your job."

The girl eyed me speculatively. Her face was oddly proportioned: a rounded nose, large, wide-set eyes, an indented chin. She could not be called pretty, but she radiated a certain impish charm.

"Only for the last trip," I said. "I went along for the ride."

"He's a good worker," my father said. "You'll have to double your efforts to match him."

The girl turned to my father, unmoved by his goadings. "Dawn, tomorrow?"

"Are you fully recovered?"

"It was just a touch of fever. I'm all right now."

"Dawn," he said.

Marie departed, and we finished off the last of the bat's blood. I felt extremely weary now; the babble of conversation in the saloon was having a soporific effect on me.

"I had better be getting home," I said.

My father nodded, his eyes half-closed.

I rose. "Thank you once again. It has been a good six days."

He made no immediate reply, but as I was walking towards the door, I heard him say: "Take care, son."

Chapter Eight

Wendi had visited the villa in my absence and removed her belongings. She had left a short, almost cheerful note to thank me for my "understanding" and "consideration," adding that she would contact me "when things have settled down a little." There was no mention of the annulment of our liaison.

The last six issues of the *Chronicle* were lying in the newspaper chute. I left them on the living-room table and went straight to bed. I slept soundly and in the morning over breakfast I began working my way through each issue. The breach in the M'threnni parapet had been repaired overnight by the aliens but the terminus had not been opened and the latest shipment still lay uncollected at its centre. The authorities had mounted a vigorous search for the perpetrators of the bomb attack and the jail-break—evidently with rapid results: the headline for the 11th read:

LEAGUE SEDITIONISTS APPREHENDED BY MILITIA

I read the report.

The rebels believed responsible for the recent bomb-blast on Round Island were yesterday taken into custody by the Civil Militia following a raid on a South Bank hostel. The hostel was known to be a meeting-point for members of the outlawed Humanistic League and the three suspects were found to be in possession of a number of explosive devices. All three have admitted planting the bomb and are expected to appear in court tomorrow. The arrest of those involved in the raid on Helixport Penitentiary is believed to be imminent.

The rest of the report gave further details of the operation. I went to the next day's paper, yesterday's paper, and scanned the follow-up report. Half-way down the page I came across the following:

The three people held in custody have been named as Samuel Koster, an electrician, Nita Duprez, an unemployed school-teacher, both of Helixport, and Jax 52176883, late of Silver Spring, recently serving as a trawlerfoil mate.

I read no further, but left my breakfast half-finished and drove to the Complex where I requested an immediate interview with Helmine. Within ten minutes I was being ushered into her office.

Helmine was sitting at her desk, attending to her nails with a file. I ignored her calculated air of indifference and came straight to the point: "One of the rebels responsible for the bomb-blast is an old friend of mine. I would like to see him."

Without looking up, she said: "Take a seat, my boy."

I sat down and leaned across the desk to stress my impatience. "The one called Jax. We grew up together in Silver Spring."

The file made tiny rasping sounds and a fine mist of powdered nail was collecting on the dark polished surface of the desk between her elbows.

"We are aware of the connection," she told me. "Immediately we learned their names we checked out their backgrounds in detail. Nothing was overlooked."

She inspected the nail, and, satisfied, peered over her fingers at me. "Where have you been these past six days?"

"I took a holiday. I needed a break."

"Where?"

"West Helixport. I went for a ride down the canals."

"With who?"

"What business is this of yours?"

"It's very much my business." She pointed the file at me. "You are admitted to the M'threnni tower, and a few days later you disappear. Don't you think we should be concerned?"

"I didn't think my movements were being monitored," I said indignantly. "Perhaps you'd like me to report in to you every hour?"

"Who were you with?"

"My father. I helped him on a supply run."

I waited, and she began work on another nail. Her little strategems for slowing the pace of any conversation were infuriating because they were so transparent.

"I'd like to see him," I said.

Helmine ran her tiny purplish tongue over the freshly manicured nail.

"I think a meeting would be appropriate," she said. "I'm sure you have a lot to talk about."

This time I deliberately waited for her to speak again.

"Find out where Eilan and her cohorts are hiding," she said. "We have been unable to trace them and the prisoners refuse to talk."

"You want me to betray him."

"It's not a question of betrayal; it's one of duty. These people are a danger to our society. They must be located and put away where they can do no harm."

"He's my friend."

"*Was* your friend. You haven't seen him in over a cycle. Don't let memories blind you to the realities of the situation now. He is a renegade; you are a citizen of Gaia in good standing and as such you must put the fate of the people at large before that of a single individual." She leaned forward in her chair, matching my posture with a sudden show of earnestness. "I am not exaggerating when I say that we are going through an extremely dangerous phase at present. There is no telling how the M'threnni might react to the attack on the terminus. We must ensure that nothing of this nature ever happens again. The League is like a malignant growth; we must cut it out, cauterize it."

I considered at length.

"No, I can't do it."

She sighed and leaned back in her chair. "There is no doubt that we *will* obtain the information we seek. It is just a matter of what method we use."

"You'll torture them?"

"Of course not. Do I look like a fiend?"

The sight of her thin, angular body and her gaunt, shrew-like features almost prompted me to say: "Yes."

"But the prisoners will inevitably suffer some discomfort," she went on. "The degree of their resistance will naturally determine the severity of our interrogative techniques."

So, it *would* be torture; I knew Jax well enough to be sure that he would never betray his friends under anything but the most extreme pressure. At that moment my dislike of Helmine was transformed into active loathing.

"Very well, I'll do it," I said.

She opened a drawer and took out a silvery, cylindrical object which I recognized as a tape-recorder. She laid it at the centre of the desk-top. "Slip it inside your tunic. It will ensure that we get everything."

"No," I replied. "I'll report everything verbatim. You have to trust me."

"No recorder, no visit."

Again I considered, then snatched up the device.

The meeting was arranged for the third hour of zenith that day. A civilian floater stood waiting outside the main entrance, manned by a gruff, hostile-looking driver who scarcely acknowledged me as I climbed inside. Leaving the approach road, we turned eastwards rather than continuing north towards the penitentiary. I resisted the impulse to ask the driver where we were going.

We drove for about twenty minutes in a straight easterly direction, then crossed Estuary Bridge and turned left on to the narrow concrete road which ran through the impoverished south-eastern suburbs and out on to Needle Point. We passed the desalination plant to the right, an array of towers, tanks, gantries and walkways, gleaming brightly in the harsh zenith light. The road wound on to the head of the Point where it terminated in front of a compound which surrounded the squat stone tower of the old lighthouse. The lighthouse had been built during the early days of the colony to guide the trawlerfoils home, but it was long defunct. A small outbuilding of recent construction stood opposite it.

The guard on duty at the gate took the authorization papers from the driver, flicked through them, and said: "You're expected."

She opened the gate and we drove through and pulled up outside the outbuilding. An officer emerged and nodded to the driver.

"You get out here," the driver said.

The officer took me over to the tower and unlocked the arched metal door in its base. The door opened without the expected creak and we climbed a zig-zag flight of stairs until finally (I counted seventy-two steps) we reached the top. A short corridor led to a door secured with three bolts and a guard sat on a stool beside the door, listening to a music-tape. He switched the machine off when he saw us, rose and saluted the officer. Unbidden, he began to unbolt the door.

"We will be waiting here," the officer said, "and checking in on you from time to time." He indicated a spy-hole in the door.

I wondered whether he had told me this to reassure me or to warn me.

The guard drew back the last bolt and opened the door sufficiently for me to squeeze through. The door closed behind me and a single bolt thunked into place.

The room was small and windowless. The little light which penetrated it came from a grille-covered hole at the centre of the ceiling. I guessed that a flight of stairs had once led up through the hole to the beacon itself. This had once been a maintenance room; now it was a cell.

As my eyes adjusted to the dimness I was able to make out three bunks against the far wall and a small table and three chairs to the right of the cross-hatched circle of light at the centre of the floor. The air was sultry, smelling strongly of sweat and urine.

I activated the recorder. "Jax?"

For a moment, nothing. Then: "Who is it?" There was no hint of real interest in the question.

"It's David."

A shadow moved on the middle bunk, became a body as it stepped into the skylight's cone of illumination.

His hair was longer than I remembered, a luxuriant bush about his head, and a thin moustache lined his upper lip. He was taller and even sturdier than he had been as a youth, and the adolescent softness of his features had given way to a lean intensity of expression which I found a little disconcerting. He looked dishevelled and grimy, but otherwise fit.

"Hello, Jax," I said as he moved towards the table.

He leaned on the back of a chair and squinted at me.

I took the chair opposite and sat down.

"This is a surprise," he said.

"A not unpleasant one, I hope."

He said nothing.

"Where are the other two?"

"Moved out a while ago. I thought perhaps they'd been taken for interrogation, but that didn't really figure, leaving me here. I wasn't expecting a visitor."

"I asked to come when I saw your name in the *Chronicle*. You never did get your surname, eh?"

"There are more important things."

"You never went back to Silver Spring? They told me you'd run away."

"I never intend to go back."

"But you made it to the trawlers, though." I was straining to keep my voice friendly and informal. Jax looked extremely wary, even hostile.

"Yes I made it." He swung the chair around and sat down, resting his arms on the back. "What's up, David?"

"What's up? I wanted to see you, that's all. Have you forgotten that we were once friends?"

"How did you get permission? No one outside the militia knows we're here."

"I work for the government. It was a favour."

He gazed at me with open disdain, obviously seeing me as an enemy.

I took the recorder from my pocket, switched it off and laid it on the table. I had my back to the door so that the guards could not see it.

"They want me to find out where Eilan is hiding," I whispered. "I'm supposed to record our entire conversation. Our glorious leader Helmine's plan."

There was a silence.

"There could be another inside your tunic," he said.

"No, Jax. I wouldn't do it. I went along with everything because I wanted to see you and because they're going to torture you if you don't tell them where she is."

He gnawed his thumbnail. "So now you're using gentle persuasion instead of deceit. No chance, David. I'm not going to tell Helmine and her storm-troopers anything."

"I'm not asking you to tell me anything. Make up a story. For the benefit of—" I tapped the recorder "—this. Say you don't know where she is or give some false location. Anything."

He stared at me for a moment. "Why *did* you come, David?"

"I've told you. I wanted to see you. We used to be the closest of friends, remember?"

Again he was silent, but I sensed a softening in his attitude.

"When did you join the League?"

"A cycle back."

"Why?"

For a moment I thought he wasn't going to answer. Then he said: "I joined the League because they're committed to ridding Gaia of the M'threnni. It's as simple as that."

"But why?" As a youth, Jax had had no interest whatsoever in the aliens.

"Because of Annia."

"Annia? You mean the aliens killed her?"

He shook his head. "Annia isn't dead, David."

"Not dead? But I saw her urn."

"You may have seen *an* urn, but it wasn't hers. The M'threnni have taken her as a Voice."

The story was brief but no less shocking for that. Two days after Annia's last visit to Helixport, she and Jax had been out at our old hideout on the rocks just after dusk. From out of the darkening skies had come a small, pebble-shaped craft which had descended soundlessly and landed beside them. A circular portal had opened in the snout of the craft and a M'threnni male had emerged. Without warning, Annia had begun to walk towards the craft and before Jax was able to react, the alien had taken her on board. The portal had closed and the craft had taken off abruptly, vanishing into the night.

"She went as if she was hypnotized," Jax told me. "I was too dazed to stop her. It was as if something was holding me back. I rushed down the mountainside, found Caril and told her what had happened. Caril hurried me off to the elder Robert and I repeated the story.

"Do you know what he said? He told me that I had to swear to tell no one else about it. I was practically in tears. I asked him if they'd get Annia back and he said, no, no, she's gone, there's nothing we can do. You must forget it; we'll tell everyone she died of a fever and you must say that too. I didn't understand any of this and eventually I exploded with rage. I tried to attack him, but he and Caril held me down and they must have got someone to sedate me because I blacked out.

"The next thing I remember is waking up in the isolation

room at the surgery. The door was locked. Caril came to see me over zenith but I wouldn't talk to her. Robert came that evening and went over the same thing again. He said that he didn't expect me to understand, I was young, but it was important, extremely important, that I said nothing to anyone about the M'threnni taking Annia away. It had to be a secret between me, him and Caril. I promised solemnly. That evening they let me go back to dorm and in the middle of the night I got up and sneaked down to the loading bay. I hid myself in a crate of butterfruit and climbed out through a window in a warehouse just off Capitol Square the following day. They took her, David, and no one did a thing about it.''

I sat back and began thinking. Everything fitted. The alien Annia and I had encountered outside the Institute had doubtless known that his Voice was dying and had gone abroad in the city to seek a replacement. He had chosen Annia. Perhaps he had probed her mind while we had been watching him; this would explain her subsequent stupor. Jax's disappearance and the elders' failure to inform me of Annia's ''death'' both hinted, in the clear light of retrospect, that something unusual had happened. And the exaggerated courtesy which I had been shown on my return to the commune was clear evidence of Robert's guilt. He had lied to me, and, more importantly, Caril had lied too. The gift of Annia's gasglobe had been a propitiatory gesture, an attempt to absolve herself of the deceit.

Jax had never risked contacting me after his flight to the city for fear of being tracked down. He had gone instead to the harbour and had eventually been taken on as an apprentice on the trawlerfoils. There had been a modicum of consolation for him in that, I guessed.

Annia, less scrupulously dutiful than I, had told Jax about our encounter with the M'threnni at the Institute and I now told him of my visit to the tower and of my speculations regarding the M'threnni-Voice relationship.

''Perhaps they can sense sympathetic minds,'' I suggested. ''Perhaps there's a certain empathy which makes one eligible to be a Voice.''

"Eligible? Cursed. Annia would never have gone with the alien of her own volition. She was interested in the M'threnni but not to that extent. She's a prisoner in that tower, just like all the other Voices."

A silence fell. I heard the spyhole flap being drawn back, then closing again.

"Jax," I said quietly, "you must tell me where Eilan is hiding. If I can contact her, let her know where you are, then maybe the League will be able to do something." I deliberately left the sentence vague.

He considered, watching me in the silence, still unsure of whether he could trust me. And why should he? I thought. I had come as Helmine's emissary. I was a servant of the government. My clothes attested a comfortable affluence which I'm sure was an anathema to him. How much *did* we have left in common?

"*Alien Star* in the harbour. Ask for Roger." He said the words so quickly, in a mumble, that I only just caught them.

Briefly, we discussed our strategy. I started the tape again and we resumed our conversation at the point where I had switched off the machine. We engaged in minor pleasantries, reflected on times past, talked of what we had been doing since we had last seen one another. Jax gave me a vague and doubtless grossly inaccurate account of his association with the League, mentioning no names. I asked him where Eilan was hiding. He pretended to prevaricate, but I insisted that I had been impressed by Eilan and her philosophy and that I wanted to join the League. He then "confessed" that he didn't know where she was, that those involved in the bomb attack had not been made privy to the details of the raid on the penitentiary in case of their capture. The irony was, he said, that Eilan was unlikely to have approved of their actions, despite her release; she had always been opposed to violence. That was the problem with the League; for all their good intentions, most of the members were mealy-mouthed and afraid to take direct action against the M'threnni or the government. I told him that I was inclined to agree with Eilan; violence was never really justifiable. He inferred cowardice. I countered by saying that his aggressive tactics were immoral and immature. He told me that I was still the spineless child he had once known. I replied that he was as reckless and stupid as ever. He repeated that I was a child.

"Then a child has fooled you," I said triumphantly. "Everything you have just told me will be reported to the authorities." I tapped the pocket in which the recorder lay. "It has all been recorded."

With an extremely authentic roar of rage, Jax leapt over the table and began, gently, to throttle me. I cried out, and within seconds the door burst open and the two militia men were upon Jax, dragging him off me. I picked myself up and hurried out of the room.

I was returned to the Complex where I handed over the recorder to Helmine. I sat in an adjoining room while she played it through and then I was admitted to her office.

She sat upright in her chair, her hands folded on the edge of the desk, the recorder lying in front of them.

"Interesting," she said, peering somewhere over my head. "I was surprised to hear that the three saboteurs were not aware of the plans of the others, but this would seem to fit in with the fact that our investigations have failed to uncover any of their accomplices on the South Bank." She looked at me as if inviting some comment. I said nothing.

"It would appear that your friendship has not stood the test of time," she said, rolling the recorder to and fro across the desk-top with her index finger.

"He annoyed me," I said. "He used to call me a child when we lived at Silver Spring. I always hated it."

"It is regrettable that you saw fit to reveal your deception, however. It has destroyed any hopes we might have had of obtaining further information from him."

"I think he was suspicious of me from the outset. He radiated caution and a subtle hostility. It was a painful meeting."

"What did you talk about?"

I indicated my puzzlement. "It's all on the tape."

She shook her head. "I think not. The conversation recorded here lasts just over fourteen minutes, whereas the guards estimate that you were inside the cell for close on twenty-five.''

I thought furiously. "We talked about an old friend of ours. Annia. She's dead now, but we remembered her in somewhat, er, sensual terms. I thought it would seem disrespectful to an outsider—embarrassing, too—so I excised it on the way here. It had no relevance to the main thread of our conversation.''

Her steely eyes fixed upon me in silent indictment. Clearly, she did not believe me.

"I think your usefulness to us is at an end," she said. "You may leave.''

There was an undertone not just of coldness, but enmity in her words.

I went home, feeling a mixture of exhilaration, foreboding, doubt, confusion. I sat in the garden for an hour or so, turning over recent events. I was agitated. I felt I had to *do* something, but I didn't know what. Jax, a rebel; Annia, a Voice. It was incredible, and somehow exciting. I was, above all, elated that Annia was alive, despite her imprisonment in the tower—if imprisonment it was. I also envied Jax, despite *his* imprisonment and the possible threat to his life. I envied his strength and his commitment. Would Helmine attempt to force the information she required out of him and his comrades? Yes, he was in danger, and I knew I should act. Yet still I vacillated, afraid to make any move that would irrevocably commit me aginst the authorities. Jax had called me a spineless child only in subterfuge, but the description galled, for it contained an element of truth.

I went into the villa and came across Mark's letter. Rather than waste the evening in futile brooding, I decided that I would deliver it.

Mark's friend was a man called Rex, the proprietor of the Chimera Dream Parlour, a luxurious and respected establishment on Sussex Street. He greeted me warmly, read through the letter, smiling, then thanked me for delivering it. We sat down over a glass of wine and he offered me the use of the parlour as a gesture of thanks. I immediately accepted.

He took me to a small room towards the rear of the establishment. It was delicately furnished with cream and brown tiles and buff-coloured walls along which hung numerous watercolours showing aspects of city-life. I lay down on the sumptuous leather couch and Rex fitted the chrome headpiece over my head. I stared at the nearest painting, a rendition of Round Island from the northern bank; it was a delicately accomplished mood-piece.

"They're all originals," Rex said proudly, doubtless assuming that I recognized the artist, although the scrawled signature was meaningless to me.

"Do you want programmed or free association?" he asked.

"Free association."

He left, and the lights began to dim. I closed my eyes and let my thoughts wander where they may.

I drifted again through the pearly mist, as I had done on my only other visit to a parlour, a bodiless, questing mentality. Then the mist began, subtly, to change hue, a gentle blushing which soon became roseate, then rubicund, then thinning slowly until it was simply a dim red light. Pale walls surrounded me and I recognized the place: I was inside the M'threnni tower, in the warped cubicle where I had talked with the Voice. There was a dark portal in one of the "walls" and as I looked at it, Annia stepped through.

She was dressed in the white shorts and vest of a fruit-picker and her hair was tied back in a familiar pony-tail. But her eyes were black and circular, the eyes of a M'threnni.

She stepped forward and stood there with her hands folded across her stomach, an alien impassivity on her features. I tried to speak, but for a moment no words came. I had to drag them from deep within my throat.

"Annia," I said finally. "They told me you were dead."

She made no response.

"Do you remember me? It's David. David from the High Valleys."

Silence.

"They told me you were dead," I repeated. "At the commune. They lied."

The black eyes bored into me. She did not move.

"I saw Jax. Remember Jax? He's a prisoner now. Captured by the authorities after the bomb attack on Round Island. He told me you lived."

Still there was no flicker of reaction.

"The alien we met outside the Institute the day the old woman died. He came for you afterwards? You serve the M'threnni now?"

I waited, but she would not speak.

"Annia, please say something."

She stood as still as a statue.

"Speak, damn you!" I shouted.

And speak she did. She opened her mouth, stuck out her purple tongue and began to assail me with a torrent of M'threnni clicks, hisses and squeals, each one sounding like an obscenity, each one a grotesque betrayal of her humanity. It was hideous, and I couldn't bear it. I backed away, moving towards the portal, averting my eyes from her. I flung myself through it, disappearing into the darkness . . . .

. . . a darkness which enfolded me like a warm blanket, inert and comforting. I could have happily stayed there for ever, hidden from everything. But it did not last; slowly the darkness evaporated to reveal another chamber, this one stone-lined like Jax's cell. I sat before a desk and behind the desk was a shadowy figure whose features I was unable to discern. I could not say whether it was masculine or feminine: the question of its sex did not occur to me. I knew only that it was autocratic and domineering and that I was afraid of it.

I tried to get up from a seat but I could not move. The figure began to shout at me, telling me to do this and not to do that, to behave in this manner and not in that. I cannot remember the contents of the instructions—they might have been gibberish—it was the tone to which I reacted. Panic gripped me, and although I attempted to protest, my words carried no weight, were drowned in the thundering tones of reproval and denunciation which flooded in almost palpable waves across the desk. My agitation increased; I trembled with fear. I closed my eyes and shook my head as if I could deny the voice its existence by these acts alone. To my surprise, its strength did begin to wane, slowly but perceptibly. I clenched the edges of my seat and redoubled my efforts to shut out the diatribe, all the while quavering with fright. . . .

I opened my eyes. Rex was standing over me, tugging at my shoulders. He helped me sit up, then fetched a glass of water. I drank it down in one.

"I had difficulty in bringing you back," Rex said. "Was it a bad dream?"

"I had two. Both were somewhat disturbing."

"I should have taken proper precautions, used a sympathetic placement sub-programme. I didn't realize you were in an anxious mood-state."

"It's all right. I asked for free association." I rubbed my eyes. "Besides, it was all my own invention. Just a mind-dream."

"Ah, yes, but the product of very real stresses and anxieties within your psyche. Something is obviously troubling you."

I swung my legs off the couch and stood up, shakily.

"Rest a few minutes more," Rex said. "You look a little groggy."

"No, I'm fine," I replied. I could feel the strength slowly returning to my body.

Rex was still fussing. "I do apologize. I should have evaluated your psychic equilibrium before I allowed you to dream."

"It's quite all right," I insisted. "Paradoxically, those nightmares have provided me with the impetus I needed to resolve a conflict of loyalties."

And it was true. Immediately on wakening I had begun to analyse the symbolism inherent in each dream. The first one was easy: I was obviously worried that Annia had been made irrevocably alien by having been chosen as a Voice. The interpretation of the second dream had required a little more thought but had provided me with a more important realization. The figure behind the desk clearly represented someone of authority, be it Helmine, the elder Robert, Lionel of the Institute, or even the manager of the Dome Baths. All my life I had been intimidated by people behind desks or tables, people who had ordered me around, directed my life to their own ends. I had obeyed because I was weak and afraid of authority. Well, no more. This time I would rebel.

Rex accompanied me to the door. I peered through the window and saw a floater parked just down the road. A man sat in the driver's seat, staring casually towards the parlour. I was sure that he was one of Helmine's minions, keeping track of my movements. Helmine must have been certain by now that I had lied to her; a simple check with the driver would have revealed that I had not spent any time erasing sections of the tape during my return to the Complex. She was hoping I would lead her to the League.

"Do you have a rear exit?" I asked Rex. "I'm being followed."

He nodded solemnly, no doubt deciding that I had paranoid tendencies best dealt with by humouring me. He led me back through the parlour to a small side exit which gave out on an alleyway.

"Good luck," he whispered, as if he was sending me off on a secret mission.

Which, although he didn't know, he was.

Chapter Nine

On leaving the parlour, I wandered through the sidestreets and arcades of the city centre until I was convinced that no one was following me. I then visited my bank and withdrew five hundred checks before taking a bus down to the harbour. It was past dusk when I arrived and I decided that I would search for the boat Jax had mentioned in the morning. I obtained a room in a small hostel at the top of Griffin Lane, one of the steep and narrow streets which rises above the harbour. The room was cramped and ill-kept, but it would suffice: I did not plan to stay there long.

After breakfast the following day I went down to the waterfront and spent most of the morning roaming along the wharves and jetties, looking for the *Alien Star*. Unlike the barges, which are never christened, most of the trawlerfoils had colourful names: *Windracer, Galatea, Green Phoenix, Merrimac*. The fisherfolk did share some characteristics with the bargemasters, though, most obviously a fondness for ale and ribaldry. Saloons lined the waterfront, comparatively empty that morning for most of the fleet was out at sea; but the previous night the noise of their laughter and conversation had carried to me in my musty room until well past midnight.

I could find no trace of the boat; doubtless it was out at sea. Over zenith I sat in one of the saloons, sipping a mug of the spiced ale which the fisherfolk favoured. I talked with no one; I simply sat there and watched the trawlerfoils return from their labours, cutting white swathes through the water before docking at the jetties, their holds bulging with glistening silverfish and livid great-eels. The crews immediately retired to a saloon to slake their thirsts, leaving their cargoes to writhe spasmodically and with steadily decreasing vigour in the afternoon sun. One or two empty boats departed, and I followed their progress out over the calm, glassy sea until they bled into the shimmering, heat-soaked horizon of water and sky.

After zenith I traversed the wharves again, but there was no sign of the *Alien Star*. No more foils would be in before dusk, so I idled away the afternoon by wandering around the immediate hinterland of the bay. I had visited the area on a number of occasions during the course of my work, but the narrow, cobbled streets and the buildings, all constructed of the dark grey stone which constituted the bay itself, formed a complex maze in which it was possible to wander for hours without retracing one's path. The harbour, although no older than the rest of the city, appears more ancient by dint of this abundance of stone, more solid and timeworn than the concrete and tile of the city proper.

Returning to the waterfront at dusk, I was still unable to locate the *Alien Star*. It was possible that the boat was out on a deep-sea mission, seeking blackfin and thresher, in which case it might be gone for days. I had been loath to approach anyone for help because I was afraid that any queries might provoke suspicion and hostility—the fisherfolk were in general somewhat mistrustful of outsiders—but now I had no choice. My clothes identified me as a resident of the city, and while I had seen no militia all that day, it was possible that they were looking for me. I had to get off the streets.

A trawlerwoman was passing by en route to a saloon, so I

approached her and asked her if she knew of the *Alien Star*. She did not check her stride, but merely pointed. She pointed not towards the wharves but towards Prospect Place, the broadest of the hilly roads which feed the harbour. I wandered off in the direction she had indicated and half-way up the hill I saw it: a red, four-pointed neon star above a hand-painted sign which told me that the *Star* was not a boat but a restaurant. I must have passed the place several times that day.

I took a table near the door. The restaurant had been decked out in the popular image of the M'threnni. The walls and ceiling were various shades of pink, the floor carpeted in maroon, the table-cloths crimson. Imitation M'threnni sculpture—dangling plates of polished aluminium stirred constantly by currents of air—reflected with kaleidoscopic confusion the roseate glow from the genuine lightsticks on each table, and fake M'threnni drapes hung from the walls, their violent sheen too bright to be convincing. The overall effect was bizarre and tasteless. Only a few tables were occupied, which tended to comfirm my supposition that the décor was positively invidious to gastronomic comfort.

A waiter arrived with a menu.

"I'd like to see Roger," I said, making no attempt to take it from him.

He nodded curtly and retreated into the gloom. A minute later, a plump, middle-aged man approached my table. He reminded me strongly of a representation I had once seen of Napoleon, an old war-lord of Earth.

"I was given your name by someone with League connections," I said quietly.

He sat down opposite me and waited for me to continue. When it was clear that I was not going to say any more, he said: "I see. What brings you here?" His voice was smoothly polite, the voice of a cultured man.

"I want to get in touch with Eilan," I said. "I have information which I think might be of use to her."

He said nothing, but rose abruptly. "Would you follow me, please?" His tone was at once mannerly and imperative.

I followed him through the kitchen, across a yard, and up a fire escape which led to the rooms directly above the restaurant. He knocked hard on the door and a few moments later it was opened by a tall, heavily built man whose face I could not see because it was in shadow.

"I have a visitor for Tomas," Roger said.

The tall man disappeared into the shadowy corridor. Roger and I stood waiting on the fire escape. The window at the end of the corridor reflected a dull red glow from the neon star outside. It occurred to me that there was good deal of irony in the thought that remnants of the League were hidden above a fake M'threnni restaurant.

The tall man returned and said: "I'll take him."

Roger departed and the tall man closed the door behind him. He led me down the corridor to a small room which looked out over the street. It was an office, evidently used for accounting purposes. A man sat in a swivel chair at a desk, his back to me.

"Sit down," he said without turning around. I took the vacant seat immediately to his right. The tall man closed the door softly and leaned against it.

The man at the desk swung his chair through ninety degrees and regarded me. He was short and wiry, with a hook-like nose and sunken cheeks. A down of fine hair covered his scalp and bristle littered his chin.

"Who are you and what do you want?" he said.

"My name is David and I'm—I used to work for the government. I came here to contact the League with a view to joining them. I was given Roger's name by Jax."

If he was surprised, he did not show it. "Where is he?"

"Not in the penitentiary. He and the other two are being held at the old lighthouse on Needle Point."

He waited, so I went on: "I was allowed to visit him only by promising Helmine that I would extract from him the whereabouts of Eilan. I carried a recorder with me to tape our conversation, but Jax and I faked it so that he claimed that he didn't know where she was. However, Helmine is suspicious, and she put a watch on me. I managed to elude him before coming here."

"What is your connection with Jax?"

"He's an old friend of mine. We grew up together. I learned from him that a mutual friend of ours was taken as a Voice by the M'threnni. That, and Jax's situation, are what finally prompted me to seek out the League. Jax and the others are in grave danger. Helmine has threatened to use force to extract the information she wants."

He glanced towards the man at the door. The memory of my dream at Rex's parlour returned to me and I smiled involuntarily. Here I was again being confronted by someone at a desk and again they held the upper hand.

"Something amuses you?"

"No, not really," I said. "I was just reflecting on the inexorable grip of the hand of fate."

He let this cryptic comment go by unchallenged. "What do you think you can offer the League?"

"I've already given you some valuable information. But there is more. Several days ago I was admitted to the M'threnni tower."

This time he was unable to hide his interest.

"We heard that someone had been allowed inside," he said.

"I was working with the haulage teams at the time of the explosion. A M'threnni female and her Voice emerged to investigate it. They took me back to the tower and questioned me. I believe that I have learned something of the M'threnni-Voice relationship as a result."

"Indeed? What?"

"I'd like to speak with Eilan."

"She is not here. What have you learned?"

"I believe that the aliens speak directly through the Voices by usurping their mentalities."

He did not greet this revelation with the surprise I had imagined; he merely shrugged. "It's possible. Anything's possible."

"I thought this knowledge might be of use to the League to consolidate their claims that the M'threnni are a malign influence."

"We are in no position to air our views. The League has been outlawed. If you join us, you become a criminal in the eyes of the authorities."

He waited, then said: "Is this all you have to say?"

"I have no further information to offer, if that's what you mean."

There was a pause.

"Will you attempt to free Jax and the others?" I asked.

He smiled. "Assuming you were a spy sent by Helmine, do you think I would be witless enough not to realize that your purpose in coming here would be to flush us out into the open, to lead us into a trap?"

"I am not a spy. I came here in good faith."

"Nonetheless, it must be obvious to you that we cannot accept your story on good faith alone. It will have to be checked."

He turned to the man at the door. "Take him to the cellar."

The cellar was tiny, a cool stone vault, empty and featureless. A short strip of violet neon fixed loosely to the ceiling and speckled with fly-droppings provided an eerie, crepuscular illumination. The tall man (his name was Mal) provided a sleeping bag, a few morsels of bread, a plate of cold, mashed silverfish, two pears and a jug of water. He left, bolting the door securely.

I set the food aside, lay down on the sleeping bag and, much to my surprise, soon dozed. I awoke late at night, feeling hungry. Switching on the light, I saw that a battalion of ants had found the fish. The bread and the fruit were untouched, however, so I ate them, drank some water, and lay down again. Sleep did not come easily this time, and I spent several hours gazing into the darkness, thinking profit-less thoughts. There was nothing to be gained, I told myself, from speculating on whether I had made the right decision in contacting the League; it was done, and there could be no turning back.

An hour after dawn, Mal returned with more food—the same staples as my meagre supper, but healthier portions.

"There's a restaurant over my head," I complained. "Can't you get me something better?"

"You're a non-paying customer," he told me. "Eat it and like it."

The hours dragged past. I removed the neon tube from its fitting, polished it with spit and the edge of my sleeping bag, then refixed it so that it glowed more brightly. I found a few nails scattered about the floor and passed an hour or so making patterns in the grime. I did push-ups, lean-backs, ran a thousand paces, going nowhere. Mal brought me lunch: a more varied fare this time. I asked him how it went and he replied that he did not know. I asked him for something in which to urinate; he indicated the empty water-jug, and left.

I counted the stones which made up the walls, then divided them by the number on the floor. I removed my shoes, stood against the door and used a nail to scrape a line across the door corresponding to the top of my head. Designating the upper half of my thumb as four centimetres, I slowly progressed upwards from the floor to the mark in thumb-steps; it was grossly inaccurate. I pressed buttons at random on my watch and tried to guess what numbers would come up. I practised yoga; I meditated; I made up nonsense rhymes and recited them to the walls. Mal entered in the middle of one of these, carrying my dinner. Bored? he asked. When will I be let out? I wanted to know. He shook his head, which might have meant that he didn't know or simply, never.

I begged him for something to read, and about a half-hour later he returned with the latest edition of the *Chronicle*. On the fourth page I found it: a short paragraph which indicated that I was missing, believed kidnapped, and that the militia were seeking my whereabouts. A reward was being offered for information leading to my ''release.'' The amount, five hundred checks, was sufficient to arouse a healthy general

interest, but insufficient to reveal just how important it was
that I be tracked down. Nowhere in the report was the League
implicated in my disappearance. Helmine was moving cautiously.

I read the paper from cover to cover, so consumed was I by
ennui. I prepared "ink" from spittle and dust, used a small
nail as my stylus, and laboriously attacked the word-puzzle
which was one of the *Chronicle's* regular features. Much to
my annoyance, the compiler was someone with whom I had
shared an office at the Complex; I knew his *modus operandi*
well and had completed the puzzle within fifteen minutes.
Time was consuming me.

At suppertime Mal took pity on me and provided a few
book- and music-tapes. I listened for a while to a synthesizer
fugue, then picked a book at random from the pile Mal had
left. It was *Awakenings* by Carlos Muller, an account of a
child's experiences on a commune in the Low Valleys. Despite the fact that he described an upbringing similiar to my
own, I found the book tedious; Muller's prose was turgid and
the narrator's voice, a deep bass, monotonous in the extreme.
Switching it off, I turned to another tape with the intriguing
title of *Foreplay,* its author unnamed. It turned out to be a
brash comedy of sexual manners set on twentieth-century
Earth. It was clumsily written, but possessed of vigour and an
odd charm which the female narrator exploited fully. I derived considerable pleasure from the book, and none of it was
cerebral.

It grew late and I began to doze fitfully. And then Mal was
shaking me awake. He told me that it was morning and that I
was to come with him.

Morning it was, but not yet light. We hurried down the
still, deserted streets, reached the waterfront and walked
along it until we came to a motorboat moored at a small jetty.
Tomas stood at the wheel. Mal ushered me on board, then
left. Tomas started the engine and we headed out to sea. As
soon as we were out of sight of the bay, he swung the boat in a
northerly direction and eventually veered back towards the
shore until we were following the duned coastline. Dawn had

broken by now, a hazy, copper-coloured dawn, still and silent, save for the purr of the boat's motor. I did not ask where we were going. I sat back, enjoying a peculiar sense of freedom after the confines of the cellar.

We had been at sea for about two hours and I was ensconced in a daydream when a sudden change in the pitch of the engine stirred me. Tomas was swinging the boat towards an indentation in the coastline, a tiny cove surmounted by an arc of dunes. He disengaged the engine in shallow water and we waded ashore.

A dark, semi-cylindrical building stood between two dunes, reflecting the sunlight to a dull metallic blur. The dunes had encroached around the building, enveloping the wall on the windward side. The entrance had evidently been cleared of sand and carefully landscaped so that it would look artificial.

I recognized the place from an old photograph shown in one of my history lessons: it was Landfall Three, one of the six base-camps which had been established in different parts of Gaia just after the *Auriga* made orbit above the planet. The survey teams had been equipped to check out the immediate area with a view to determining the best site for settlement. The team at Landfall Five, on the northern bank of the Tamus, had eventually won out and the other camps had been abandoned with the landing of the *Auriga*. Landfall Five itself had been preserved as a site of historical interest and lay just south of Union Plaza.

Tomas rapped twice on the door and shouted his name.

We were admitted by a bearded man whose face seemed vaguely familiar to me. The hut was divided by a central corridor lined on both sides by open-plan laboratories, workrooms and sleeping quarters. The bearded man led us to the largest of the laboratory areas towards the far end of the building. Its benches were cluttered with an array of electronic equipment, some of which, I saw, was still operational. A fair-haired woman and a tall, ungainly youth were brewing tea on a hot-plate. Eilan sat in an armchair, an unopened folder in her lap.

Tomas provided the introductions. Eilan greeted me warmly and apologized for my incarceration in the cellar.

"Thomas is sometimes a little over-zealous in his caution," she told me. "But you must understand that we could afford to take no risks. We have been forced to behave like frightened criminals. It is regrettable, but necessary under the circumstances."

The youth's name was Islor, a toothy, freckled fellow who grinned hugely and patted me on the shoulder several times as if I was a long-lost friend. By contrast, Junith, the fair-haired woman, was cool in her reception: she neither smiled nor attempted body-contact, but acknowledged my presence with the curtest of nods. Her skin was extremely pale, as if she had spent all her days avoiding the sun. The bearded man was called Wolther, and as soon as Tomas announced his name, I remembered him. During one of my visits to the quarries in southern Gaia, the foreman in charge had taken me along to see a blasting and I recalled Wolther crouched at the base of an overhang implanting explosives. I had talked with him briefly afterwards (he had been like a ghost, his entire body covered with a film of fine, cinereal dust), although he didn't remember the occasion when I mentioned it to him.

Islor poured tea while I reiterated my reasons for contacting the League. Eilan was fascinated by the details of my visit to the tower and intrigued by my ideas about the M'threnni-Voice relationship. This gratified me enormously, since it was the first sign of goodwill that anyone connected with the League had hitherto shown me. She then informed me that they planned a raid on the lighthouse to free Jax and his comrades. Would I play a part in this operation? Although there was no hint of obligation in her tone, I knew that I had no option other than to accept.

I described the lay-out of the lighthouse and the surrounding area as well as my memory would allow, and then Eilan outlined the plan of attack. Two boats would approach from the sea by night and make a landing on the southern side of Needle Point where we would not be visible from the lighthouse. Wolther and Islor would take the first boat, with Tomas, Junith and myself following thirty minutes later. Wolther and Islor would set explosives around the perimeter of the desalination plant further along the Point and as soon as the guards had been drawn away from the lighthouse by the explosions, Tomas, Junith and I would move in and free Jax and his two comrades.

"Do you think three of us will be enough?" I asked. "My disappearance has been noted and Helmine must have guessed that I have contacted you. She may be expecting an attack on the lighthouse."

"Oh, she will," Eilan said, smiling somewhat unctuously. "But not, perhaps, for a day or two. We move in tonight."

It was a still, clear night, the bed of stars in the sky providing sufficient light for navigation, but insufficient (or so we hoped) for any guard gazing out to sea to make out our incoming boat. Tomas sat on the prow, peering ahead to the ragged black outline of the Point. I wielded the starboard oar; Junith, the port. My arms ached with the exertion and it seemed like an eternity since we had set off from the trawler-foil which was resting further out to sea, awaiting our return. I voiced no complaints, however, for Junith, pale and sickly though she looked, pulled steadfastly, and I was determined not to be outdone. The ocean gleamed under the starlight like an expanse of liquid metal; our oars plopped and swished through the water, and slowly the shoreline loomed nearer.

As we drew into a small cove at the base of a rocky ridge, I saw Wolther and Islor's boat moored in the shadows less than fifty metres away. Tomas leapt ashore and wrapped the guy-rope around a pinnacle of rock. Gratefully I released the oar and began to massage my shoulder muscles. Junith climbed out and Tomas hissed at me: "Hurry!" Clumsily I disembarked and began to follow them up the slippery, weed-choked rocks.

We had landed, as planned, midway between the lighthouse and the desalination plant. Finding a convenient niche between some rocks, we lay down and waited. A small searchlight atop the outbuilding threw a cone of light across the compound. The gates were closed and a guard attended them. I looked westwards, towards the desalination plant, its towers and chambers lit at intervals by red and white lights; a thin plume of white smoke or steam billowed languidly into the air from one of the towers. The road between the plant and the compound was deserted.

The pistol I was carrying in my belt was jutting into my groin. I removed it and examined it in the starlight. Ever since Tomas had handed me the weapon several hours earlier I had felt uncomfortable. "Do you expect me to use this?" I had asked him, and he had simply replied: "It may be necessary." It was only then that I had realized how naïve my hope had been that we might be able to spirit Jax and his comrades away without having to confront any guards. I was not a pacifist, but I had never considered the possibility of inflicting permanent damage, let alone death, on anyone. The gun terrified me. It was one of the heavy, snub-nosed discharge pistols carried by the militia and capable of delivering pulsed electronic charges of variable intensity. I set the dial on low, so that the gun would deliver nothing more than a debilitating electric shock. Medium intensity charges could stun a person, while the charge from a high intensity bolt would be fatal. Only the militia were allowed to bear arms, so the guns must have come by some circuitous route from Helmine's troops: another irony. That we possessed them at all tended to confirm my suspicion that the League had better resources than most people imagined.

A guard emerged from the outbuilding, wandered around the compound and stopped to talk to the guard at the gate. He then completed another circuit and went back inside. No sooner had he closed the door than a flare of white light illuminated the peninsula, followed an instant later by the thump of an explosion, then several more bursts of light and noise. Orange-rimmed smoke shrouded the desalination plant.

Several figures emerged from the outbuilding, some clambering into floaters, others running ahead to the gate, which was hurriedly being opened by the guard. They took off down the road towards the plant and within minutes the compound was deserted save for a solitary guard stationed between the outbuilding and the lighthouse.

"Quickly," Thomas whispered.

We went down the incline, crouching low, keeping pace with the group on the road, moving towards the compound as they moved away. The guard, growing restless, began a tour of the perimeter and disappeared behind the outbuilding. We approached the gate and walked boldly through, our pistols tucked into our belts behind our backs.

We were half-way across the compound when the guard reappeared. Tomas immediately strode over to him and said: "Where are the others: I gave orders that a full complement of guards were to remain on duty here."

The guard, who had pulled out his own pistol, looked confused. "There was an explosion at the plant. They have gone to investigate."

"I can see that, you idiot," Tomas said. Junith walked past the two of them and stopped just behind the guard.

"Well?" Tomas said. "Have they left you here alone?"

"No, there's one—who are you, anyway?"

He began to raise his pistol, but Junith turned sharply and clubbed him over the head with the butt of her gun. He stumbled forward, dazed but not unconscious, and Thomas grabbed his weapon away. He wedged it into the small of his back and began marching him towards the outbuilding. The door opened, and a female guard emerged. Junith levelled her pistol. There was a sharp, loud crackle and a bolt of white light flashed across the compound, hitting the woman in her midriff. Her body jerked as if hidden strings had been pulled and she slumped to the ground.

"Get over to the lighthouse and stand guard," Tomas directed me.

I fled across the compound, my heart pounding with fear and tension. I crouched beside the door and pointed my pistol towards the gate, praying that no one would appear.

The seconds dragged by. Finally Tomas and Junith emerged from the outbuilding and hurried across to me. Tomas had the keys.

"What have you done with them?" I asked as he unlocked the door.

"Tied and gagged them. Come."

Junith stood guard at the door while Tomas and I moved slowly up the steps, our backs flattened against the wall. We had expected to encounter at least one more guard in the tower itself, but there was no sound or movement above us, and when we reached the landing, it was deserted. This was strange, I thought; surely they wouldn't have left the cell unattended:

Tomas unbolted the door and opened it.

"Sam!" he whispered. "Nita! Jax!"

There was no reply. Tomas switched on his torch and the eye of the beam flashed over the bunks. Jax and his two comrades lay asleep. Tomas knelt beside the lower bunk in which the woman lay and shook her gently, lifting her head. Her eyes opened, but her pupils were only just visible beneath her upper eyelids, as if she was staring at her eyebrows. Tomas flashed the torch in her face but there was no reaction. He shook her more vigorously and her mouth lolled open.

He set her down and moved to Jax's bunk. Raising him to a sitting position, he slapped his cheek. Jax murmured, his eyes opened and I saw that they were the same as the woman's: raised in moronic supplication to the heavens. Tomas removed his support and Jax flopped back on the pillow.

"What is it?" I asked.

"Let's go," Tomas said, moving past me.

I grabbed his arm. "What's happened to them?"

"They are as good as dead," he said in a level tone. "We can do nothing for them. Let's get out of here."

I blocked his exit. "I'm not leaving Jax."

"Then stay here with him!" he said, pushing me aside.

I went over to Jax, dragged him off the bed and forced him to stand. Drugged, I told myself. He's drugged.

"You can walk," I said, leading him towards the door. He

moved his feet, ponderously, mechanically, and we reached the top of the stairs.

"Steps," I said, leading him down. He stumbled and I was only just able to support him. But his legs would not work again. I took his weight on my shoulder and began to drag him down the stairs. Once or twice his feet moved, as if some dim consciousness of their function was trying to surface, but their movements were so uncoordinated as to be of no help to me.

At length we reached the bottom. To my surprise I found that Junith and Tomas were waiting for me. Junith put one arm under Jax's shoulder and together we propelled him across the compound and out through the gate. Tomas ran at our side, his pistol at the ready.

Two guards were coming down the road from the plant. They saw us and broke into a run. Tomas knelt and fired. The light-bolt cut a searing path down the road, forcing the guards to dive for cover. Junith and I began to drag Jax up the rocks while Tomas gave covering fire behind. Several balls of light rent the air over our heads; the fire was being returned. We reached the ridge and began tumbling, helter-skelter, down the slope to the cove.

Junith and I bundled Jax on board then took the oars. Junith yelled to Tomas, who appeared moments later on the crest of the ridge. Suddenly his figure was starkly silhouetted as a ball of white light exploded just in front of him. He keeled backwards and came careening down the slope, arms and legs flailing, before finally coming to rest sprawled across a weed-covered boulder only metres away. I leapt ashore, scrambled over the rocks and, hoisting him by the armpits, dragged him towards the boat. Junith took his legs and we heaved him on board.

Frantically Junith and I pulled off, thrusting and lifting, thrusting and lifting, our progress from the shore inexorably slow. Within minutes several guards had appeared on the ridge and they began firing at us. Lightballs hissed through the air and exploded into the water on either side of the boat. From their size I knew that the guards' weapons were set to maximum intensity. If a bolt hit the boat, we were all dead.

Slowly, slowly the coastline receded. Thrust and lift. Thrust and lift. At some point I became aware that the boat was no longer being illuminated by hostile flashes of light; no cascades of water drenched us; the air did not crackle overhead. I looked up in time to see the last bright explosion of water some distance behind the boat. We were out of range and the guards had ceased fire. For the first time since we had landed on the Point, I thought it possible we might escape.

But I continued to row as obsessively as ever, pouring all my thoughts and energies into the act. When Junith tapped me on the shoulder and told me to stop, I had no idea of how long we had been at sea. An hour, perhaps, or perhaps only ten minutes. Tomas was lying in the prow of the boat and Junith went over to him.

"Is he all right?" I asked.

"He's burned but he's still breathing."

"I'm all right," Tomas said in a cracked voice. "Help me up."

Junith helped him sit. Jax was still slumped in the bottom of the boat like a man in a stupor of drunkenness.

"You risked our lives for a corpse," Tomas said. He was staring out to sea.

"What's wrong with him?"

"He's been brain-blanked."

So Helmine had carried out her threat. "Is there nothing we can do for him?" I asked, knowing that the question was futile.

"Helmine used no delicacy in her attempt to extract the information she required," Tomas said through clenched teeth. He was obviously in great pain. "Enforced memory retrieval burns out vital neural pathways and only a rudimentary consciousness remains. Reason cannot be re-imprinted on a blanked mind. The only kindness you could do him now would be to put him out of his misery."

I regarded Jax for a long moment, then took the pistol from my belt.

"It won't work," Junith said. "It's not charged."

I stared at the gun, then at her.

"We could not take the risk," she said, removing her own pistol and making adjustments to the barrel aperture before passing it to me. The aperture was now the size of a pin-hole and would deliver a thin, concentrated beam of energy which could cut effortlessly through flesh and bone.

Telling myself that he was dead, already dead, I lifted Jax, hung his head over the edge of the boat and put the barrel of the pistol under his chin. Turning away, I pressed the trigger. There was a brief, loud hiss, like a jet of water escaping from a nozzle, and Jax's body jerked, went limp. I threw the gun to the floor of the boat, then heaved the body over the side. It hit the water with a splash, brine splattering my face. A muted frenzy of despair and self-loathing passed through me like a shiver. I turned away from Tomas and Junith, feeling nauseous and utterly spent.

Presently Junith activated her torch and began flashing it out to sea. I heard the low throb of the trawlerfoil's auxiliary engine and then I saw the dark bulk of the foil itself less than fifty metres away.

We manoeuvred the boat alongside the foil and a rope-ladder uncoiled from the deck. We climbed on board. Eilan ushered Tomas off to attend to his burns, while Junith conferred with Alma, the foil's captain. I slumped against the railing, thinking dire thoughts. Had I not fled from Helmine, Jax might never have had to undergo brain-blanking. I had not only "executed" him on the boat, but had effectively sentenced him to death when I had escaped Helmine's surveillance and fled to the harbour. By attempting to save Jax, I had only hastened his demise.

I became aware that Junith and Alma were arguing about something. "We have to leave now," I heard Junith say.

I went over to them. "What is it?"

"Wolther and Islor have not returned," Alma said. "They should have been here an hour ago."

"If we stay here any longer we'll never get away," Junith said to Alma. She turned to me. "Alma thinks we should wait until they show up."

"What does Eilan say?"

"She's with Tomas. *We* have to decide."

I considered. Alma looked worried; Junith, grimly determined.

"If we get caught," I said, "all this effort will have been for nothing. At least we can salvage our pride by escaping. I think we should go."

Alma nodded solemnly, accepting the majority decision without further argument. She went up to the bridge and a moment later the engines fired.

We moved off, rapidly picking up speed, the solar panels at the rear of the craft beginning to glow. The prow of the craft lifted from the water, the engines increased their whine, and a breeze rose cool and fresh on our faces as we plunged into the star-filled night.

Chapter Ten

I awoke. Bright sunlight was streaming into the cabin, and the hammock in which I was lying swayed gently with the rise and fall of the foil. Tomas lay asleep on the bottom bunk, his face swathed with bandages. Quietly I threaded my way past the row of empty hammocks which had been set up in anticipation of a larger complement of passengers (the foils normally carried a crew of four) and thrust my head through the porthole: the ocean stretched unbroken to the horizon.

I wandered down the narrow passageway to the galley and found Eilan at the stove, stirring up some vegetable broth. While I washed (my hands were covered with cuts and abrasions from the hurried descent down the rock-face and my watch had been broken), I asked her where we were going.

"The Antipodean Isles," she told me.

I studied my lathered hands. "Why there?"

"It's necessary," Eilan said. "We have to get as far away from Helmine as possible. After last night's raid she'll stop at nothing to track us down."

The soap was stinging my eyes. I rinsed my face and found a towel.

"We could hide out in the mountains," I said.

"How would we eat?" She began to fill a bowl with broth as if to demonstrate her point.

"What about the western shore, beyond the mountains?"

She filled a second bowl and brought them both over to the table.

"A desert of rock," she said. "The Antipodean Isles have plant and animal life. We can survive there and it's highly unlikely that Helmine will pursue us half-way round the world. Do you want bread?"

"I think it's ridiculous," I said, sitting down at the table. The smell of the broth was extremely inviting; I was famished.

Eilan took a hunk of brown bread from the larder. "It was all decided before we began the operation."

"I was not consulted."

"No one knew except for Alma and myself." She broke off a handful of bread and passed it to me. "In that way, unless we were all captured, Helmine would not be able to trace us." She looked up at me. "Besides, you could not reasonably expect to be involved in policy decisions at such an early stage. None of us knew you and we could not be certain of your loyalty."

"The events of last night will have hardly served to confirm my worth to you."

"No, you acted bravely if somewhat foolishly in trying to save Jax. In your position I would probably have done the same thing myself." She sat down and began to eat her broth.

After a while I asked: "How is Tomas?"

"He'll recover. But his optic nerves were permanently damaged by the blast."

"You mean he's blind?"

"He doesn't know it, yet. But yes."

I pushed the half-empty bowl away. "It's my fault. If I hadn't insisted on getting Jax back to the boat, it wouldn't have happened."

"You can't be sure of that. Besides, he knew what risks were involved." She pushed the bowl back to me. "Make a meal of that, instead of your guilt."

I ate without enthusiasm. Jax dead, Tomas blinded, Wolther and Islor in Helmine's clutches. The entire operation had been a disaster.

Eilan brewed tea, which we drank from tin mugs.

"Has Alma been at the wheel all night?" I asked.

"She refuses to sleep. She says that there is no one else to steer the foil."

"Is this true?"

"Strictly speaking, yes. In our original plan we anticipated that Islor and Jax would take turns at the wheel. But in reality her objection is only technical. We are in open water, the weather is good, and it is simply a matter of holding the foil on a firm easterly course." She spat a tea-leaf back into the mug. "Alma is worried about Wolther. They have been in liaison for twelve seasons. Theirs is a close bond."

"What of the others left on the mainland? Helmine must know by now about Landfall Three and the *Star*."

"Judging by the resistance which Jax and the others put up to the mind-probes, I doubt that she has learned anything useful. In any case, Landfall has been abandoned." She refilled her mug with tea. "As for the others, well, there are only a handful left. Very few maintained their allegiance to the League after Helmine sabotaged the parlours."

"The fire-bombing was her doing?"

"Of course. You don't think we would have been stupid enough to wreck a successful campaign with such a suicidal move?"

I nodded; there really was no limit to Helmine's deviousness and ruthlessness.

"The others will be looked after," she said. "Roger has friends in high places."

"Why did you decide to take on Helmine in the first place?"

She smiled, wrinkles multiplying on her face. "Like you, I had an encounter with a dying Voice."

She got up and took two more bowls from the shelf. She filled them with broth and carried them outside to Junith and Alma.

I waited until she had returned. "When?"

"When what?"

"When did you meet the Voice?"

"Six seasons ago." She put her hands on her hips and stretched, straightening her back.

"I'd like to hear about it."

"I'm sure you would," she said, flopping into the canvas chair beside the stove. She leaned back, as if collecting her thoughts.

"I was working for the government at the Complex," she said, "and it was my habit to take a stroll along the riverside after finishing work. One evening, just after dusk, I noticed a body lying in the shallows downstream from Round Island Bridge. It was a woman, a hairless woman garbed in the muddied robe of a M'threnni Voice. At first I thought she was dead but when I went down to her I was able to detect a faint pulse. She was in a coma, and fading rapidly. I managed to carry her back to the Complex and took her up to my laboratory.

"There was no one else about and so . . ." She paused, sighed. "It's a shameful thing to have to admit, but I made no attempt to save her life. I told myself that she was dying, that I could do nothing for her, so why not conduct an experiment?

"I had been doing some research into the clinical applications of brain phase monitoring—attempting to correlate certain dream images with certain types of psychosis—and my lab had effectively been converted into a dream parlour. It was an opportunity too good to pass up. I hooked up a dual series system and connected the dying Voice to one headpiece and myself to the other so that I could directly monitor her mental activity.

"There was little apparent activity. The Voice *was* dying and all her mental processes were shutting down. At first all I could detect was a fuzz. But then I became aware that at the core of this static there was some activity and as I probed it I discovered that it was like a vortex, an eddy of thought which spiralled so fast that I could hardly penetrate it. But I could tell that it was not a purely human mental process: there were undertones of an incomprehensive flux which had to be alien in origin.''

She stared at me. ''You are right, David, the M'threnni do exert a dominance over a Voice's brain, but it's an indirect one. They don't speak through the Voices in the sense of using them as mental puppets; they implant a nucleus of alien thought-patterns in the cerebral cortex, thus enabling the Voice to *think* like a M'threnni.''

She shook her head slowly, as if she still found the idea hard to accept.

''And then what?'' I asked.

''The Voice died. All activity faded into nothingness. I unhooked myself and got up. When I looked down at the Voice I was overcome with a revulsion for the aliens who had not only penetrated her mind, but left her to die like an animal. She must have been dumped in the river, or had fallen in and somehow managed to struggle ashore. In that moment of hatred I decided that I would do my utmost to secure the removal of the M'threnni from Gaia. I could no longer countenance working for a government which effectively supported the aliens and I knew that I could never work changes from the inside, so I resigned my job and joined the League.''

''The League was already in existence?''

''Oh, yes. Has been almost since the M'threnni first arrived.'' She smiled faintly. ''I just put a little organization and backbone into their efforts.''

''But why didn't you reveal all this during your campaign against Helmine?''

''I had no proof. After the Voice died I took her back to the river and returned her body to its intended grave. I didn't want anyone at the Complex to know of it. I thought I'd be in a better position to reveal all when the League gained office. I was hoping that by then we would have the full weight of public opinion behind us and thus be able to force the aliens to leave Gaia.''

''You might have learned something from an examination of the body,'' I said.

''Dead Voices have been discovered in the city on a number of occasions in the past. What do you think happened to the one you encountered? It was doubtless taken away for autopsy like all the others. Nothing significant has been learned from physical examinations of the bodies. The Voices all died of ailments associated with old age but otherwise appeared physiologically normal.''

So, there *was* a comspiracy of silence surrounding the Voices. Jon must have known of this, yet he had said nothing during our seminars. Little wonder that the authorities wanted to keep public knowledge of the M'threnni to a minimum. A general disregard for human life was tolerable in view of the aliens' material aid; but a calculated callousness was another matter altogether. No doubt this was why Eilan had been confident that if the League gained power they would be able to compel the M'threnni to abandon their base on Gaia.

Alma was resolute throughout the day and night but finally, towards dawn on the second day, exhaustion overcame her and she fainted at the wheel. Junith and I carried her below and left Eilan in charge of her second patient.

While Alma rested, Junith and I took turns at the helm, six hours at a stretch. As Eilan had indicated, it required little effort to keep the foil on a straight easterly course; there was no wind and few tidal streams. Within a day Alma had recovered but we maintained our rota, for piloting the foil at least helped break the monotony of the voyage. For days on end there was nothing else to do except stare out at the placid, leaden ocean.

Junith, when not at the wheel, spent much of her time in the radio room, poring over some kind of receiver. It was an unusual piece of equipment, occupying one whole wall, and unlike anything I had ever seen before. Junith refused to explain its function to me, and Eilan was similarly non-

comittal when I questioned her. Obviously I would have to
wait a little longer before I was made privy to all the secrets of
the League.

By the sixth day Tomas was sufficiently recovered to be
pressing Eilan to remove his bandages. That evening, when
Eilan and I accompanied him back to the cabin after dinner,
he announced: "If you don't take them off, I'll remove them
myself."

Before Eilan could even frame her objections, he added:
"I know I'm going to be blind."

"You know?" I said.

"It's obvious. That blast seared my eyeballs. I couldn't
see a thing when we were on the rowing boat. I knew it would
be permanent."

Eilan and I exchanged glances, then she got up and began
to unpeel the bandages from his head. She worked carefully
and removed the final layer with particular delicacy. Tomas
winced once or twice, but he did not cry out.

His face was not as badly burned as I had expected. His
forehead, cheeks and nose were reddened and festering in
places but the burns were second-degree and would eventually heal. His eyebrows and eyelashes had been seared away
but his eyes looked quite normal apart from a slight misti-
ness. And yet they were dead. They were dead because they
had had to absorb not just a tremendous burst of heat, but of
light as well. It was the light that had blinded.

The semblance of a smile formed on Tomas's blistered
face.

"Perfect," he said.

"Perfect what?" I asked.

"Perfect darkness."

The morning of the eight day was overcast and Alma announced that she was stopping to overhaul the engines. The
foils were powered by a series of solar batteries which lined
the stern of the craft and vaporized sea-water drawn in
through four conduits in the hull. The batteries could store
sufficient energy to power the craft throughout the night but

their efficiency tailed off after more than twenty hours without direct sunlight. This in itself was sufficient reason for stopping, but it also gave us the opportunity to dismantle the panels and get inside the insolation chamber. Salt residues built up within the chamber over a period of time, reducing the engine's efficiency and I knew that it was normal practice to carry out the descaling operation every ten days or so.

It was several hours before the batteries had cooled sufficiently to permit their removal. Clad in green rubber coveralls, Alma then descended a ladder into the encrusted chamber armed with canisters of descalant. Junith and I donned gill-masks and dived under the boat to clear debris from the conduit grilles.

Junith entered the rear, starboard conduit; I, the rear port. The conduits were roughly five metres deep and about half as wide so that access was easy. The gill-masks would allow us to stay underwater for ten to twelve minutes, sufficient time to complete our task. I moved towards the grille in the murky half-light, took a knife from my belt and began cutting away the debris which had been sucked into the conduit during the voyage. It was mostly algae, greenkelp and a few dead jellyfish; I stuffed them into the bag tied at my waist. They came away easily and within minutes the grille was clear. I moved to the inner port conduit. As I approached the grille I could see that a large body was blocking it, an obstacle which, though covered with weed, I took to be a piece of driftwood, shaped in a warped parody of a human body. I began stripping it of its coating of weed and suddenly, to my horror, I discovered that I was holding a man's arm. I recoiled in fright, back-pedalling frantically, but the body detached itself from the grille and drifted after me like a green mummy. On one of the fingers of the outstretched hand a circlet of copper gleamed.

I flapped my arms and legs vigorously, cursing the inertia of the water. Finally I was out of the tunnel and pushing upwards towards the gleaming horizon. I broke surface, tore away my mask and began gulping in air. For several minutes

I rested against the side of the boat and then Junith surfaced, swam towards me and noticed my distress.

"What is it? What's happened?"

With confused, disjointed utterances I told her. When I had finished she said nothing, but slipped her mask back on, turned head over heels and disappeared beneath the water. Some time later she reappeared beside me and said: "He's gone."

She was wearing Jax's snake-ring on her right thumb. I thought perhaps she had recovered it to offer it me as a memento, but she made no move to do so. Despite feeling vaguely outraged that she had plundered my dead friend's body, I said nothing; I was still trembling with the irrational conviction that Jax was determined to follow me to the Antipodean Isles and punish me for killing him.

I was shaken for the remainder of the day and Eilan broke open one of the bottles of wine which she had been saving for our journey's end. She gave me sufficient to drink that I slept soundly that night. Early next morning, before we resumed our voyage, I went underwater and examined the four conduits. They were all clear, as was the water round about; but several days were to pass before I could think of Jax without experiencing a tremor of unease.

We continued on our way. Tomas's face began to heal but he talked little, despite all our efforts to engage him in conversation. Before joining the League he had been a shuttle pilot, a profession now irrevocably lost to him. Junith continued to spend most of her free time alone with her receiver. She did not seem to want for companionship and would only appear on deck when it was her turn at the wheel or when there was an essential task to perform. Alma, once she had recovered from the loss of Wolther, showed a stolid good-humour throughout the voyage and I always felt relaxed in her company. She seemed quite content with her lot and I guessed that she was one of those rare people who have no inner demons urging them on. Eilan and I discovered a common

interest in Earth history and we spent many hours deliberat-
ing on the variegated past of our ancestral planet. We did not
talk of the M'threnni or of Gaia; perhaps we sensed that we
had temporarily put both behind us and that they were better
left untalked of until the immediate future resolved itself.

Alma sighted land towards dusk on our twelfth day at sea
and we mustered on the bridge. There it was: a smear of
darkness on the horizon. Alma increased our speed but we
soon realized that we would not reach the island before
sunset. So, as the descending suns burnished the ocean with
their bloodshot stare, Alma cut the engines. We would ride in
at dawn tomorrow.

That night we celebrated our arrival with a feast of fish
freshly caught the day before. We drank the wine which
remained and talked well into the night. We were all in good
spirits. I demonstrated several card tricks which my father
had taught me; Alma told jokes, chuckling to herself long
before she reached the punch-lines; Eilan recited ribald
poetry with a gusto far removed from her normal sedateness;
Tomas surprised me, too, by singing several songs in a clear,
forceful tenor. He seemed to have regained all his earlier fire.
Only Junith did not join wholeheartedly in the festivities. She
drank a little wine and retired to bed early. At length the wine
dulled our sensibilities sufficiently that the rest of us stumbled off to our bunks and hammocks, weary but content.

We reached the island soon after dawn the following day. We
moored the foil about sixty metres from the shore and
launched a rowing boat.

No humans inhabited the Antipodean Isles, although they
had been well-mapped and photographed from the *Auriga*
soon after it arrived in orbit over Gaia. The islands bore more
varied and abundant plant and animal life than the mainland
but were rejected as the initial site for habitation because it
was felt that none were large enough to allow for a controlled
expansion of the colony; and spreading the population over
several islands would have destroyed the cohesiveness essential if the colony was to prosper. Sporadic visits had been

made in the past with a view to exploiting the islands' natural resources—particularly the wood obtainable from the forests—but their remoteness from the mainland had prevented any of these plans from reaching fruition.

The boat ground on to a shingled beach and we clambered out. Immediately beyond the beach the forest began, a dense olive curtain of squat trees and vines. Junith scooped a handful of pebbles from the beach and tossed them casually at a queer-looking bird which was strutting along the high-water line. The bird, of tawny plumage, had a squat rotund body, a long, slender neck and two large, mournful white eyes which sat atop its pointed head. It waddled forward to inspect us, its head dipping up and down, and it emitted a throaty warble which sounded uncannily like someone gargling water.

Junith took a stick of bread from her pouch, broke off a piece and offered it to the bird. Its eyes wobbled like eggs in a saucer, its mouth opened as if in a yawn, and suddenly its whole body jerked forward, snapping the bread from Junith's hand so swiftly that she jumped back in surprise. The bird hurried off down the beach, burbling loudly. It dunked the bread into the water, then swallowed it whole.

We moved inland. The vegetation was thick and in places impenetrable so that we had to use our gutting knives to cut our way through. The canopy overhead was provided by broad, palm-like fronds while the vegetation of the forest floor comprised pendulous bushes, giant ferns, liana and innumerable species of exotic flowers, all vying for the mottled greenish light which filtered through the trees. The air was hot, humid and fragrant. Tiny brown creatures scuttled across our path and we heard the strange cries of unknown animals: chirrups and screeches, squawks and hisses. We stayed close to one another as we moved through the undergrowth. I noticed that the bird we had encountered on the beach was trailing after us.

The vegetation thinned abruptly and we emerged in a clearing at the base of the escarpment of dark rock which formed the backbone of the island. The hillside was pockmarked with caves, like some great geological sponge, and white bird-droppings stained its upper reaches. Near the mouth of one cave was a small pool fed by a stream which burrowed out of a cleft in the rockface.

Alma, Junith and I were discussing who should sample the water when Tomas said: "I'll do the sampling. I'm the most expendable person here."

There was a trace of self-pity in his voice; but resolution, too. He had been silent since our landing, letting Eilan lead him by the hand through the forest; but he had obviously been feeling that he was a burden to us. Here was his chance to do something useful.

None of us made any objections so Eilan led him over to the pool. He knelt, scooped out a handful of water and splashed it against his lips. He repeated the motion, almost like a child at play, then rose.

"No taste," he said. "So far, so good."

We spent the remainder of the morning exploring the immediate area before finally deciding that the place beside the pool would make the best site for settlement. The cave behind the pool was deep enough to provide temporary shelter from the elements and unknown predators until we could construct some sort of cabin. Alma climbed to the top of the escarpment and called to us that she could see the far shore a few kilometres away. Later we were able to verify that we had come upon one of the smaller islands of the cluster.

Over zenith we sat in the mouth of the cave and discussed our plans. We all agreed that our first priority was a cabin; it was odd, in retrospect, that no one suggested that we continue to live on the foil—though perhaps not so odd considering that we were all heartily weary of ship-life. We had sufficient supplies of food to last at least another month but Tomas was eager to sample the vegetable life of the island. We agreed, but stipulated that he should try only one new item each day so that if he fell ill the culprit would be more easily identifiable.

Junith and I went down to the forest's edge and collected a handful of the large purplish fruit which grew on one of the bushy plants. While the rest of us feasted on ship's rations, Tomas ate the fruit. He was lavish in his praise of their flavour and succulence—so lavish that I was almost tempted to try one myself. The mottled bird wandered fussily about us as we ate, snapping at the crumbs which escaped our mouths and burbling incessantly. Junith fed it generous scraps of her rations and eventually, surfeited with food, it fell asleep at her side.

We decided that we would start work on the cabin immediately. After zenith Alma, Junith and I returned to the trawler to fetch tools. We had only two axes, a few knives and a handful of fish-hooks and it was eight days before the frame of the cabin was complete. First we cut a swathe through the forest from the beach to the escarpment, uprooting plants and shrubs, and chopping down the slender-boled trees which formed the forest's canopy. Then we laboriously carved out four deep holes in the bedrock beside the pool and set a stout trunk in each. We cut the remaining trunks into sections about eight metres long and bound them together with dried vines and liana, then bound these sections in turn to our four corner-posts. Finally we strung the dried, waxen leaf-fronds across a skein of branches to form a rough but watertight roof. We worked from dawn to dusk every day, only stopping when it grew too hot or when our blistered hands needed attention or when we were simply too tired to carry on. Eilan prepared our meals and attended to our wounds, while Tomas sat cross-legged at the mouth of the cave and called to us occasionally, asking us how it went.

On the evening of the eighth day we moved in. The interior of the cabin was still rough—just four windowless walls— but at least we now had a roof over our heads; it was a haven, however crude, from the wildness of the island. In the deepening gloom we sat down on a carpet of dried leaves to a meal of salted pork, mashed beans and rice. Tomas had a supplementary vegetable on his plate: a white-fleshed tuber which Eilan had discovered in the forest. Physically he appeared none the worse for wear from his diet of island food but the pall of his blindness was evident on his face. Eilan had also prepared a liquor from some berries which Tomas had earlier verified as edible. It was tart on the palate, but full-blooded, reminding me strongly of unripened roseplum juice.

Eilan and Alma were discussing how best the interior of the cabin should be structured to suit our needs: a kitchen in that corner, a fireplace beside that wall, sleeping quarters over there.

"How long will we have to stay here?" I asked. It was a question which had been bothering me ever since I had been told our destination, and now that our most urgent needs were met I felt that it was time to broach the matter.

"Until we can safely return to the mainland," Eilan said.

"That could be never."

"No, a season at most."

In the darkness I could not see her face. "How can you be sure? Helmine will not forget that quickly."

"Helmine will have other matters on her mind. A ship from Earth is on its way to Gaia."

Eilan said this so casually that it was a moment before the words registered on me. "A ship from Earth? When?"

"We're not exactly sure. In ten or eleven months' time, we think."

"They've already made contact with Gaia?"

"No. We located them first. Or rather, Junith did."

"But how? If they're that far away I can't see how the ship could have been detected in the first place."

"Junith?" Eilan said.

Junith's shadow spoke. "For the past two and a half cycles I've been monitoring the M'threnni freighter arrivals and departures from Round Island and I've discovered . . ." She paused. "Let me start from the beginning."

I heard the rustling of leaves and someone stood up. It was Tomas. He excused himself and went outside. He was slowly gaining in confidence in moving around on his own. It occurred to me that in the darkness of the cabin we were all as blind as he. But no, for we could dimly make out shapes and sense movements. The difference was small but inestimable.

"According to our understanding of the universe," Junith began, "no physical object should be able to travel faster than the speed of light since the mass of an object, and hence its inertia, increases exponentially towards infinity as it approaches the speed of light. And yet we are faced with the fact that the M'threnni freighters, which evidently originate outside our solar system, must possess plus-light capabilities. I was intrigued, so I did a little research and came across some work done by the late twentieth-century Earth mathematician William Smith. Smith calculated that an object possessing mass and travelling at plus-light speeds should be emitting vast amounts of energy in the form of pulsed gravitational waves. It's possible—the mathematics is complicated but not insurmountable—to relate the frequency of the pulses to the speed of the craft: the higher the frequency, the faster it's travelling. I built a receiver capable of picking up these gravitational pulses and began monitoring the M'threnni freighters—"

"You built it yourself?"

"It's not a new technology. Similar equipment was developed on Earth in the light of Smith's calculations to search for the hypothetical faster-than-light particles known as tachyons. None were found, which isn't very surprising, for when I checked Smith's calculations I discovered that his mathematics, while basically sound, embodied a factorial error . . . ."

I could hardly believe what I was hearing. Here was Junith, whom I had always regarded as a pale, sickly ghost of a human being, expounding with great enthusiasm and obvious expertise on the work of one of the foremost theoretical physicists of Earth. She had found a mistake in his arithmetic. . . .

". . . The strength of the emitted radiation," Junith was saying, "is, in fact, ten million times weaker than Smith had anticipated—which explains why the researchers missed it: their receivers just weren't sensitive enough.

"I modified my equipment accordingly and when I came to monitor a departing M'threnni freighter, there they were:

faint but detectable pulsations emanating from the craft soon after take-off when it became invisible—that is, when it breached the light-barrier. I monitored the decaying signals for over two hours, until they became too faint to register on the receiver. I was able to calculate from this that the M'threnni homeworld lies at a distance greater than two hundred light-years from Gaia, somewhere in the constellation we know as The Shield. If we could build more sensitive equipment it might just be possible to monitor the ship all the way back to its home-star, but at present that's beyond us."

She paused, and I heard someone snoring softly. Alma had fallen asleep.

Undaunted, Junith continued: "Calculations based on the frequency of the pulses show that the M'threnni freighters are capable of travelling at a velocity greater than fifty times light-speed. Again, with our present equipment we can't put an upper limit on it—we simply don't have the resolution."

"Does Helmine know anything of this?" I asked.

"Not unless she had a spy planted in the middle of the League," Junith said. "I did most of this work under Eilan's auspices."

"I'm a patron of the sciences," Eilan said wryly.

"After this discovery," Junith went on, "I took to scanning the skies for incoming M'threnni ships; the principle is the same, only the reverse of what I've already described. Naturally most of the time the receiver was aimed in that area of the sky where we believe the M'threnni homeworld to be located. However, about a month ago on a whim I aligned the receiver in the direction of Sol. To my surprise I discovered that I was picking up similar signals to those from approaching M'threnni craft, but of much lower frequency. The obvious conclusion is that there is a ship on its way from Earth, travelling at a speed about five times that of light."

Alma was snoring more loudly now. Eilan reached out and evidently pinched her nose, for she snorted and fell silent.

"We can deduce the time of arrival from the intensity of the pulses," Junith said. "The figure we arrive at is ten or eleven months hence."

It was a startling revelation.

"How many people know about this?" I asked.

"At first I told only Tomas. Naturally Eilan was also informed as soon as we had freed her from prison."

Of course; the League's sudden boldness in moving against the authorities made more sense in the light of this disclosure. Tomas must have organized the raid on the penitentiary because he knew that there was no longer anything to be gained from playing a waiting game.

"We told no one else," Eilan said. "Not even our fellow League members. We could not risk the news leaking out. It would simply have given Helmine more time to consolidate her position."

"What about the M'threnni?"

"Well, we must assume that they are aware of the incoming ship. Who can say how they will react?"

Who, indeed. The arrival of people from Earth would no doubt signal the beginning of a new era for the colony. With starships of plus-light capability, Earth would be able to maintain continuous contact with Gaia. What place for the M'threnni then?

I was intrigued by the revelation of Junith's genius. When I was next alone with Eilan I asked her about Junith's background. At first, with her usual prudence, she refused to tell me anything, but I persisted and finally the story emerged.

Junith had been an exceptionally gifted child. It was clear from an early age that her intellectual abilities far outstripped those of her crèche companions. Indeed, Eilan told me, there was a suspicion, never verified, that someone had tampered with the fertilization programme, artificially enhancing her intelligence quotient. This was illegal; only the sexual characteristics and the physical health of a newborn baby could be determined beforehand. At the age of three she had been taken from her nursery and raised by a team of educational psychologists under conditions designed to maximize her intellectual development. But her emotional needs were neglected; she had no friends her own age and her tutors lacked warmth. She grew into a remote, diffident adolescent. At fifteen, she ran away and lived for a cycle in poverty and squalor on the South Bank. Then, one day, she was discovered on Round Island Bridge. Apparently she had climbed the parapet and unsuccessfully attempted to gain access to the tower. She had never spoken of the incident but Eilan theorized that she had been attracted to the aliens because she knew their mental abilities must far outstrip her own.

"All her life she had been performing in an intellectual circus," Eilan said, "and perhaps she felt her only recourse was to be taken under the wing of a being who would demand nothing of her beyond servitude. In any event the aliens rejected her and she loathed them for it. Soon after her abortive assault on the tower she contacted the League. Joining us fulfilled two of her basic needs: the first, to revenge herself on the M'threnni; the second, to oppose a government she blamed for her unhappy childhood. She has a hatred of authority inculcated from those early days. Should the League ever win power, I think she would leave us, too."

We explored the rest of the island. It was predominantly forested with some swampland and areas of savannah. Shingled beaches hemmed the entire coastline. The animal life mostly avoided us but we glimpsed variants of the springers who populated the lower slopes of the mainland, in addition to leathery, tree-crawling primates and shy, mottled quadrupeds who peered at us through the foliage but fled if we approached them. The most ubiquitous creatures were the burblers, those inquisitive, flightless birds whose ambassador had already been adopted by Junith. They were utterly fearless and utterly trusting and soon our cabin was besieged by them. In desperation we roasted a few and chased the rest off with torches lest we lose our sanity under their incessant warbling. During this purge Junith locked her pet away in the cabin.

Tomas suffered a minor stomach upset from some fungi he ate but apart from that, everything else he tried appeared edible. There were numerous varieties of fruit and vegetables in the forest and Eilan began to add them to our diet. We made spears and bows and arrows, and hunted the animal life. The springer meat was strong and salty, the tree-crawlers tough and unpalatable, the quadrupeds rich but somewhat greasy. The burblers provided most of our meat, the taste of their flesh similar to that of chicken. Only Junith refused to partake of it.

Gradually we improved the cabin, carving out windows, building interior walls and lining the floor with strips of wood. We removed the bunks from the trawler and set them up in our separate bedrooms. We added an annex to the existing structure to be used as a bathroom and toilet. The roof fell in and we repaired it with a sturdier frame of branches. We carved stones into blocks and constructed a chimney which exhibited an efficiency far beyond our expectations. We built stools and tables which frequently collapsed at first but grew stronger as we improved our woodwork. We could have commandeered all our furniture from the foil but we wanted to maintain the craft in as pristine a condition as possible so that we could make our eventual departure from the island with a minimum of fuss—and besides, it was fun to experiment with joints and angles; we had plenty of time on our hands.

About a month after our arrival, however, tragedy struck. Alma, Junith and I, returning late one afternoon from a fishing expedition, arrived back at the cabin to find that Tomas was dead. Eilan had been away for most of the afternoon, hewing the thick savannah grass which she was weaving into carpets. Tomas had taken a knife from the kitchen and slit his throat. Eilan had found him lying in a pool of caking blood against the rear wall of the cabin; he had been dead for over an hour.

We had all been aware of how deeply his blindness had affected him and initially we had endeavoured to ensure that someone was with him at all times. But Tomas had grown as weary of this stricture as we, and had asked to be allowed to spend some time on his own. We had agreed, assuming that it was the first sign of his recovery from the trauma. It had proved a fatal mistake.

Eilan maintained a fragile composure as she greeted us with the news. Tomas's body lay in the shadows beside the pool, covered with a brown woollen blanket. A cloud of flies had found it, and none of us was able to summon the courage to step forward and draw back the blanket from the face.

That evening we constructed a rough bier and in the morning we carried the body out to the foil. Nobody spoke as we made our lugubrious voyage out into deep waters; we committed the body to the ocean without ceremony or speech. Our silence was a small measure of the common guilt we felt.

Another month passed. We used the foil to explore the other islands of the archipelago, carefully charting their positions and contours until we had eventually built up quite a comprehensive map. Of course charts more accurate than ours existed on the mainland but that did not deter us—they had been obtained from an orbiting spacecraft whereas we were working in the spirit of the ancient mariners of Earth. If we had been forced into exile, well, then, we would make our exile an adventure.

The other islands were much like our own, save for the larger ones which held a greater variety of plant and animal life. We encountered a relative of the tree-crawling primate which inhabited our island, this species less hairy and predominantly land-based. These creatures, discovered by earlier explorers and christened homuncules, had been the basis of much speculation on the mainland; some anthropologists felt that they were the precursors of intelligent indigenous life, while others argued that the planet lacked sufficient land-mass for the evolution of man-like creatures. Still others claimed that all Gaian life-forms were originally extrinsic to the planet and had been brought here by the M'threnni. Gaia had been a virgin planet, they said, until impregnated by alien seed. The homuncules were a timid, nervous species who darted through the savannah, semi-erect, in groups of up to twenty. They ate berries and seeds, and showed no sign that they possessed anything beyond the most rudimentary intelligence. Soon after their discovery several specimens had been brought back to the mainland but had died within months of their instalment in Helixport Zoo.

On the whole we adapted well to island life and I must admit that for me it was as happy a period as I had ever spent. Forced to provide for our most basic needs, our lives became determined by expediency and whim, a refreshing contrast to the ritual demands of city-life. I grew a beard and let my hair go untrimmed. Most days, when we had sufficient firewood and food in store, I wandered around the island or went swimming or took a rowing boat out on an aimless voyage. Eilan and Alma, too, spent most of their time outdoors, but Junith, strange Junith, seldom emerged from the cabin. She would sit for hours with her pet bird, fondling and petting it, and constantly feeding it scraps of food until it grew grossly fat. Occasionally she would go out to the foil to check on the progress of the incoming starship but she rarely spoke of her findings unless directly asked, and even then she would seldom say more than: "It's still on its way."

The weather remained good throughout our first two months on the island, a succession of bright, cloudless days. One afternoon, however, I was returning from the interior of the island when I noticed that clouds were massing in the east. A light wind soon sprang up, quickly ripening into a gale. As I hurried through the forest I could hear large drops of rain splattering the leafy canopy overhead and by the time I had reached the cabin the rain had increased to a downpour and the wind was still rising.

Eilan and Alma had gone off to investigate a hot-water spring on one of the larger islands. Junith sat in the living-room beside a hissing fire, her bird asleep on the hearth. She did not greet me as I entered the cabin, nor did she show a flicker of interest as I stripped off my sodden clothes, rubbed myself down, and donned a fresh pair of shorts. I added more wood to the fire and put some water on to heat, dropping a handful of berries into it to provide a flavour (we had used up all our tea, one luxury that I really missed).

The wind was gusting through the cabin with considerable ferocity so I put up the shutters which we had prepared for such an emergency; but some of the firewood must have been green, for now acrid smoke billowed into the cabin. I extinguished the fire, filled a mug with the tepid berry-juice and sat down on my rickety but serviceable stool. After some minutes water began to drip on my shoulder. I looked up; the roof was leaking badly in several places. The bird awoke and began waddling around the room, showing increasing signs of agitation. As the wind continued to rise the walls of the cabin began to sway.

Junith looked at me with unspoken alarm.

"I think we had better—" I began, but never finished, for suddenly there was a great slurping sound and I was knocked to the floor under a weight of water, branches and leaves.

Slowly I disentangled myself, wincing as broken twigs bit into my flesh, and got to my feet. Junith was also up, scraping mud and leaves from her body. The four walls of the cabin were in violent motion, oscillating with the gale, and the door, its latch broken, battered itself against the jamb. Hurriedly I took Junith's arm and we ran out of the cabin and up the incline to the cave. Scarcely had we reached it than the entire cabin was torn from its foundations by the wind, the corner-posts snapping, the walls parting from one another, the individual logs splitting apart to be carried down the hillside, tumbling and bouncing in a frenzy of motion.

Junith and I cowered in the cave, watching the storm vent its anger on the island. The trees buckled into arcs under its onslaught, grasses and shrubs prostrated themselves, the very ground shivered. A bright vein flashed in the skies and thunder rolled in from afar. Junith clung to me, her hair matted to her face, her tunic stuck to her body like a second skin. We had moved as far inside the cave as we could; here the rain did not penetrate and there was a residual warmth from the earlier half of the day. Junith's bird, its feathers in wet dishevelment, came waddling into the cave and hid in a cranny. Junith buried her head in my chest while I gazed dully out at the unrelenting violence of the gale. I began to stroke her hair, to clasp her closer to me.

Our island life had been celibate up to now. Tomas had been too morose over his blindness to engage in any coupling, and I had not sought, or been sought, as a bed-partner. Eilan was old enough to have rescinded the pleasures of the flesh some time ago, while Alma was almost twice my age and inspired no lust in me (besides, I respected her liaison with Wolther, irrespective of the possibility that he was dead). This left Junith, whom I had desired in an abstract fashion on numerous occasions but had never approached because she radiated frigidity. But now circumstances had thrown us together and she seemed responsive to my touch.

I lifted her head and kissed her on both cheeks, then ran my lips along the ridge of her jawbone. Although her mouth lolled open, she did nothing either to encourage or deter me; she seemed in a daze, almost unaware of me. I laid her flat and drew her tunic from her pale, thin body. She turned her head away while I undressed and stared out through the cave at the storm. She did not protest as I straddled her and began kissing her neck and breasts, and when I entered her she gave a short gasp, but that was all. She was barely moist, as though she felt that desire would only interfere with the mechanics of the act. It was a strange passionless coupling; not once did her breathing quicken; not once did a murmur of pleasure issue from her throat; not once did she turn away from her glazed contemplation of the storm. When finally I was spent, it was with no sense of elation or completion, but with a feeling of shame. I felt as if I had raped her.

The storm continued to rage, and after a while Junith fell asleep. By now my shame had transformed itself into a resentful anger at her indifference to my attentions; I felt slighted and demeaned. With a sudden resolve I leaned forward and gently eased Jax's snake-ring from her thumb. I found my shorts and put the ring into one of the pockets.

There was a smear of blood on my genitals, I saw, a smear duplicated on Junith's thighs. At first I took it to be some kind of vaginal haemorrhage; but no, my penetration had not caused her pain, I was sure. Then I recalled a phrase used by many girls to describe their defloration at their majority ceremonies: they called it "the letting of the womb-blood." Junith was a virgin.

It was over four hours before the storm abated, and four more before Alma and Eilan returned. I had been worried that perhaps they had been taken unawares by the storm while at sea, but Alma was experienced in reading the weather and she had moored the foil in a leeward cove before the storm had reached the islands. That night we slept on board the foil, and the next day we set about rebuilding the cabin, this time setting it in the mouth of the cave where it would be better protected from future storms.

The days bled into one another in an indolent, timeless succession. Since the storm, Junith seemed changed. She no longer confined herself to the cabin, but wandered all over the island, sometimes spending the night in the forest. She abandoned clothing, going everywhere naked, and soon she was as brown as the rest of us. As the months passed her body gradually ripened, her modest breasts increasing in size, the swell of her abdomen growing by degrees more pronounced. Alma and I were mystified by this transformation: was the forest working some strange metamorphosis on her? Although this was a ridiculous proposition, it was not easy to dismiss it lightly for by the end of the ninth month of our stay on the island the distension in her abdomen was so marked that it seemed as if she would eventually explode. One evening, while we sat around a fire outside the cabin, I asked her if she was well.

She was sitting in a low-strung chair which I had constructed for her, the size of her belly having made it increasingly difficult for her to attain a position of comfort on the stools which we normally used. Her pet-bird, as always nestled in her lap, burbling gently under her attentions. She looked at me and said, as if surprised: "I'm quite well."

"But your stomach is—swollen."

"I am carrying a child within me."

Only Eilan looked unsurprised. She had kept her counsel while Alma and I had speculated on the changes in Junith's physique; I believe she had a general fondness for being secretive.

"How is this possible?" I asked.

"It's possible," Eilan said, "because Junith never underwent the sterilization procedures designed to prevent both vaginal bleeding and the possibility of pregnancy. It's a simple procedure—an injection administered at puberty which stops the release of ova and eliminates menstruation. Junith's wardens were too busy with her education to pay any attention to her physical growth."

"I always felt ashamed because I bled," Junith said. "For all my fine education my tutors never saw fit to teach me the basic facts about my body."

Which explained her coldness and reclusiveness, I thought. I tried to imagine what it would be like to feel that something as natural as, say, urinating was an unhealthy and inexplicable process. It was impossible to contemplate.

"There have been other pregnancies in the past," Eilan said. "On the South Bank, where people are sometimes lax in their duties towards their youth, a number of females have conceived over the past few cycles, though the embryos were all aborted before—"

"My child will be born," Junith said with a whispered vehemence.

Eilan smiled. "I was not suggesting otherwise. Even if you did not want the baby, how could it be avoided? We are several thousand kilometres away from the nearest hospital; and in any case, your pregnancy is far too advanced to risk termination. Your child *will* be born."

My own reaction to this revelation was simply one of awed silence. The child growing within her had been fathered by me, but the very idea that it would be delivered from her body

seemed totally preposterous and not a little repugnant. I knew
that child-bearing had once been the norm among women on
Earth but nonetheless it seemed a gruesome and insanitary
means of propagating the human species.

A further month passed, during which time Junith began to
pay increasingly frequent visits to the foil to monitor the
signals from the approaching Earth-ship. Alma and I would
ferry her out in the rowing boat, treating her with extreme
delicacy, as if the child inside her was as fragile as an egg.
Since the announcement of her pregnancy she had become
noticeably more friendly; the terrible burden of self-shame
which had isolated her from other people had at last been
lifted.

One afternoon she returned from the foil with Alma, and I
saw that both of them were smiling.

"The ship's decelerating!" Alma called.

Eilan, who had just emerged from the cabin, put her hand
on my arm and said: "I think it's time we went home."

Chapter Eleven

Ten days later we approached the harbour. The journey home
had been uneventful apart from the progression of Junith's
pregnancy. The birth of her child was now imminent and we
had all been hoping that she would not enter labour on the
boat since none of us had any notion of what to do in such a
situation. Thankfully the child remained obligingly within
her womb throughout the voyage.

A rising tide of anticipation had infected all of us as the
days had passed and we had drawn closer and closer to the
mainland. Whenever possible Alma had kept the engines
under full power; we had been blessed with fine weather and
had made good time. Two days out from shore we had begun
to encounter other foils out on fishing expeditions but we had
not attempted to contact them. We would sail, unannounced,
into the harbour to meet whatever fate awaited us.

Around mid-morning we moored at a central wharf in the
bay. There were few people about; most of the trawler crews
were out at sea, and those on shore were using the period of
lull to take a siesta before the fleet returned at zenith. A few
people from the city were wandering along the promenade as
we disembarked but they paid us no attention, not even

glancing twice at Junith. We crossed the street and began climbing Prospect Place.

It was Spring, I realized. Our months on the island had gone by with no sense of the progression of the seasons. It occurred to me that there should be a new mayor in Helixport now; but Helmine had already secured a second term of office and if her stranglehold on the government was as strong as it had been when we had left I saw no reason why she should not still be installed in power.

This speculation was given ominous credence when we reached the *Alien Star*. The restaurant was closed and its windows were shuttered. We stood on the opposite side of the road, debating whether we should knock on the door. Then suddenly a voice called: "Eilan!"

A Napoleonic head was poking out through one of the windows above the restaurant. It vanished, and moments later the door was being opened and Roger was beckoning us in.

"Where have you been?" he asked, hugging Eilan. "We searched everywhere for you. I had given you up for dead."

"Holidaying on the Antipodean Isles," Eilan said. She told him of our sojourn on the island as he led us through the dining-area.

The restaurant was a shell. All the fittings had been removed, the carpet rolled up along one wall, the chairs and tables stacked into one corner. We went down a narrow corridor and thence into a private room where Roger evidently resided. A long L-shaped sofa, black and sumptuously padded, ran the length of two walls, and we settled ourselves upon it while Roger went to his drinks cabinet and selected a crystal decanter filled with a dark red liquid.

"Grape-wine all right for everyone?" he asked.

We all agreed that it would be eminently acceptable. Grapes did not grow well in our climate and could only be properly reared in hothouses; the wine was thus costly and highly prized.

"So much has happened since you've been away," Roger said, filling the glasses. "I don't know where to start."

He handed out the drinks and took a seat on the corner of the sofa. He was obviously intrigued by Junith's swollen midriff, but his propriety was stronger than his inquisitiveness and he did not comment on it.

"Tomas?" he asked.

"Dead," Eilan said. "What of Wolther and Islor?"

"Alive and well. They are presently out at sea fishing."

For the first time since we had reached the shore Alma visibly relaxed, a smile of pure relief forming on her face.

Wolther and Islor had made a successful retreat from the Point after planting their explosives, Roger told us, but Islor (who was evidently a little dim-witted) had forgotten to withdraw his oar so that when they arrived back at the boat the oar was gone. After a frantic but fruitless search they had eventually cast off, but the single oar had made linear motion impossible. Every few strokes they had switched the oar to the opposite rowlock, describing a tortuous path from the shore. Their progress was slow and by the time they had made the rendezvous the foil was long gone. Weary and disconsolate, they had drifted with the current and had finally been cast up on a deserted beach some kilometres south of the Point. They had quickly vanished into the night and had eventually found their way back to the harbour where a friend of Roger's had made provisions for hiding them.

"You had been arrested by then?" I asked.

"Oh yes, I was arrested. Held in solitary for four days. But there was no direct evidence of my involvement with the League and Eldon pulled strings on my behalf. He's always disliked Helmine. I was released after ten days."

Roger did indeed have friends in high places; Eldon was a former mayor of Helixport and a highly respected politician. He had retired two seasons previously but clearly still wielded a considerable influence over governmental affairs.

"What of Helmine?" Eilan inquired. She still looked tense, cautious, as if she expected the good news we had already received to be counterbalanced by some dire revelation.

"Ousted," Roger said with relish. "She overstepped herself. At the end of the last cycle she tried to get the Senate to endorse her for a third term. But there had been a growing unease about the possibility of a dictatorship throughout Winter—Helmine's strong-arm tactics and her blatant disregard for civil liberties were becoming more and more apparent. So Eldon mobilized his support and when Helmine attempted a third endorsement, he swooped. I had already hinted that we believed that she was responsible for the fire-bombings which had been blamed on the League and he produced conclusive evidence of this. She was impeached and quickly removed from office. She's in jail now and Nathan is mayor. The new Senate is far more democratic and is seeking to embrace all shades of opinion. The constitution is being rewritten to increase its number to ten. There's a place for you if you want it.''

Eilan showed a modicum of surprise. ''This seems a remarkable turnabout.''

Roger grinned broadly. ''Not as remarkable as my last two items of news. The M'threnni have left Gaia and a starship is on its way from Earth.''

The news of the incoming starship had broken a month previously when astronomers at the Hart Observatory in the Crescent Mountains had detected a new object of the twelfth magnitude during a routine sky-scan. At first they had assumed it to be a comet but attempts to calculate its orbital period had revealed that it was on a direct course for Gaia and that its point of origin could be traced back to the star Sol. The starship was now clearly visible in the night sky and its arrival was anticipated within a matter of days.

If this news had been sufficient to create a stir, what had happened next had been equally surprising. Just four nights ago a M'threnni freighter had arrived on Round Island and had taken off some ten hours later—a much longer stopover than normal. When dawn broke, no cargo lay waiting at the centre of the terminus but a group of Voices. The M'threnni had departed the island, abandoning their human servants. The Voices, all apparently catatonic, had been removed to the hospital and were currently under observation. All attempts to gain access to the tower had so far met with failure.

Roger continued talking, telling us how his clientele at the restaurant had fallen off drastically since the departure of the M'threnni, thus forcing him to close down for refurbishment. I was only half-listening. Annia had been released from the tower and she was at the hospital, mere kilometres away. I had to see her.

It was too early for lunch, but Roger must have decided that our island-leanness was a sign of undernourishment for he dispatched a waiter to a nearby bakery and the man returned with a tray of honeyed pancakes. They seemed such a delicacy after our primal island diet that we wolfed them down within minutes.

The talk went on. Eilan wanted to know more about the proposed changes in the constitution but Roger could tell her little. She asked about the current status of the Voices: what was being done with them and what results had been obtained? Roger didn't know. I sensed that she was eager to bring herself up to date on current affairs, that she would have liked to leave immediately for the city but felt constrained by Roger's hospitality. I was wondering how best I could slip away when there was a sudden cry from Junith. She was holding her belly and gulping in air.

Eilan rose quickly and said to Roger: "Fetch your floater. We have to get her to the hospital."

Roger exited at speed while Eilan attended to Junith, loosening her garments and laying her flat on the sofa.

"Can you hold out?" she asked. "We'll be at the hospital within ten minutes."

Junith swallowed more air. "I'll try," she gasped.

Roger returned to say that the floater was waiting outside. By now Junith was somewhat calmer and she was able to walk out to the vehicle. I insisted on accompanying her and Eilan to the hospital. Eilan, who must have been aware of the dual nature of my motive (I had told her all about Annia), raised no objections. Alma required little persuasion to stay behind to greet Wolther and Islor.

As Junith was easing delicately into the front passenger

seat of the floater I noticed that her pet bird—which she had insisted on bringing home with her and had promptly forgotten as soon as we had stepped ashore—was waddling along the embankment, pursued by two small girls. The bird, ill at ease amongst the stone and concrete of the harbour, flapped its stunted wings in a pathetic attempt to escape the attentions of the youngsters. Finally they cornered it on a narrow jetty and began waving their arms with glee. For the bird, their exuberance at discovering such a quaint creature was nothing more than a threat; it cowered on the edge of the jetty, burbling pitifully.

Roger drove at speed to the hospital, paying scant attention to the surrounding traffic; he was thoroughly unnerved by Junith's condition. Junith herself was somewhat calmer now. Her labour-pains had ceased and she rested her head on the seat, her eyes closed and a hand across her belly.

Eilan, who was obviously familiar with the hospital, brushed aside the nurses and orderlies who attempted to block our path and took Junith directly to an empty operating theatre. Within minutes a doctor had appeared and after brief and whispered consultations with Eilan, he departed to find some literature on obstetrics.

Eilan came over to me. "You can do nothing here. Junith's in capable hands."

"I'd like to see the birth," I said.

"Junith doesn't want it. She insists that only I and the doctor be present."

I looked across at Junith. She was staring wide-eyed at the ceiling and she looked frightened.

"Come back in a few hours," Eilan said, putting her hand on my arm and smiling, as if she knew what I was going to do next and was silently endorsing it.

I wandered down the white corridors, wondering where the Voices might be quartered. I knew that strict security measures would surround their enclosure and that, unannounced, I was unlikely to gain admittance. I went down to the main entrance hall and asked the receptionist if Doctor Wendi

Carver was on duty. He checked his roster, then referred to his watch.

"She's about to come off for the morning. Shall I page her for you?"

"Please."

Wendi arrived about five minutes later. I was sitting in one of the semi-circular couches which lined the main entrance when I saw her emerge from one of the ward-corridors. She was dressed in a pale blue smock with silver ribbing and she wore a navy-blue scarf about her forehead, tied into a knot above her left ear.

She stopped at the receptionist's desk and he pointed in my direction. She walked over, a frown of puzzlement on her face. Then, as she drew near, she broke into a smile.

"David! I didn't recognize you with all that hair. How are you?"

"I'm fine," I said, rising. "You look very prosperous."

I was referring to the silver neckband and the crystal cheekdrops which she wore: she radiated affluence.

She smiled winningly, as if inviting me to expand my observation into a direct compliment.

"I thought you might have gone back to the High Valleys," she said. "I went back to the villa a few times, but it was always empty. What have you been doing with yourself?"

"Oh, nothing much," I said. She was obviously unaware of my involvement with the League. "Do you remember Annia?"

"Annia?" she said, pondering. I couldn't tell whether or not she was pretending to have difficulty in recalling the name.

"The girl from my commune that I thought was dead."

"Oh yes."

"Well, she isn't. The M'threnni took her as a Voice. I think she's now under observation here at the hospital. I'd like to see her."

"I see," Wendi said, staring towards the entrance. A man in a wheel-chair was attempting, rather unsuccessfully, to manoeuvre himself through the swing-doors. Wendi called to a passing orderly and he went over to help him.

"You realize, David," she said, "that all the Voices are completely uncommunicative? She won't talk to you."

"I'm prepared for that. I'd just like to see her."

She studied me for a moment, perhaps wondering (as I was) whether Annia, whom I was now convinced she did remember, had been the spectre that had hovered over us throughout our liaison, finally forcing us apart.

"I'll see what I can do," she said, and went off.

I sat down again and watched a young boy playing with a spinning top across the hall. He was unable to flick the top with sufficient vigour to get it going, so I went over and started it for him. The top careered off across the tiled floor, the boy chasing after it with whoops of delight. I studied the arabesqued tiles. Green and cream, the interwoven patterns seemed to go on for ever . . .

It was some time before Wendi eventually returned. She was accompanied by a heavily bespectacled middle-aged man with all the authoritative mien of a "senior consultant."

"This is Doctor Jacobsen," Wendi said. "He's our senior neurophysiologist and the overall head of the team who are studying the Voices."

"You must understand," Jacobsen said without preamble, "that these people—the Voices—are exhibiting all the classic signs of catatonia. All our efforts to engage them in any form of communication have so far been unsuccessful. They show a complete lack of interest in the world around them."

"That has been explained to me," I said.

"Several of these people have already been visited by friends, and nothing fruitful has come of it. It can be quite distressing if the person was once close to the Voice."

"It seems a singularly inappropriate name, given their present condition."

Jacobsen did not appear to appreciate the irony; his severe features remained set in their granitic mould.

"I'm prepared for the worst," I said with a hint of impatience. "I'd like to see her."

Jacobsen stared at me for a moment, then nodded.

The Voices were quartered in an isolation ward on the top floor of the west wing. The only access was via an elevator. A militia woman stood outside the door, talking to a male nurse. The door itself held a large sign, red letters on white, saying: NO UNAUTHORIZED ENTRY. Wendi told me that the sign was common to all wards in this part of the hospital and had not been put up especially for the Voices. Nonetheless, they had been securely cocooned in the most inaccessible area. We did not enter the ward, but Jacobsen allowed me to peer in through the circular window.

The beds were all empty and the Voices were gathered at the far end of the ward. A series of couches had been arranged around the glass-faced wall and the Voices were sitting or standing in the sunlight, attended by three yellow-frocked female nurses. I counted nineteen, ten men and nine women. About two-thirds of them were elderly or middle-aged, the rest somewhat younger. They all wore white patients' tunics, their left sleeves rolled up to accommodate the nutrient pads fixed to their upper arms. None of them moved or showed the slightest awareness of their environment; they were frozen like holo-figures, their hairless faces utterly blank. It was a *tableau vivant* of the eeriest kind.

"How many are there all together?" I asked.

"Twenty-three," Jacobsen said.

The same as the number of days between the freighter shipments, I recalled. Coincidence, or some magic number for the M'threnni?

"We've arranged for you to meet Annia in private," Jacobsen said. "Wendi will sit with you."

I turned away from the window. "I'd like to see her alone."

He shook his head. "Impossible. The Voices must be under qualified supervision at all times. If you wish to see her, then you will do so under our conditions or not at all."

Annia was sitting in a private bedroom just along the corridor. I say "sitting," but the verb is inexact, since it suggests some conscious act on her part. She had *been sat* in the chair—presumably by the orderly who now stood at her back, his face almost as impassive as hers.

"This is Annia, I take it?" Wendi said.

"Yes," I replied.

"We didn't know her name until you arrived today. She was the only one who fitted the age criterion. She appears to be youngest of the group."

"No one from Silver Spring has been to visit her?"

"No." She motioned to the orderly and he departed. We took seats facing Annia's chair.

Over a cycle had passed since I had last seen her, and she was no longer a young girl, but a young woman. Her head was as glabrous as an egg, her skin far paler than I remembered. Her face expressed—not inertness, but neutrality, as if she had fallen asleep with her eyes open. She stared straight ahead at the wall, giving no indication that she had even registered our entry.

"None of them have spoken so far?" I asked.

"None," Wendi said.

I noticed that the pupils of Annia's eyes were abnormally contracted, as if the sunlight, which was streaming through the window to her right, was far too strong for her.

"Annia?" I said. "Annia, it's David. Do you remember me?"

As if in a trance, she continued to stare at the wall.

"Annia," I said more loudly, "I thought you were dead. At the commune, they told me you were dead."

I had a feeling of déjà vu; then I realized that I was paraphrasing my dream parlour conversation with her.

"Perhaps they're all deaf," I said inanely to Wendi.

"No, they can hear sounds. They just don't react to them. They don't react to anything."

I pulled my chair up to her and took her hands in mine. They were cool; not cold, but cool. I had deliberately blocked her line of sight so that she was now forced to look directly at my face. But if her eyes focused automatically, there was no sign that she recognized me or even acknowledged my proximity.

"Annia, you have to fight this," I said. "Whatever they've done to you, you have to fight it." I squeezed her hands in emphasis of my words. "You can come back, Annia. They're gone now, the M'threnni have gone. You can be whole again."

Nothing; I might have been addressing a statue. Her hands remained limp in mine. I looked down at them and saw Jax's snake-ring on my own finger. I slipped it off, raised her right hand to the level of my chin, and slid the ring on her middle finger. Her eyes moved to the ring, then back to my face.

"It's Jax's ring," I said. "Remember it? Jax is dead, Annia." I waited a second, then added: "I killed him."

Even this dramatic half-truth failed to stir her. But she had looked at the ring; for a split second she had shown some awareness of the world around her.

I turned to Wendi. "Did you see it?"

"Yes," she said, smiling. "I saw it."

Junith was still in labour, so Wendi and I had lunch together at a restaurant near the hospital. She must have been intrigued by my confession of murder to Annia but she said nothing of it. I, in turn, did not ask her about her life since leaving me; but she confessed, unprompted, that she was now in liaison with the banker, Theo. She described him as a kind and considerate man—adjectives which by their very blandness telegraphed that she was not completely happy with him. I felt a little uneasy; I didn't know whether she was offering me an olive-branch or an invitation. I moved the conversation on to generalities. We talked of the departure of the M'threnni and the imminent arrival of the starship from Earth. But Wendi had no real stomach for such weighty matters and we discussed them in bantering tones, with Wendi speculating that Gaia might become a holiday resort for Earthfolk, and I countering this by remarking, with totally unfelt humour, that the M'threnni had probably fled from Gaia because they disliked tourists. But when we left the restaurant, Wendi took my hand momentarily and said: "I'll help all I can with Annia, you know."

I returned to the villa and found that it had lain idle since my departure. The garden was derelict; storm-sand had drifted across the untended flower-beds and the pool was clotted with weeds. The house itself remained as I had left it—dustier, perhaps and disused, but inviolate. There was a pile of *Chronicles* on my desk in the living-room; put there, no doubt, by Wendi during one of her visits. They were dated up to a month after my departure for the Antipodean Isles. I dumped them, unread, in the disposal chute.

I was surprised that the villa had not been relet in my absence; the properties on the estate were keenly sought after. Perhaps Helmine had put the place under surveillance following my disappearance in the hope that I would eventually return there. No doubt when she was deposed, the house had been left empty to await my return: a reward for the exiled hero.

The solar heater was still operational so I took a long, hot bath, relishing the luxury. Afterwards I fell asleep in my favourite chair and when I awoke it was early evening.

I returned to the hospital, stopping off on the way at a barber's to get my hair trimmed. I decided against having my beard shaved off; it could remain a while longer.

When I finally arrived at the hospital I discovered that Junith had given birth to a boy. She had been placed in a private room on the northern corner of the main building; a host of doctors and nurses stood in the corridor outside, enthusiastically discussing this strange phenomenon of endogenesis. As I threaded my way past them I was tempted to announce loudly and proudly that I was the father.

Junith herself was attended by Eilan alone, her baby (somehow I could not really think of it as *our* baby) nestling on her breast. She looked quite composed, and was obviously enjoying all the attention she was receiving. We talked for a short while, and I took the baby from her and held it in my arms. It began to cry; a raucous, uninhibited bawling. Although strictly ugly in the manner of most newborn babies, I must confess that the child kindled in me something which I can only describe as a glow of paternal pride. But Junith was soon asking for the baby, and I handed it back to her. It was clear that she considered the child hers and hers alone. I raised no objections.

"What will you call him?" I asked.

"Island," she said.

Inwardly, I winced.

Later that evening Eilan was contacted by Nathan and the following morning she met with the Senate. It transpired that she had been offered, and had accepted, a provisional seat on the governing body, to be confirmed when the new constitution was officially ratified. As a political entity, the League no longer existed, but Eilan had emerged as something of a folk-hero following Helmine's disgrace. Her return to the mainland had been announced in that morning's *Chronicle*, coupled with the news that she would be invited to join the Senate—a conspicuous public relations exercise by Nathan. Although there was less of an ideological rift between Eilan and the Senate now that the M'threnni problem had been resolved by the aliens' voluntary departure from Gaia, she had insisted that a substantial portion of the city's capital budget for next season be earmarked for development on the South Bank as a condition of her acceptance of the Senate post. She told me that Nathan and the others had agreed with a minimum of fuss; they were more concerned with presenting a united front to the imminent arrivals from Earth.

It promised to be a busy time for Eilan. In addition to her new responsibilities on the Senate, she was also advising the team of specialists who were investigating the Voices, having at last made public her own findings with the dying Voice. The doctors were unable to instigate an immediate programme of brain phase monitoring on the Voices as there was a temporary injunction on the use of the headpieces following the outcry against Helmine's abuses. However, Eilan's work, coupled with my own subjective impressions of the M'threnni-Voice relationship, at least provided some formal basis for the development of appropriate therapeutic techniques. It was possible, we reasoned, that the core of M'threnni thought-patterns in each Voice's brain had somehow short-circuted the rest of the cerebral cortex, just as an electric shock may induce temporary amnesia. The most fruitful approach might simply be to expose the Voices to as many stimuli as possible in the hope that they might help break down whatever alien-induced traumata had caused their mental seizures.

It was not going to be easy, however. When I visited Annia that afternoon I took along with me her old gasglobe in the hope that it might stir some response in her. I put it into her hands, but she did not look at it or react to its faint warmth. I conducted a halting monologue for about ten minutes, with equally negative results. I leaned forward and kissed her gently on the cheek, but still she remained inert.

I went to see Eilan and asked her if it would be possible to take Annia out into the city for a few hours each day. She considered, then told me that she would broach the subject with Jacobsen.

The next day I arrived at the hospital to find a small crowd of saffron-robed people sitting on the grass outside Junith's room. There were about twenty of them, all members of The Children of the Divine Light, one of the eccentric South Bank sects. They were staring towards the window of Junith's room with reverent expressions on their faces. I saw that Junith was sitting at the window, her child in her arms.

"What do they want?" I asked her when I reached her room.

"They believe that my child is the fulfilment of a prophecy."

I remembered the prophecy. The mainspring of the Children's doctrine was the belief that the goddess Capella would one day visit Gaia in human form to purge the planet of its sins—a singularly unoriginal religious notion. The prophecy had been made by one of their founders who, while witnessing a rare dual transit of the two minor suns across the

face of each of the major components (thus creating the effect
of "pupils" embedded in Capella's "eyes"—an auspicious
time for prophecy) had had a "vision" of a girl child torn
from the body of a woman who was destined to become the
saviour of Gaia. No matter that Junith's child was a boy: was
it not the miracle birth? Junith's son was their Messiah;
prophecies could always be modified after the fact. Judging
by the way in which Junith was displaying the child for their
benefit, it seemed as if she was quite happy with this chosen
role.

Annia was still unresponsive to my attentions, but Eilan had
persuaded Jacobsen to allow me to take her for a short ride
under his supervision. We drove northwards on the highway,
passing the Institute with its black crystal. Annia did not even
glance at it. On the way back, however, a floater passing by
in the opposite direction reflected a dazzle of sunlight into our
eyes, and Annia turned her head away. She continued to stare
through the side window and for a few minutes it seemed as if
she was actually registering what was passing by. Jacobsen
said nothing, but I knew that he had been impressed for he
later gave me permission to take Annia out (under Wendi's
supervision) for up to two hours each afternoon.

That evening, just after dusk, Eilan and I went over to Round
Island to inspect the terminus. The investigators at the tower
had tried every measure short of using explosives to attempt
to gain access to it, but without success. The entrance portal,
whose location I remembered well, could not even be seen;
there was just the smooth, unblemished ivory exterior,
diamond-hard, heat-resistance, and inert to the variety of
acids and other corrosives which had been sprayed on it.
    There had been some nervous speculation that the aliens
had first expelled the Voices, then sealed themselves in the
tower. But no; the M'threnni were gone, I was convinced.
The faint breeze which had been blowing when we had
crossed Round Island Bridge blew equally strongly inside the
terminus; there was no muting of the elements as before.

Round Island had once been an alien outpost, its entire environment strange; now it was just a collection of exotic artifacts, as exposed to the external world as the humblest rock.

Eilan and I stared up at the darkening sky, where the incoming ship from Earth now outshone all the stars. Its light was faintly bluish. Eilan told me that the Senate had decided earlier that day to make Round Island the landing point for any descent craft. It was a decision, I reflected, with all sorts of symbolic undertones.

Chapter Twelve

The ship from Earth entered planetary orbit two days later. Attempts to communicate with the craft had met with an ominous silence up to that time, but soon after it attained orbit a radio message was received:

"Greetings from Earth. We are pleased to find a settlement on your planet. Our ship embarked upon this voyage with the express hope of finding a thriving colony. We congratulate you on your success. We propose to launch a lander in two hours' time, and we await your landing instructions."

The message seemed oddly stilted, possessed of an excessive formality which was a little difficult to understand. We had assumed that the people from Earth would be delighted to find human life on Gaia; but the terseness and stolidity of their greeting suggested that they did not regard it as a particulary momentous event. Perhaps, I thought, they had made contact with other colonies established during the first phase of instellar exploration; in addition to the *Auriga*, six other ships had been launched towards stars known to have orbiting Earth-type planets, four of them closer to Sol than

Capella. Their current mission might be just one in a series of reconciliations.

The radio controller gave the landing instructions, then sat back to await a reply. A few minutes later, it came:

"Acknowledged and understood. Estimated time of landing one hour forty-six minutes hence." The ship's radio went dead.

The Senate members, who were gathered in the control centre of the shuttle terminus for the occasion, looked at one another with bemusement. Was there to be no further dialogue before landing, no introductions, no exchange of information? An awkward silence ensued.

"We had better get moving," someone said at last. "There's not much time."

I had gained an invitation to the control centre at Eilan's express request. She had also insisted that I was to be present amongst the welcoming party on Round Island. Since our return from the Antipodean Isles, I had been helping her with a variety of work, effectively acting as her personal secretary-cum-confidant. While she was fully committed to the Senate, I think she wanted someone around her whom she knew she could trust, someone of proven loyalty.

The descent craft was due to land on Round Island at nine hours, the midpoint of zenith. The welcoming committee—which consisted of the City Senate and numerous senior commune members from the High and Low Valleys and the Plains—gathered on Round Island a half-hour before. The banks of the Tamus had been thronged with people as we had crossed the bridge in a stately motorcade flanked by militia floaters. Nathan began to organize us into a triangular array with himself at the apex and Eilan and a representative from each of the three outlying districts in the second rank. There were twenty-nine of us in all, and I, as the only unofficial member of the party, stood at the end of the fourth, rear line next to Julia, the youngest Senate member. I had scanned all the faces, but saw no one from Silver Spring. Well, then, I thought, I would be their ambassador.

We stood with our backs to the arched entranceway. Work on the tower had been temporarily abandoned and it lay unattended on the opposite side of the terminus. A large red cross had been painted on the centre of the obsidian landing area.

It was an extremely hot day. There was not a breath of wind, and the twin suns, basking in a cloudless sky, shed their vernal heat with an unremitting intensity. Several of the older members had brought along parasols, but these had been discarded under Nathan's orders for reasons of protocol. Hats were not allowed either. We simply had to stand there and bear it.

After what seemed like an age of waiting, an excited murmur from the crowds on the shore carried to us. Someone in the row in front of me pointed skywards. I looked up, and there it was: a black dot in the blueness.

We watched in silence as it fell, rapidly growing larger and finally acquiring a distinct shape. It was a solid trapezium, a squat, lopped pyramid. The sound of its engines carried to us: a low thrumming like the purring of a cat. A series of slit-like portholes could be seen along one flank and below them some designs in yellow which did not appear to be numbers or letters.

The ship eclipsed the suns, casting a dark, fleeting shadow over our expectant faces. We clapped our hands over our ears as the now-loud bleating of its engines assailed us. Landing-pads like inverted golf-tees extruded from each corner of the craft as it dropped diagonally towards the red cross. It was travelling too fast, I thought; but even as I did so, the pitch of its engines heightened and it decelerated rapidly until it was hovering like an insect over the landing point. Then the purring died away and it settled gently over the red cross.

It was a small craft, about the same size as a trawlerfoil. The yellow designs on its flank looked vaguely familiar, but I could not place them. Its fluted windows were in shadow, so that its interior could not be seen. Although no weaponry was evident, it was ominously military in appearance, like a metallic bunker.

A ladder dropped from the underbelly of the craft and a moment later a man dressed in black stepped out. Two others, wearing mid-blue uniforms, followed him. They paused to stare at the tower, then emerged from the shadows and began walking towards us.

The man in black was of Caucasian origin, fair-haired and ruddy-skinned. But his companions were sallower, dark of hair, and their eyes bore the epicanthic fold characteristic of the Mongoloid race. They were orientals, and the yellow designs on the craft were Chinese characters.

"Welcome to Gaia," Nathan said, stepping forward to greet them.

The men in blue smiled and bowed their heads. The man in black said: "Thank you. On behalf of the crew of the *Da Jwang,* we greet you."

His accent was a little strange, but it was perfectly clear that English was his native language. *Da Jwang;* the words struck a chord in my memory. Of course; not Da Jwang, that was the phonetic version, but *Ta Chaung.* It was one of the hexagrams of the *I Ching,* the Chinese Oracle of Changes. Wendi, with her fascination for prophecy, had had a copy of the book, and we had consulted it when we had decided to apply for parentage. But I was unable to recall the meaning of the hexagram.

Nathan announced that this was a proud and momentous day for Gaia. After thirty cycles of isolation we had been reunited with the peoples of our ancestral planet. It was an historic occasion. He felt at once proud and humble that fate had chosen him to be the one to greet our visitors. He hoped that a permanent link would now be established with Earth and he looked forward to the beginning of a new era for both our planets.

Thankfully it was a brief speech.

The man in black nodded, then spoke to the other two. In Chinese. Clearly, he was translating Nathan's speech. One of the orientals replied in the same tongue, then the fair-haired man spoke again in English:

"Your welcome is as warm as your suns. Our aims are in accord with yours. It is our purpose to forge an unbreakable bond between our two worlds. You have much beauty here. Your twisting white tower is a feast to the eyes."

"We did not build it, I must confess," Nathan said. "It was constructed by aliens."

This revelation was hastily conveyed to the two Chinese, and they began talking excitedly amongst themselves. The man in black looked on, but said nothing.

I was disquieted. Something told me that Nathan had been precipitate in revealing the origin of the tower. There was something exclusive about the Chinese, something that went beyond their lack of understanding of our language. They seemed to huddle together like children exchanging secrets. It was strange that they did not speak English, for it had been the international language when our ancestors had departed Earth. And the United States had been the dominant nation. Had the Chinese now attained primacy?

One of the Chinese addressed the fair-haired man, and he turned again to Nathan. "This is very strange to us. Do the aliens live inside the tower?"

"They did until recently," Nathan said. "I'm sorry to say that they fled with the approach of your starship."

"But they communed with you until then?"

"They supplied us with materials necessary for our survival, but there was no direct contact. They remained secluded on this island, cut off from the rest of our city."

Again the information was conveyed to the Chinese. They were both middle-aged men, strikingly alike to me in appearance, their faces evincing an unattractive suavity. Again they conferred, this time more briefly, before giving the fair-haired man the text of their response.

"My companions are intrigued by these aliens," he said. "How long did they dwell here?"

It went on for several minutes, this gentle probing by the men from Earth. Finally, when Nathan was in the middle of explaining the M'threnni freighter operation, Eilan stepped forward and said: "Where are your women?"

The fair-haired man did not consult the Chinese. "There are just us three."

"And none on board your mother-ship?"

"Oh, yes. Of course. Why do you ask?"

"It's nothing. Do you have a multinational crew?"

He stiffened slightly. "We have people on board from a number of different nations. I, myself, am from the same region of Earth as many of your ancestors: North America. My companions are citizens of the Pan-Asian Confederation."

"And they financed this mission and built the starship?"

"That is correct. You are one of the mayor's advisers?"

Eilan ignored the disparaging tone. "A colleague. Does your enterprise have multinational backing?"

"It has the backing of the Confederation, which represents two-thirds of the Earth's population."

"Including your homeland?"

"Yes."

"What, then is your status?"

"I am the official interpreter for this mission." He looked at Nathan, obviously wanting to continue his conversation with him.

"And what is the status of your homeland within the Confederation?"

He stared at her for a moment, then said: "It is a self-governing protectorate."

"I see," Eilan replied. "Thank you." She withdrew.

One of the Chinese addressed the fair-haired man, who spoke back, then listened again before turning to Nathan.

"Could we perhaps continue our conversation in a shaded place?" he said. "We are unused to the fierce heat of your suns."

"Of course," said Nathan, obviously pleased that some positive action was called for. He had seemed thoroughly perplexed by Eilan's conversation with the interpreter.

Quickly, Nathan led our visitors along each rank. The two Chinese insisted on shaking hands with each person—a ritual which caused a little confusion because some of the delegates were unfamiliar with it. A permanent smile was fixed on their faces, and they nodded continuously as if their heads were attached to their necks by pivots. The interpreter wore a more solemn expression, and he did not offer his hand to anyone. Briefly, Nathan introduced everyone, giving their names and their official status—a purely formal gesture since the fair-haired man was not translating. When it came to my turn—and I was the last in line—Nathan merely said: "This is David, an aide of one of the Senate." One hand, then another gripped mine, and two heads, with their identical smiles, bobbed up and down in front of me. And than Nathan was leading them off to the array of floaters parked outside on the bridge.

The three Earthmen sat with Nathan in his floater at the head of the motorcade. As we crossed the bridge, cheers erupted from the bank, and when we emerged from the underpass beneath the Complex, New Broadway was filled with hosts of flag-waving people. About half the flags were Gaian, the other half an equal mixture of Stars and Stripes and Union Jacks. Little did they know, I thought, that the hegemony of th English-speaking peoples had passed away, that the once dominant United States was now little more than a colony of some sprawling Asiatic empire. The two Chinese waved periodically to the crowd, smiling all the while. Smiles of irony? I wondered.

At length we arrived at Capitol Square, which had been closed to the public for the day. Armed militia stood on guard at each of its three entrances.

No one had known how many guests we would be entertaining, but the news that only three Earthmen had landed must have been swiftly relayed to Nathan's staff, for when we entered the banquet room, a single long table which would accommodate everyone had been set up with all the pomp the occasion demanded. Pewter vases of freshly-cut flowers vied for pride of place with M'threnni lightsticks mounted on elaborate silver candleholders; the table-cloth was immaculately white, and the cutlery gleamed. Nathan had insisted that only official delegates should attend the dinner and I had previously agreed to slip away after cocktails. Following the exchanges on Round Island, however, I was beginning to regret this concession; I wanted to see how things developed. I consoled myself with the thought that I would be seeing Annia instead.

I went over to Eilan and spoke briefly with her before I left.

"I don't like it," she told me. "Something's not right."

"I agree," I said. "They seem a little remote, don't they?"

She nodded. "Especially considering the amount of goodwill that Nathan is radiating." She gestured with her glass towards the far end of the room. The french windows had been opened and Nathan, the Earthmen and half the delegation were standing out on the balcony overlooking the square. Nathan was talking and waving his arms with great animation, while the two Chinese (the translator stood in the background like a shadow) looked on with their perennial smiles. Smiles that were thoroughly devoid of humour or goodwill.

"We expected Americans," Eilan said. "Nobody actually said so, but subconsciously we all assumed that the people on board the Earthship would be like us. Evidently there have some changes since our ancestors left the planet."

"Perhaps that's why they seem a little—cool," I said, searching for a glimmer of optimism. "Perhaps we're a little strange to them as well. Maybe they're just overwhelmed by the occasion."

"Perhaps," Eilan said, still staring towards the balcony. But she obviously didn't believe it.

I finished my drink. "I must be off," I said. "It's visiting time."

"Oh, yes," she said, turning back to me. "Keep up the good work. If anyone can break through to Annia, it's going to be you."

"Jacobsen told me yesterday that he thought Annia had the best prospects for rehabilitation of all the Voices."

"I would think so," Eilan agreed. "She seems to be the youngest."

"Will I see you later?"

"Who can say? I'll contact you if anything crops up."

I set my glass on a tray. "Well, have a good dinner."

"It's sure to be an interesting one," she said.

Wendi and I took Annia back to the villa that afternoon. On the pretext that she had some shopping to do, Wendi went off to the city centre and left me alone with Annia.

In my spare moments I had been attempting to renovate the garden. I sat her on a chair in the sunlight and while I was attending to the weeds, I told her all about the arrival of the Earthmen. She did not respond, of course, but I had decided that it might be therapeutic to converse with her as if she was a normal human being. Junith's pet bird, which I had rescued, half-starved, from the harbour the day after our return and had installed in the gaden, wandered around the fringes of the lily-pool, rooting amongst the grass. It seemed quite content in this miniature approximation of its island habitat, although it had developed an unwelcome taste for mistflower buds, thus forcing me to tether it to a post on a long string which did not quite extend to their beds. On one occasion, the bird waddled up to Annia's chair and she looked down at it momentarily. I said nothing, but I felt elated. It was coming; slowly, it was coming.

Towards sunset, a courier arrived with a message from Eilan.

Important news, it read. *Come to the Star. Eilan.*

Roger had provided Eilan with a small room above his restaurant until she could find accommodation nearer the city centre. I arrived there just after dusk. Only it was no longer the *Alien Star.* Roger had had the sign replaced with another: it was now *Sol Three,* and a stylized globe of the Earth hung from a bracket in place of the red neon star.

"We're opening in three days' time," Roger told me as he led me through the main eating area. Several artists were at work painting murals on the walls. I recognized the Pyramids of Egypt and the Colossus of Rhodes.

"We're doing the Seven Wonders of Earth," Roger explained. "Should prove popular, yes?"

"You had better make room for the Great Wall of China," I said.

"Eh?"

"They're Chinese. The men from Earth."

"Oh, yes. Eilan told me. I've been looking for designs for Chinese lanterns. I'm told they're really attractive."

When I tapped on Eilan's door and opened it, I saw that she was lying on top of her bed, asleep.

"Forgive me," she said, rousing as I entered. "I must have dozed off."

"It's a hangover from our life of exile," I said; we had fallen into the habit of taking a nap most evenings while on the island.

She went over to the wash-basin and splashed water on her face.

"How did it go?" I asked. "You're back earlier than I expected."

She patted her cheeks with a towel. "Our guests found the Gaian day rather too long," she said. "Before dusk they were exhausted and they asked to be returned to their ship." She put the towel back on the rack. "Nathan was disappointed, of course. He tried to persuade them to spend the night in his residence, but they were adamant. They told him that they were under orders to return to their ship by sunset." She settled herself in an armchair and invited me to sit down. I perched myself on the edge of the bed, since there were no other chairs.

"There are good reasons why they left in such a hurry," Eilan said. "We talked for several hours after dinner, and a number of interesting facts emerged. Firstly they told us that of the seven prospective colony planets to which our ancestors had sent ships, four had already been investigated, and all but one were lifeless. Apparently there's a thriving colony on Delta Pavonis Four. Contact was made about a cycle ago, and a permanent link with Earth has already been established.

A similar link with Gaia is the object of this mission. They are quite willing—indeed, eager—to initiate supply flights, but there is a condition. They want to establish a permanent base on Gaia—which seemed quite reasonable until they told us its size: they want five thousand people down here. For what purpose? we inquired. For scientific and cultural liaison, they told us. We pressed them, and at length they revealed that one of its prime functions, would be 'ideological instruction.' Earlier they had shown a great interest in our political organization, and they now informed us that it was based on American Federalism, a system which has been found to be 'untenable' in the long term. They would not explain exactly what form of government they have, but it certainly doesn't appear to have any democratic flavour. What they were effectively saying was that they intended to reform our society in their own image; Gaia would become another constituent state of their Confederation—a colony in all senses of the world. We refused outright. They told us that the people on Delta Pavonis Four had come to see the wisdom of their proposals—a veiled threat if I ever heard one. Nathan began to waver, but several of us got together and made it perfectly clear that we were not prepared to allow any interference in our internal politics. It was shortly after this that they decided that they were tired and had to return to their ship."

"What about the M'threnni?"

"Naturally they were fascinated by them. None of the other colonies ever encountered aliens. They were completely surprised. No doubt it will give them added incentive to establish a base here."

"So what happens now?"

"I don't know. After the Earthmen left, we spent a few hours arguing over the wisdom of our decision. Quite a number of people thought we should have accepted their proposals—we've been so dependent on the M'threnni, they find it impossible to conceive that we could exist without outside aid. Eventually I grew weary of their bickering and I walked out."

"You resigned?"

"Oh, no. I'm waiting to see what happens next. Assuming that we stand fast, then the Earthmen must either agree to our conditions or force us to comply with theirs."

They did, in fact, do neither. That same night, a number of landers descended on Round Island, and the following morning one of them, obviously armed, was positioned at the island end of the bridge, blocking the entrance to the terminus. Attempts to contact the mother-ship met with no response, so Nathan led a small delegation across the bridge. They were refused entry by the guards on duty, who did not speak English but brandished sinister-looking rifles in an unequivocal fashion. Nathan and his party retreated to the shore and again attempted to contact the Earthmen via radio. They would not reply.

Ten days have passed since the Earthmen first landed, ten days of anxious waiting. The Earthmen have barricaded themselves on Round Island and have refused to communicate with us. It appears that they have gained access to the M'threnni tower and are currently investigating its interior. The Senate dithers, but does nothing. What can it do? The Earthmen possess superior weaponry and could doubtless annihilate the whole of Helixport from their mother-ship if they so desired. We await some ultimatum, some ultimatum which we will be unable to refuse.

Despite our weakness, there are those amongst us who are foolish enough to suppose that we could resist. The Children of the Divine Light view the Earthmen as the incarnation of the promised Force of Evil from which their Messiah will deliver them—the M'threnni having inconveniently disburdened themselves of this role by their abrupt departure from Gaia. Already they are rallying their support, with Junith, who has found her role at last, in their vanguard. Any one of them might be capable of an irrational act which could bring the full wrath of the Earthmen down upon us.

What of the M'threnni, our vanished mentors? Of them,

there is no sign, nor, I believe, will there be. They have
retreated to some distant star where no human will ever find
them. My own belief, for what it is worth, is that they are
supremely rational beings, devoid of all the worthy passions
which we humans hold dear, but lacking, too, our mad-
nesses. That is why they hid themselves inside the tower, and
that is why, when they knew they could hide no longer, they
fled. Perhaps the Voices are the outcome of their attempts to
eradicate the base emotions of humanity. If so, then it is a sad
testimony that the end product is something less than human.
But these are speculations only, and cannot approach the
truth. The Earthmen probe the tower, but I do not think they
will discover much. The essence of the aliens is their mys-
tery.

All is not bleakness, however. Inside my garden, the
flowers bloom, and for two hours each day I bring Annia
there, and she, too, is blossoming. Whatever method the
M'threnni used for depilating the Voices, it was not permanent, for Annia's hair is beginning to grow back. A soft, fine
stubble now covers her head, and her eyebrows are sprout-
ing. A subtle but noticeable animation in her features accom-
panies this growth; she is coming alive again. Yesterday,
when I was crouching in front of her, tying a loose buckle on
one of her sandals, she reached forward and gently touched
my beard; at the same time, her lips parted momentarily as if
she was about to speak. Some day soon she *will* speak, I am
sure, and that will be the most joyous moment of my life.

And so we wait, and I have been filling the empty hours in
composing this account. It is a tale full of incompletenesses,
a story which ends, perhaps, with beginnings. But what
beginnings, what destinies await us, I would not venture to
guess. I am content to sit in my garden and let events unfold
as they will. Meanwhile Gaia turns, and each day Capella's
golden eyes look down upon us.

A Note on Gaia

The fifth planet of the Capella star-system, Gaia has a period of rotation of 35.84 hours and a revolutionary period of 968.1 rotations. Its diameter is 12,400km and its surface gravity 0.95G. The planet has only one major land-mass, a roughly semicircular island (also called Gaia) about twice the size of the Iberian Peninsula which straddles the equator in the Western Hemisphere. An archipelago of small volcanic islands, the Antipodean Isles, on the opposite side of the globe is the only other surface feature.

The Gaian calendar comprises four seasons (each season approximately equivalent to a Terran year) which make up a complete cycle of the planet. Gaia has no appreciable axial tilt, the high eccentricity of the orbit accounting for the seasonal variations in temperature. The seasons are sub-divided into twelve months, each of twenty days' duration, with two additional days designated Newseason's Day and Midseason's Day. Thus a typical Gaian date 8.7 Summer 29 would refer to the eighth day of the seventh month of Summer in the twenty-ninth planetary cycle, dated from the time of the first landing.

WHY WASTE
YOUR PRECIOUS
PENNIES ON GAS OR
YOUR VALUABLE
TIME ON LINE
AT THE BOOKSTORE?

We will send you, FREE, our 28 page cata-
logue, filled with a wide range of Ace
Science Fiction paperback titles—we've
got something for every reader's pleasure.

Here's your chance to add to your personal
library, with all the convenience of shopping by mail. There's no need to be without
a book to enjoy—request your *free* cata-
logue today.

CONAN

ALL TWELVE TITLES AVAILABLE FROM ACE
$2.25 EACH